CLOCKWORK DRAGON

Book IV of the Troutespond Series

Elizabeth Priest

Text Copyright © 2020 Elizabeth Priest
Cover Art © 2020 Bede Rogerson
Cover Design - Ben Keen

First published by Luna Press Publishing, Edinburgh, 2020

www.lunapresspublishing.com

ISBN-13: 978-1-913387-08-2

*To the (mostly) not evil twin - don't worry,
the Green Man isn't really in this one.*

Contents

Results Day

Here's something you don't know.

If you search my name on the internet—go on, type it in: Tanya Pomphrey—you get, apart from some moderately famous hockey player in Milwaukee, some newspaper articles from the local rag about my success with the Maths Challenge or my chess tournament achievements. Some stuff about those times I ran away. I don't have a huge internet footprint under obvious usernames, and American Tanya Pomphrey takes up the first two pages.

If you search for my friend Ally, you get junk from Facebook which would be a much better way to stalk all of us, and a link to her mum's mail-order Wicca supplies website. Half the content of that is a long, rambling blog that gets more hits than the shop, and Hester Guardian loves telling the world about all the silly little things Ally does. I haven't told Ally this yet.

If you search for my friend Teb's full name, you get zero hits because she doesn't exist anymore. I guess she doesn't know that either.

If you search for Alana, my new mysterious friend, you get millions of hits, and they're all about her. I bet she checks all the time.

Apparently she was a TV star as a kid, rising to fame on a sort of kids' chat show thing, presenting it as a precocious and adorable four-year-old with gap teeth and her hair in pigtails, all dressed up like a little cowgirl pretending to play banjo as some other kids pranced around. I bet she still has nightmares about the puppets.

Teb hates Alana. She thinks the last traces of the American accent are fake and that Alana has 'attitude' problems.

Here's some of the articles that I found:

"'Little Lana's Father In Fatal Car Accident

Agent to the child star and producer of the *Little Lana Show*, Greg Larbie (30) died last night when his car plunged hundreds of feet from a mountain road in the Los Angeles area. Production of the show will halt while an inquest is made concerning millions of dollars missing from the company's accounts..."

"Little Lana To Leave LA

TV's Little Lana is leaving the show, and America, 'perhaps for good' as one executive exclusively revealed to us. Her mother, Suzanne Larbie, flew into the country last night and took Alana out of the care of the CEO of the network hours before he too was arrested in the scandal which is shaking Hollywood. 'She's coming home to England and damned if I'm letting her act again,' Suzanne said."

"Where Are They Now? Child Stars and What They Did Next

- 7. 'LITTLE LANA'; Alana Larbie presented the *Little Lana Show* for three years, from age four to seven, warming hearts around the world with her folksy charm. The show ended with her father's suicide by vehicular accident and the exposure of massive fraud within the production company, who were selling faulty merchandise and the rights for Alana's songs to up to five hundred different buyers.

WHERE IS SHE NOW? Alana moved to England and lives a life of obscurity with her mother, who swore she would never act again. Aged eighteen now, she will be going to university later this year. Sources close to her claim, 'She was really hot but kind of scary. She was expelled from this school because of witchcraft. Haven't really seen her since then. Don't write my name down—she might curse me.' A strange turn from such a cute start, but her life has been filled with dark twists and turns..."

I like that last one. I used to think that the strange men who hung around in the tea shop near St Troute's school were government agents, and Ally and I used to play at tailing them through the streets, but I guess I know now that they're reporters hoping to catch Alana. They vanish pretty fast. She probably *is* cursing them.

In any case, I suppose all this shows is that lives can be interesting—and yet so very boring. Very actively boring. Alana had struggled her whole life since to live in the most uninteresting way possible. You might almost not believe it of her to hear her story—past the childhood fame and into her teenage years, to the parts all my friends were acquainted with involving a few more demons and cosmic entities, she was working for balance, stability and tranquillity in the universe. Teb seemed to think there was something more sinister afoot, but that is genuinely all Alana has ever wanted... All she ever wants. Fortunately she wouldn't need to proclaim her goals so loudly if the universe didn't work in opposition to itself. For the Piper there was some unknown god of Chaos walking the sunny streets of Troutespond, and for Alana there was me.

*

It was day twenty-six of our "Let's never talk about it again" pact. So far, we hadn't talked about "it". I don't think Ally was even sure what "it" was anymore. I was doing my best not to accidentally act suspiciously when I was genuinely just musing on the plot of a new book I liked and they mistook fiction for reality, and so far no one suspected me of anything. All in all, whatever our pact had been about when we stopped Teb running off and leaving us (for the third time), it seemed to be trundling along fine now. Teb was even (mostly) getting along with Alana.

The sun was beating down on the school playground, doing its "hottest day on record" impression that we were all grimly familiar with. Still, there was a festival attitude among the members of our sixth form and their parents. Someone had hung a banner across the front of the school: "A LEVEL RESULTS DAY: GOOD LUCK, TROUTESPOND!" Someone who wasn't me had scrawled in green marker underneath, "were going to need it." I figured with grammar like that, they certainly did.

The local press was in a huddle in a quieter corner of the playground, and in most people's anxiety they hadn't noticed the photographers. The arrival of a film crew from the county news team drew eyes, though, as they pulled their van straight into the playground. Normally they camped out at St Troute's Catholic school, because the traditional images of jumping teenagers looked better if they were all wearing matching blazers.

When Teb pointed them out, Ally said, "Hey, there are your friends, Alana!" and pointed loudly. Ally clearly remembered some incident that I had missed.

I was guessing it was that time Teb got herself onto the six o'clock news, pleading for my return during one of those instances when I vanished. I had definitely had other engagements at that time. Teb made me watch it a dozen times just to laugh at the snippet of Ally babbling something in a frenzied panic and accidentally insulting me on national television. I wasn't sure what part Alana had played in it that Ally was singling her out over Teb, because it had seemed mostly a teasing between them, not Alana.

Alana grimaced. "They really aren't." She pulled Ally, the tallest of us and therefore the best human shield, around slightly to block herself from view as a sweating cameraman heaved his equipment from the mud-peppered van out onto a tarmac pavement reflecting so much sun it seemed white. There was a heat haze making mirages between us and the tennis courts. A couple of boys from my classes, who seemed a lot less bothered about the results than most, were kicking a football back and forth, running through the mirage completely unafraid of being drowned in its imaginary waters.

Parents gossiped loudly and little siblings wove between legs, unaware of the weight on their brothers and sisters' futures. Teb's little brother screamed as a girl made a grab for him and he fell over, making a quite impressive somersault before landing splat on the playground. For a moment the Nandakishores were distracted from their conversation with my dad. Sarika flinched, wanting to run to her son and hug him despite his honour as a man (well, nine year old), but Mahesh put a hand on her arm as Avinash got to his feet, shook himself off, and with a battle cry chased after the girl, determined to get revenge. Kind of all gender normative but also cute.

"Idiot," Teb said, shaking her head, her flippy ponytail swinging back and forth. She'd finally cut her hair and was back to looking like a hipster rather than some sort of terrible warrior-queen. The fire still lurked behind her purple eyes if you looked hard enough, but our 'don't talk about it' pact was keeping anyone from looking closely. Besides, she was really getting into gold eye shadow right now and it was hard to argue with that.

"It's cute," Ally said, a wide, dopey smile on her face. Avi was the only little sibling any of us had, and he was rather spoiled from having so many extra older sisters.

I carried on looking around the heat-baked tarmac and picked out Warren at last: he was dwarfed by his friend Mackerel, who loomed widely as well as tall. I probably ought to have looked for him first, then down to spot my boyfriend. Rose-tinted glasses don't actually have great focus powers. I waved furiously, but at that moment Teb's barely-even-qualified-as-ex-boyfriend Chris King came over to the small group, and Warren could only shrug apologetically to me from across the playground.

Things had got all sorts of awkward and confusing between those two, and Warren and I had agreed to try and keep ourselves as a couple separate from Teb or, well, any group of people of any size that incidentally included Teb. Any hope of mixing our group of friends with the boys was long dead and, with the end of school, would now just be a pointless headache. With no common room to share there was little chance of accidentally bumping into each other or 'coincidental' arranging of the only two free tables being next to each other.

Mr Plebsy, the headteacher, had been working his way around the various chatting groups of parents, doing a sort of pincer movement along with Mr Westcott, the head of year, to leave no group unharassed. Now he headed our way. I hailed him with a salute as he drew near, and the group looked around curiously to see why I was doing it. I swear, none of them have eyes in the back of their heads. Hester stopped trying to engage Mrs Larbie in futile conversation (Alana had tried everything to make her not come, but there were some things it was impossible to shake a parent from doing with you, if only because it cut down avenues from hiding results between here and home). Danny and my dad paused their conversation about the game last night. No dramatic tension involved.

"Ah, welcome, welcome," Mr Plebsy said. "You must all be so proud," he added, shaking hands with them all—"Mr and Mrs Guardian... Looking good. How's business?" He moved to the Nandakishores before hearing the answer properly and assured Mrs Larbie it was good of her to come before spending too many of his overtaxed pleasantries on them. When it came to my dad, he was all, "Ah, Paul... Paul, Paul Paul... I don't know how you have a hair left on your head."

My dad, who had a very impressive bald spot, nodded rather morosely. "I've been channelling it all into the moustache, Michael." It was little wonder Daddy and Mr Plebsy—and every other authority figure in a twenty mile radius—got along so well. He had spent the last decade at least of his life being hauled out to answer for me and they probably had a support group.

"A fine moustache it is too," Mr Plebsy nodded, self-consciously stroking his own. "Who would have ever thought we'd all get to stand here together today? Now, Ally and Teb, they're smart girls, and Alana... Well, she came from a very good school. But it's Tanya that's the brains of this little outfit, wouldn't you say?"

"Yes sir," my friends all chorused, although Alana gave me a rather chilling look, welcome on the hot day. I wasn't scared of her, and Ally and Teb had been with me since we were three or four and knew this very much to be the truth.

"Shame, really," Mr Plebsy continued. "Perhaps we should have put Tanya in a better school. Some scholarships would have been easy enough to apply for... And maybe I'd have gained back five years of my youth..." he chuckled feebly, rubbing his thick head of white hair. "Well, I suppose we find out today if her, er, active imagination has finally overcome her test scores. I believe Mr Westcott intends to make an example of her."

"You'd never have got rid of her, sir," Ally said loyally. "Not without taking me and Teb with her."

"You are all smart girls," he repeated, looking rather more uncertain. The Guardians didn't seem too fussed at all about hearing Ally compared to me in negative terms, well aware their daughter was a dreamer and, while full of compassion and weird ideas, not a genius by a long shot. Sarika looked rather more put-out.

"My Teb is a very clever girl!" she protested. "She is doing five A Levels! More than Tanya, and all the sciences too!"

Now very flustered, Mr Plebsy ran a handkerchief over his forehead and nodded a lot, saying, "Yes, yes... Excellent student, that girl. No doubt done very well. Five As predicted, right? No doubt she's got some of them! Well, I must hurry—so many people here! Such a good showing. Good morning to you all, good luck girls!" and he hurried off to bother the next group of parents, apparently convinced that we all had a choice about if we wanted to be here or not.

My gaze had drifted and I caught sight of Jess Standerwick arriving a little late. She was an odious girl, but she'd really not had a good time at our prom and had been keeping a very low profile since then. She crept in wearing large sunglasses and drab clothes and didn't look too long at anyone. I would have felt sorry for her, but though she didn't know it I was the cause of her humiliation, and she had totally deserved it.

I waved at her as she passed, but she blanked me out.

I wondered what she actually remembered of that night.

Mr Westcott, looking stiff and uncomfortable as one of the few people in a proper suit in this unnatural weather, reappeared from the school building as I got back to scanning the crowds, and now he was followed by our friend Cathy, our history teacher's fiancée. She was carrying a large cardboard box full of brown envelopes. Or, perhaps, a box of hopes and dreams, which sold for an awful lot more if you knew the right market, which she did. I wondered if she was considering absconding with the box and making a profit.

When Mr Westcott got to a table set up to one side of the school building, he picked up a megaphone that had been carelessly left unguarded in public and cleared his throat into it impressively loudly. The "Hhhruumhumhum!" echoed across the playground, and many people jumped, having not seen him coming. A few babies started crying. Avi came running back to Sarika and flung his arms around her waist, burying his face in her shoulder. I could tell now that in a couple of years, when he chose secondary schools, he was going to opt for the long commute to Bilsworth or Waitington. You know, if our horror stories we'd teased him with for years hadn't already put him off.

Mr Westcott cleared his throat again, quietly to himself, to fix the damage the big attention grabbing growl had done, and hurried through a brief speech I was sure he'd spent all of a few seconds working on before this moment. "Good morning, sixth formers and parents! It falls on me as the head of year of this sorry lot to hand over the results as wired to us this morning by the exam boards. Try not to weep unduly; the labour market always needs plumbers and bricklayers, all well-paying, skilled careers..." He paused again, checking the reactions. To be honest, if he hadn't gone out of his way to persecute me for a series of crimes which might not have immediately seemed to be my fault, whatever result the investigation turned up, I might have thought he was one of the more awesome teachers for his cruel humour, but it got directed at me too often. The motivational part of the speech over, Westcott moved onto the practical part: "We've been shoving your results into envelopes as fast as we could print them out all morning, just so you can rip them open again in a few seconds. We'll do this in an orderly fashion; I'm sure you saw the riots on the news last year. Johnathan Acton..."

John jumped a bit like he thought Westcott was accusing him personally for starting the riots, implied in the head of year's announcement, then realised he had only been called to collect his results and shuffled out of the crowd, blushing and trying to shrink away from every eye on him. Cathy handed him the envelope with his name on, a massive grin on her face that showed her pleasure at helping out, but John only slunk back into the crowd with raised shoulders and sunk head.

"C'mon, open it!" someone yelled, but I could understand why he hadn't. The thoughts of his terrible performance in the exams was hanging on his mind like a dark cloud, as with many students here, and he did not want to open it while the cruel whims of the alphabet had put so many eyes on him. I had a feeling he hadn't done as badly as he thought, but he wasn't to know that.

It took four more students being called up before a single envelope was opened, and then the tense mood was punctuated with shrieks and the warm buzzing of friends and family. The cameras began clicking, and Mr Westcott raised his voice unnecessarily, so it rang out deep and guttural probably across the whole village.

Ally was the first of us to be called up. She sauntered up to Cathy and took the envelope with a hello and some small talk. The letter had been opened and read before she finished walking back up to us with a grin on her face. "Yup, C, B, B, A… I knew I was going to pass—I got an acceptance letter from my university this morning before I left."

"You sly thing!" Ted cried and punched her on her arm as Hester and Danny finally allowed themselves to glow with the parental pride they'd been holding back so far. Teb rounded on me: "You'd better not be hiding it from us too—I know your ways!"

I shook my head, holding up my hands. "No idea. Cross my heart."

"Alana Larbie!"

Alana nodded grimly.

"You'll be fine," Ally assured her.

"Easy for you to say," Teb put in.

It was as if a funeral march was playing as Alana walked across the playground. She was pale and clammy despite the heat, and dropped her envelope when Cathy handed it to her. She came back to us with the letter unopened and blanked her mother out of the circle as she joined us again. Suzanne immediately moved behind her daughter and stood on tiptoes to see over her head. The letter wobbled about in Alana's shaking hands for a long time. Slowly she eased her finger under the gummy strip holding the envelope closed and dragged it across at a snail pace.

"Hurry *up*, this is killing me," Teb said.

Bit by bit, Alana began working the thin bundle of certificates out.

"Teb Nandi!" Mr Westcott yelled. I think the world at large had rationalised her shorter name as just being teenage rebelliousness combined with a desire for people to be able to pronounce her name in official situations without dealing with what she described as white people stumblings. It was a reason, just not... the reason, or maybe one her pride ever would have actually made her go for.

Teb rolled her eyes. "Yeah, Alana. It's my turn." She sounded far more bored than scared, like this whole ceremony was a joke to her. She'd stressed so hard about her A Levels I had to assume this was a coping mechanism. On the day she'd handed them all in I'd had to comfort her as she dissolved into messy tears, weeping with horror at the thought of *not getting straight As*. Like the value society placed on these arbitrary letters would determine *her* fate forever.

Alana seemed to have frozen in place, the first inch of her certificate before the results came all that was poking out of the envelope.

Teb grabbed the envelope from her, yanked the papers out and flicked through them. "E for History, which figures since your coursework was two pages long and you slept through three of the exams. C, Media Studies... Um, C, English Literature, U, Art."

"Oh my god," Alana said weakly. I agreed. How did one fail Art? On the other hand, I hadn't even known Alana was *taking* it. Perhaps she hadn't noticed either. Alana snatched the results from Teb and looked properly. "Oh my *god*!" she repeated in a shriek. "That's enough! That's enough points! I'm going to university! I'm actually *leaving* this place! Oh my *god*!" She sank to the ground sobbing with delight. I saw her mother had narrowed eyes, silently furious at her daughter's delight to be anywhere but here, and perhaps a little afraid to let her out into the world. But the piece of paper had spoken, and UCAS had sorted Alana neatly into a low-ranking university of her choice. By now the damage control would be too great to stop her leaving, not least because the parents of three of Alana's friends were all watching this too, and my Daddy was like a superlawyer and would tell her where to go if she tried to stop Alana.

"Teb Nandi? I can see you gossiping with your friends over there," Mr Westcott growled, having read two more names in the meantime. Sarika was hovering at Teb's side, also trying to push her in the direction of the school.

"Alright, I'm coming!" she yelled across the playground, almost as loud as our head of year even without the megaphone. She stomped off to get her certificates with many people in the playground laughing. She went to Cathy, received her envelope and opened it right there at the table. Her eyes flicked over the certificates inside, and then she pushed them back into the envelope, not betraying a single emotion. She walked back up to us.

"Oh well, exams are stupid," she said.

"Teb!" Sarika cried. "You did not do badly?!"

"Failed everything," Teb said, smiling mildly. "Guess I'm going to University of Nowheretown."

"Good science program there," I muttered to no one. I'd like to think I made any of the goblins lurking around Teb giggle a little.

"You're joking, right?" Sarika butted in before we could derail the conversation.

Teb shrugged one shoulder and casually half-hid the results envelope behind her. "I wasn't sleeping very well before the exams. I must have messed up really badly... I mean, I have some points, but they were asking for way more than what I got."

"No!" her mother cried, flinging her arms around Teb. A moment later, though, she transferred the grip to shaking her by the shoulders. "But you studied! You're so smart! You're my clever little girl! Let me see!"

I saw the concern on Mr Nandakishore's face, Sarika's grasping hands looking for the envelope—and the brown rectangle drop from between Teb and her mother. Mahesh twitched for it but wasn't fast enough—Alana and I dived for it, grabbed it and retreated behind Ally's parents to fight over opening it while Sarika was still shaking Teb down as if some better grades would fall out of her. I let Alana take it before it ripped.

"History... A star. Maths. A. All As or A stars for the three sciences. She's a genius! She had a time turner!"

Mahesh had joined us, his kind eyes all crinkled up and confused. He had grey speckles in his dark hair at his temples; I had spent some of the morning reflecting on how while the four of us girls had begun blossoming into women, it seemed rather at the price of the youth of all our parents. Looking at Mr Nandakishore now, I knew I had no heart to do anything but tell him the truth, because I could tell Teb's actions would send that dotted white right across his head if he knew what she had been doing in her spare time.

"Is it true?" he asked me.

I yanked the certificates from Alana's hands and gave them to him.

"Don't let her know we showed you," I said. "She wants to do this. No one would tell their parents they failed for a joke."

"Not without saying '...Not!' a few seconds later," Alana amended. She was still wiping at smudgy eyeliner on her face, and I knew she wished she'd thought of doing this instead of her undignified freak-out.

"And we all know Teb's not the joking sort," I put in.

Mahesh looked at the certificates for a moment and a smile came to his face. "I knew Teb is a very smart girl," he said. "I suppose I will have to trust her choice not to go to university, if this is why she did this."

"Really?" I couldn't help asking.

"I had wondered if she was changing her mind about something: she's been very quiet on the subject lately. I wish she talked about it with us though."

"She knows what she's doing, I'm sure," Alana said. It always seemed to be Teb's actions that brought us near to breaking the "don't talk about it" rule, but then it was Teb who had the least choice of avoiding what we weren't talking about, with what she had become. Which we also weren't talking about.

Mr Nandakishore nodded and excused himself to go back to looking worried about Teb, whose bones must have rattled loose by then. He left the envelope in my possession and I slipped it into my messenger bag before Alana could tell me what I was meant to do with it.

Instead she said, "Hey, Westcott has called Warren *and* Jess Standerwick—you should have been called already. Go up to Cathy—I have to see how you did. Ally and I were debating if you had psychiced all your exams."

"No, he's holding my results back," I said. "Come on." I beckoned Alana to follow me and set off towards the school. Ally saw and trailed after, and Teb glanced around a moment later, realised she was abandoned and slipped out of her mother's grip to chase us.

I stopped directly in front of Mr Westcott, looking up at him with my best mild little smile as he called the last couple of Williamses. He paused and gave the crowd a moment to think it was over. By that point the people in the playground were ridiculously self-centred in any case, everyone having only been listening for their own name, able to keep track of the alphabet (they should have been after fourteen years of education), and once called they became much more interested in shrieking and posing for photos. But Mr Westcott's throat-clearing was aeroplane engine loud and used as a weapon of discipline in its own right—the sound of it rumbling down the corridors could clear miscreants out of a whole wing of the school. People looked up, expecting a sort of final "thank you, well done, it was a pleasure" etc. from him. Or at least what he could manage in the place of thank yous. Instead we got a little speech in my honour:

"Now... Tanya Pomphrey... Our little troublemaker who should need no introduction to any of you after her, ah, antics at the sixth form prom last month. I promised her I would find one more way to punish her before she left school and was merely accountable to society... All I have left to hold against her before she graduates is this envelope..." He waved a brown square of paper in the air and, despite the steely cool exterior, I felt my heart jump a little. I did care a great deal about getting into university... But he'd already said that he could do nothing actually harmful to me, since we'd already left school at the time of the prom—the teachers there had been overseeing rather than controlling the crowd. However, I had a feeling he was emboldened by the legal greyzone of who we were to each other right now.

"Let's see," he said, a smile stretching wider across his face, "how she balanced all that trouble and study for her exams, shall we?"

There was a worried murmur among the crowd. Warren had beaten his way to the front of it, but stopped short to see me standing next to Teb. I gave him a reassuring thumbs-up. He looked like he needed it more than me.

The rest of the playground full of parents and students were now paying a lot of attention. I had clearly made a great big name for myself over the years—the prom was not the first time in a long, long history of trouble that students would have run home to tell their parents about me. Mixed in with the locking of a French teacher in his supply closet (I had good reasons) and changing all the school clocks and computers minute by minute over a term until the day was ending two hours early (who needs a reason?) there must have been a lengthy string of all the times I'd been singled out for being brilliant. Alana's 'genius' comment stung a little because while Teb was smart and studied hard, I coasted along, just being amazing. I don't know... It never seemed like schoolwork was this big effort that everyone else made it out to be. Surely that qualified me more?

"Of course, I have it here that Miss Pomphrey was predicted nothing less than a straight run of As for all her modules... We'll see how she measured up." He slid the envelope open and shook out the certificates. His eyes ran across them with a poker face before he picked the megaphone up again. "For History, only a B. Most disappointing." His smirk was wider than I'd ever seen it. I could hardly believe how much he was enjoying this—it made me feel sort of dirty, like I was on the wrong side of something perverse.

My heart dropped when I heard the mark: I'd needed just one A to be confident, and it was in History. I would have to ace everything else to get my place at university. And now he had me hanging in front of everyone, making my personal fear public. I hadn't worked as hard at History as I could have. I'd done all the coursework on time, but some sort of empathy for Alana had stopped me being brilliant in the exams. Also she'd sat behind me and it turned out that she snored. "For Biology... An A. A low A—it says here she failed one of her modules..." Well, that just meant I'd done all the better on all the rest. "For Literature another A..." Now he was definitely scowling. Perhaps I had misread his poker face before because actually he always looked grumpy, but that time he'd meant it. "And Philosophy, an A. But that's hardly a real A level."

He thrust the certificates back into the envelope with a great deal of frustration as people applauded me, all their dislike of me washed away by a much greater dislike of Mr Westcott (and probably the creeping feeling that this had not been very legal). I barely heard them. I'd not exactly been looking for a super demanding course. I think this was all part of Mr Westcott's dislike of me, never mind everything else: he tried to make a small club of outstanding students to cajole into going to Oxbridge each year and Teb and I had soundly rejected him in favour of trendy new universities with flexible programmes, and as usual I was seen as the ringleader of that coup. I just hadn't wanted to be in some special club Ally wasn't being invited to.

As he pretty much threw my envelope at me, I finally let out a scream that made Alana's reaction seem muted and composed. "I got in! I got in!" I cried and turned around. Ally was closest, but too tall, so I turned further and spotted Alana. Throwing aside all our past differences, I planted a kiss on her cheek, then grabbed her hands and swung her about in a manic dance, a front-page making jig.

When I let go of Alana she staggered back, letting out a rare laugh. Well, she was in a good mood for once. "I think," she said, straightening her hair a bit, "we really ought to go get ridiculously drunk in celebration."

I couldn't stop laughing. "I'm good with that."

Ridiculous Drunkenness

Here's something you don't know.

None of us were born here in Troutespond (Or, well, Bilsworth General Hospital, but *close enough*).

Ally and Teb both have birthdays in April. They both moved to Troutespond just after they had been born. Danny's parents insisted on helping out with everything, to the point of making sure Hester had their doctor and used their private hospital, whatever she said about wanting a natural homebirth so Ally could start out as hippy-ish as she would eventually grow up to be. Sarika insisted on Teb being born on English soil if they were planning to emigrate there permanently, to ensure Teb would have her British citizenship. As such Sarika had flown out and been living in a council flat in London for six months, separated from her husband while he carried on working for his brother's firm in India to get enough money to pay for their house and all the other immigration stuff. He flew out to join his wife and new daughter a month after Teb had been born and whisked them away to a life of comparable luxury in Troutespond.

Both families felt like they'd ended up in a fairy tale world once the dust settled and they could begin new lives in the town. We always said how it was fate that brought them here at the same time. I also moved here when I was only three. Between playgroups and just everyone knowing everyone through their parents, we were the three kids in the class who didn't speak a word of the other kids' language (literally for Teb).

No wonder Alana fitted in so well.

I met Alana and Teb walking down from their end of the village. The final meeting point was outside Ally's house, but I saw them on the High Street and legged it after them. Of us all, I was sure Alana's Mum didn't care where her daughter went any more, Ally's mum was extremely liberal and probably had embarrassed her by trying to give her more alcohol than she'd ever want, and my dad was resigned to it, leaving Teb's parents as the only ones we actually had to make a point of not telling. But leaving the house with a sanctioned "have fun, girls!" from Hester would sort of devalue the experience, so we weren't going to stop by, no matter how tempting the thought of home-baked celebratory cookies was.

We met with bags of picnic stuff we'd blagged as a cover and booze stolen from all the nooks and crannies our parents hid it. I had a large bottle of rum, and I think Alana had half-emptied her fridge from the looks of her bulging bag. Teb had a modest bottle of vodka and a large bottle of cherryade in a new plastic bag, which made me think she had the confidence to buy alcohol at the One Stop without being asked for identification. Come to think of it, we were all eighteen already. But it was the feel of things that mattered; we'd never been properly drunk together, the lies spread about what 'actually' happened at the prom notwithstanding.

The three of us, having furtively shown each other the alcohol we'd collected, set off on the walk to Ally's. We had met just outside the tiny church, small and squat and made of stones that were last moved in the Dark Ages. Our path took us across the triangular town square between the tall Tudor houses and down an increasingly modern street—Victorian shops in a row, leading to the cluster of "new" sixties and seventies houses Ally's family had holed up in.

As we walked Teb looked at me in a way that seemed almost like the good old suspicion from the time before we stopped talking about it. "You seemed pretty excited to get into university," she said tactfully. Alana was listening a lot more closely suddenly, although she hadn't changed her pace or the casual, gently clinking walk she was using to pretend like there weren't bottles of wine in the carrier bags she was swinging at her sides.

"I'm going to Hogwarts! What did you expect?!"

"It's not Hogwarts," Teb groaned. "Nowhere is Hogwarts. And I saw the pictures—it's a modern building in the middle of a city."

"Let me have this," I begged.

"No. It's just a stupid folklore course which might happen to talk about magic and fairies. That does not mean you're suddenly Harry Potter."

Alana weighed in: "Teb, stop ruining all her hopes and dreams. We don't know how fragile her brain is. Maybe she is literally unable to believe Harry Potter doesn't exist."

"But... Argh, it's so frustrating!"

"Have you ever considered that she's just winding you up?" I'd never expected Alana to take even a tiny step towards my side… It was actually sort of amusing. But she and Teb didn't get along either… Really, I thought, if Ally and Alana hadn't got so close right off the bat, we'd never have kept her in our group. *She* had been quick to point fingers before, but if she hadn't shown up in the first place there would be no need to have a thing not to talk about. Our friendship group never would have begun to fracture in the first place. Talk about keeping the status quo, Alana…

By that point we were close enough to Ally's road that I was keeping an eye out for her. And there she was at the corner of the road, waving to us. We put on a little burst of speed and she walked a few paces forwards. "Hallo!" she called, smiling brightly, looking so excited she was practically hopping as she approached. "Did you confirm your places on the UCAS website?"

"Yes, yes," Alana said. "More importantly: party!" The relief she felt at passing was immense, a bubble all around her. Or maybe it was the absence of the dark cloud she normally carried over her head. Of course she'd been expecting to fail; she had missed months of school then transferred to our sixth form—even picking up new courses like Media because she'd thought it would be easier to make up the work than compressing half a year of maths homework into two months—so hadn't started on the back foot so much as pretty much start all over with only a few months left to do all the work in. And we hadn't helped her keep a lot of time free for study (or painting). The fact she'd scraped by at all showed her determination to get out of town *now*, the same time as us. Maybe the smartest one of the group was the one sitting on two clearly failed classes.

Ally giggled, doubling back the moment we caught up with her, and the four of us set off towards the end of her road.

The dull patch of suburban houses, like a lichen stain on the landscape when viewed from above, quickly ended, and we came to a stile. Normally we'd scramble over it easy as anything, but this time we let Teb clamber over first, holding her bag for her, then handed over all the booze before following her. We *probably* wouldn't have broken it, but as this was our first time we didn't really want to take any risks. I could sense a very high probability that Ally would have smashed something, dripped wine all over herself and we'd have had to turn back for a change of clothes and a shamefaced "We weren't even drinking yet when this happened," to her mum.

After the stile we left the town behind and entered the beginning of a long stretch of woodland; the hills that ran to the edge of the county on this side. It began with a field, sloping steeply up to a patch of trees, then some more grass, then suddenly dense, solid trees as far as the eye could see if all the trees weren't in the way. The path was very familiar, a place we'd trodden so often in our childhood I could run about in the woods in the dark and a blind panic without so much as stumbling over a root. I'd done it before.

"Are we going up to the stone circle?" Alana asked.

"That sounds like a good idea," I said, having honestly not expected her to mention it or to want to go there.

Alana's eyes narrowed, again a tiny dent in her glee as I reminded her of the things unsaid. But it was also a very nice place to have a picnic, and she wasn't going to be able to say "no, let's go sit somewhere else" without bringing up why she didn't want to go there immediately after having suggested it herself. And my feet were already leading the way up the steepest of the woodland paths.

I honestly wasn't plotting anything. Remember that every moment that led us here, it had been *Alana* accidentally putting us there. I think, in all honesty, she was either unconsciously leading us or had been led. Like me, she lay a little closer to the secret paths of fate, was more susceptible to them reaching out and brushing over her than the average person.

It took us a while longer than normal to make our way up the old paths to the stone circle with all the heavy bottles and picnic stuff that we were carrying. It was a great relief to step out from between the gnarled trunks of the old trees that ringed the circle into the warm sunlight. The others were hot and sweating, but I'd paced myself and stepped lightly, drifting along casually, and the walk hadn't been a struggle. What can I say? I'm just better than them.

Ally instantly sat down on the spot, puffing. "I was going to suggest that since we're being rebellious teenagers for once in our lives, maybe we should take up smoking just for this afternoon, you know, to get in the spirit of things, but I think I'd rather not now I know how out of shape I am..." She flopped backwards. "Do not need any more reason to wheeze..."

After an obligatory chuckle, we ignored her comments, because we knew better than to reply and find out whatever other gems she had to offer on the subject. I looked around instead. The inside of the circle wasn't hugely wide—not much bigger than your average living room. There was a massive, sofa-sized rock in the middle that made the altar table. We collapsed onto the smooth carpet of grass around it, putting down the bags with much stretching of white-and-red-striped fingers. A single sapling grew beside the stone, barely older than us, and it provided a little cool spot of patchy shade, the reverse of a tall lamp behind the sofa stone. All we needed was a television mounted on the taller standing stone. Ally dragged herself into the shade, but I was happy to spread myself out in the sun.

Alana and Teb, the more practical-minded in the group, got to work setting up the picnic and pouring drinks. Since it was those two they also bickered about how to do it properly. We weren't exactly worried about being caught drinking in public: Troutespond was hardly a major tourist destination after all. With a single signpost to the stone circle, unless there were some very determined tourists scouring an Ordinance Survey map on a quest to visit every Stone Age monument in the area, we were pretty much guaranteed to be left alone.

"Hey Alana," Ally said. "Remember when you dragged me all the way up here to do Literature homework?" All their conversations made me feel like I was eavesdropping on some private moment. Not that it stopped me from listening. Any new information I could get on Alana was always appreciated. "What a weird day."

"It paid off; that piece was probably the only thing between me and failing."

"Don't be so hard on yourself. You had a rough few months."

"A rough life," snorted the rich girl who'd gone to a posh Catholic school.

Teb scoffed openly, already mixing her drink. She offered a glass to Alana. "Well, let's get on with it, then."

*

We ate lunch, drank too much and let the afternoon pass in an amazing drunken blur.

Teb drank fastest and hardest, and her afternoon culminated in climbing atop the altar stone to sing loudly. Her voice echoed through the trees and, I fancied, right across the hills. She slipped in the middle of her ridiculous dance and landed heavily on her bum. She then spent several minutes lying spread out on the stone giggling and declaring loudly that she'd broken her back and was probably going to die here if we didn't phone the mountain rescue people. Aside from laughing at her we did nothing, and eventually she got bored and slid down from the stone, wobbled to the edge of the circle, proving that she was completely capable of moving her legs if she felt like it. She curled up on a mossy patch beside one of the fallen stones and was asleep fairly soon after that.

"Should we be worried about her?" Ally asked, biting her lip as she looked up from her work on the world's longest daisy chain.

"You already are, so why bother asking?" Alana pointed out. She got rather grumpier when drunk, it seemed. "I always knew Teb would be a lightweight... She's far too uptight normally. Give her half a chance to unwind, and..."

"Or she thinks she's indestructible," I said. "She doesn't realise drinking a whole bottle of vodka will actually make her so drunk."

"She's so skinny now," Ally pointed out. "She mustn't be able to take much of anything. That's why I'm drinking slowly!" She was only on her third half-glass of wine, and aside from some dizziness and a new loud way of talking with far more confidence than normal, she seemed pretty much unaffected. She had a dreamy smile on her face all the time anyway, as well as the tendency to get involved in projects like the giant daisy chain that she was fumbling around with. With her disappointingly responsible attitude towards alcohol, it was between Alana and me who would flake out next.

Alana had drunk heavily, but stopped after a few spills, perhaps realising that if she was working so hard to get the grass drunk she probably needed to cool it a bit. She lay on her side in an arty sort of pose, her head propped up on one hand, watching Ally with so little shame that it was an unblinking, devoted look.

I, on the other hand, had kept the bottle of rum to myself, clinging possessively to it. I'd danced a bit more with Teb while she'd still been upright, and I'm sorry to say that at one point I looked into my mostly-empty bottle and said, "But why's the rum gone?" before draining it.

As the afternoon drifted into evening, still warm, the air a little clearer, I lay back and watched the blue sky above us as it turned darker. It was spinning gently and the noises the leaves made were all rattling together offensively loudly, so the odd gust of wind made an unbearable clamour in my head.

"The trees are shouting to each other," I observed.

"See——" Alana tried to straighten up, failed, and flopped onto her back as well, so that we were lying vaguely top and tail. "See, I had this..." she waved her hand vaguely in the air and waited for the word. A bird swooped overhead, making me jump a moment too late after it had crashed by. "Theory! A theory that *you*," she said it very determinedly, pointing at me with a wobbling arm, "would made more sense when you got drink. Drunk." Her arm hovered in the air for a moment and then slowly retreated back down out of my line of vision.

"I always make sense. You just don't listen properly."

"Well maybe... maybe I thought that if I got drunk as well, then maybe like... I'd unlock a new level of understanding as well... Well, not as well. You know what I mean?"

"No," Ally said.

Alana tried a little harder to pick her words better. "I thought Tanya would make more sense if I was drunk, or she was, or one of us was."

"That's only true if I'm talking gibberish when we're all sober," I said. "I don't. You'd know what I was talking about if you tried hard enough."

"I'd need a lot more to drink before sense I could make of that last sentence, Alana," Ally said, fully enjoying being the most sensible of her friends.

"Shut up and come here," Alana said, grabbing Ally by the arm. It took no effort to pull our gently-swaying friend over, and she landed beside Alana with a surprised shriek. "Hey, just lie still and look at the sky," Alana commanded.

"But my flowers!"

"Everyone else is lying down," Alana snapped. "Stop not fitting in!"

"You are way too unsubtle," I informed her as if Ally weren't there, which, I suppose for all I was concerned, she wasn't, since I wanted to talk to Alana at that second. "Also insulting her probably doesn't help."

Still, despite my accidental sabotage of her plans, Alana got what she wanted. Ally didn't struggle up again, but shifted closer, where Alana initiated a cuddle. They lay back to do some more contemplating of the trees and sky.

My eyes sluggishly tracked back to pointing straight up, and though I made a point of observing I was not the first of us to fall asleep, I have no idea which of the remaining three went next, because after that it was all giant snails and dancing flowers in a light, drunken dream that recast the blades of grass that I lay with my face pressed against as fearsome monsters.

*

It was definitely the sounds of approaching people that woke us up. As I rolled onto my back to look around, all three of my friends were beginning to stir. You couldn't get that much synchronised waking without an alarm clock of some sort.

The perfect hot summer day that had sent us into this afternoon siesta had long worn away, and the sky was a deep blue. The dense trees made it almost midnight-dark down on the ground, all the light sucked away by the leaves and the remains of the day too weak to fill in the gaps. I felt a sudden thrill that we'd fallen asleep in the middle of a fairy space: it was probably one of the easier ways to get snatched by them if they felt capricious.

"It must be ten o'clock," Ally groaned, disentangling herself from Alana.

"I feel sick," Teb announced. Her hair was loose and tangled on the side she'd been sleeping; bits of moss were stuck to the side of her face, dark speckles of muddy brown and green. She rubbed at them and failed to knock most of her new freckles off.

"I'm still drunk," Alana giggled.

There was a crack from down the hill—probably *another* crack, from the first that had woken us.

"Shh!" I hissed. There were men coming. Three, four of them. I couldn't tell exactly—my head was swimming with remains of the rum.

"What's happening?" Ally asked, still blinking and kneading her eyes. She didn't sleep much; it was little wonder she'd fallen asleep so hard when drinking less than us. I'd often wondered why she kept herself awake at night and if she'd be less confused—a primary character attribute—if she got her full eight hours regularly.

"Theoretically just a friendly exchange with some late-evening walkers," I said. "We ought to clear up some of this litter..." I tried not to let them know how much my skin was itching at the thought of these approaching men, though we possibly outnumbered them. I scooped empty bottles into a nearby plastic bag. "We can go hole up at Ally's house until we look less hungover."

"What do you mean theoretically?" Ally asked, always finding something to worry about.

"I... I don't know if these men are good news," I admitted.

I could almost feel the chill run down three spines as they stopped clearing up for a pause. Even Teb looked up from her queasy hunch, her purple eyes wide.

With a flurry of activity we finished hiding the bottles back in their bags and Ally, being the only one tall enough, hauled Teb to her feet. Ally quickly backed off three steps in case she was sick, but Teb had more dignity than to throw up on her friends and held her head high, although her gaze was wandering around the circle with rather less focus.

We drew together like four scared hobbits in the middle of our stone circle, and with that image in my head I almost laughed out loud when a cloaked figure stepped out of the shadows beneath the trees and stopped short at the sight of us.

"Kids!" he said, in much the same way as one uttering a horrible swear word, and he backed off a few steps, the long flapping sleeves of his red cloak waving comically about. But his hood was pulled low, and his face was hidden completely in shade in this low evening light, making him more than a little sinister. I didn't laugh.

"We should go—" Ally started to say, but our bumbling hooded man came back with three friends in that instant. They fanned out, not blocking escape so much as making a point. There were still a dozen ways we could have run between the fallen stones, and two official footpaths they'd left unguarded, including the one we wanted to take to get to Ally's fastest.

In the gloom we stared at each other, the cloaked men shifting uneasily while we were more likely swaying. Teb had drifted next to me and rested a hand on my shoulder. Every few moments she shifted her weight and sometimes leaned heavily on me, other times gripping me hard to stop herself from wobbling too far the other way. Because falling over in front of scary cloaked strangers is just embarrassing.

The cloaked figures looked around. One of them shrugged a bit. I didn't know how they could see out from under those heavy hoods. They had to be baking—it was a warm night and they must have walked at least twenty minutes uphill swathed in thick felt cloth. *Dedicated* men in sinister robes.

"Oh my god," Ally muttered. "Is this actually happening? Tanya?"

I liked how I was the deciding vote for what was real or not.

The men turned their attention back to us, a spokesperson from their side elected as well. "Shoo," he said. "Go drink somewhere else tonight. You shouldn't be here." He sounded patronising, attempting to speak kindly to us but failing to disguise his scorn.

"He's letting us go," Alana hissed. On that prompt we broke formation, grabbed our bags of rubbish and empty bottles and paper plates and legged it down the hill. Alana started laughing even before we had left the ring of stones, and we didn't really get that far; just enough to put the circle out of sight, a few steep meters of the sloping path behind us. We came to a gasping, out-of-breath stop as Alana was laughing too much to keep moving. Teb quite probably went green, though it was getting too dark to tell, and staggered over to a nearby tree, grabbing a lower branch to cling to and throwing up a few times in the undergrowth.

Ally was still blinking, breathing heavily because she was woefully out of shape. As always, I seemed the only one who was unaffected. The short jog had actually cleared my mind a little, and I was suddenly curious about what we'd just seen, cursing myself for being unusually out of sorts and unable to observe more than primary colours and basic shapes with those men.

"Oh my god," Ally repeated, rather more loudly, her trademark bafflement in place. "Did we just get threatened by cultists?"

"Looks like," Alana chortled, still in the grips of her laughing fit.

"But... That sort of thing doesn't happen here! It shouldn't!"

"There's a strong Wiccan presence in the area. You should know that," I said. "If anything, it was a bit low of us to profane their ritual area by drinking there."

"They sounded mean," Ally said. "Anyway, they were wearing red."

"Red can be a good colour as well as an evil one," I reminded her. "It's a *strong* colour, that's all."

"This whole thing is ridiculous," Teb said, rejoining us with a shiny face from a layer of cold sweat. "Let's go to Ally's... I could really do with a mug of tea."

"Hear, hear," Alana said. I felt her hand clamp over my elbow and she set off walking, dragging me along for two steps of backwards stumbling before I managed to turn myself.

"I was coming," I said. She didn't answer. I looked over my shoulder several times until we'd gone around the corner and so far down the hill there was no way of knowing what was going on up at the stone circle.

*

The kettle had just finished boiling as we filed into Ally's sitting room. Hester always knew when tea was needed, even if it meant having the kettle on before the doorbell rang. Teb flopped down on the armchair, drew up her legs and closed her eyes. Alana and I took seats on opposite sofas, she on the long plush one that looked like it belonged in a real living room, me on the creaking basketlike one that still found ways to stab you with loose straw through layers upon layers of throws and cushions. It was nearer the fire, though, and Hester liked to leave the grate burning whatever time of year it was with incense strewn amongst the embers. It was very welcome after sleeping on the cold ground.

Between them, Ally and Alana told the events after we'd woken up like it was a joke. In the bright light of the arts-and-crafts-filled living room, comfortable and familiar as our own homes, if not more, it seemed really hard to take the cultists seriously. It was just another one of those ridiculous things Ally stumbled across, then spent the next week trying to convince us had actually happened, like how she's convinced her neighbour's dog always winks at her. Except this time we had all actually witnessed an Ally Moment first-hand. Maybe she always seemed so confused because after a lifetime of this sort of thing, she had no idea how to judge what was normal anymore. At least I actively sought out strange things, knew how to identify them, was excited to see them and had usually deliberately stumbled on them.

Hester seemed a little more worried. "I don't know these 'cultists' you described… I thought I knew everyone around here."

That caught my attention. Her friends list on Facebook read like a who's who of local and sometimes national paganism. If she wasn't sure what was going on, then at the very least these guys were new, at the worst another threat. "Can you ask your friends if they know who they might be?" I suggested. "Perhaps you just missed a memo?"

Hester frowned. "Maybe. I could check the county website… It has all the ancient ritual sites on it with calendars. You know, to stop double-booking."

"Ooh, yes. It'd be really useful to see the rota," I said.

"Tanya, *no*," Alana said sharply. "No investigating." When I looked at her she had a very familiar expression: suspicion. It made me more than a little nostalgic. How many good times I'd had with Alana as my opposition. It seemed like our normal way of interacting to have her glaring at me, trying to suss out what plans were boiling behind my carefully maintained calm expression.

I fell silent, not willing to push this too hard when I didn't have an agenda outside of curiosity. I mean, when *didn't* that form my main agenda? But it was not powerful enough without a secondary motivation to make it worth getting past Alana's glare.

Fortunately, there was someone else in the room dripping with plots and intrigue. Much revived by the tea and having got some of the alcohol out of her system, Teb leaned forwards with a calculated attack on her lips: "I don't see any harm in knowing. They gave us quite a fright! I say we look them up and send them a strongly worded letter of complaint."

Hester couldn't resist the idea of a stern letter, having written dozens to the local paper about everything from the poor fences around the pond to the drunken yobs from out of town who wrecked the summer fair the year before last.

"I'll go see if anyone's booked for tonight then," she said, a sparkle to her eyes. She stood up with a rustle of her voluminous skirts and skipped across the room to turn on the hulking family computer which lived in the alcove under the stairs.

Alana directed a scowl back and forth between Teb and me, not really convinced that we'd stopped working together. I thought my "Who, me?" face was getting overused to the point of being completely unbelievable. I just smiled quickly at her and looked down at the mug of tea that I was cradling. It was in a massive lumpy pottery mug that Hester had made during a brief stint in a ceramics class; she'd been kicked out for making a female fertility idol of some sort. Let me say this again: Ally's Mum is *awesome*.

The habit of winding up Alana was rather ingrained, though, so after a moment I looked back up, met her scowl and smirked. Some subversive part of me almost wanted her to suspect me. Of course, I had nothing actually planned. I was just waiting until university, when I could research properly. But there was no harm in letting Alana think I was up to something. I was already idly working out a game to play with these cultists, or at least the pretence that I was playing a game with the cultists. Let her chase after me for the rest of the summer; it would give her something to do while we weren't talking about it and keep her sharp. I knew that she had been taking time off her apprenticeship to do her exams.

By that point Hester was navigating her way around a dark green website with pretty gold writing (she'd had to put on a pair of half-moon glasses, which I swear she'd bought just because Dumbledore wore the same). She hummed thoughtfully as she ran an ink-stained finger down a column on the screen. "Well, the Brothers of the Old Moon have the circle like they do every twenty-eight days, but they're just some accountants from Waitington. I've never known them to dress up in red... Or be less than perfectly amiable to anyone they meet. They're wonderfully polite at the solstice festival."

"You really know all of them, don't you?" Ally asked, still coming to grips with just how deeply involved her mother was. She leaned over to get a better look, but Hester closed the window.

"Not all of them by a long shot, but I have my friends." She smiled mysteriously. "Does anyone want more tea?"

I curled up under one of the throws on my sofa, settling down with a crunch from the ageing wickerwork. I let their babble of conversation wash over me and pretended to be asleep as they talked about universities and grades. They brought Mr Westcott up again, thoroughly slagging him off on my behalf, before moving into more nostalgic discussion of our teachers and classes, other great stories that we had to tell. Alana fell quiet too; a new student to the school, she'd only been our friend for five months or so. I wondered if she was sleeping or pretending to, but to open my eyes would be to lose my game, so I kept them closed and finally began to drift as my brain went onto standby from lack of use. I stayed curled up on the sofa until morning.

Tourist Hot Spot

Here's something you don't know.

Teb always wears purple. You've probably picked up by now that it's her favourite colour. I'm guessing Alana's favourite colour isn't red, but Ally's is probably green based on the latest notebook she bought, and I'm rather partial to yellows and golds. I've never changed, but Ally liked every colour at one time or another, defining her mood and personality by which one she favoured (she will actually turn violent, a rare thing for her, if you bring up her pink phase, though the walls of her room still bear its scars). When we were about six or so she decided we all had to have a favourite colour. I dibsed yellow right away, especially since I wore this cute yellow dress with big pink pockets almost every other day if in my various antics I hadn't stained it to the point of an overnight soak. Ally decided she would have blue, because she didn't like red for some reason at that time. Then she made the mistake of telling Teb, "You've got to be red now, because we've picked the other two colours."

Teb instantly went into a massive rant about how there were more than three colours and we were all morons and if we ever wanted to be artists no one would buy our paintings if we only used red, yellow and blue (probably flying in the face of the trends of modern art, really) and so on and so on. It was a massive falling out (for six year olds) and Ally cried and Teb sulked and the teacher split us up for the morning. We had art after lunch, and we had those big blocks of watercolour paint, like massive pastilles. They came in weak orangey-red, a sort of grungy yellow, a really deep pink, pale and dark blue, dark green, black and a horribly paint-speckled white that no one ever used because you might as well have just rubbed your painting in a puddle on the ground. It wasn't like we ever painted on anything other than white paper anyway.

"Okay, which one of *these* colours are you?" Ally pressed, determined that we'd all have a colour. She was probably going to make us hats or something.

"These colours are *horrible!*" Teb yelled, getting us shushed again. She got a new palette and silently spent several minutes mixing and mixing and mixing paints, finally coming up with a massive puddle of an admittedly still rather horrible shade of purple. "See, I made my own colour!" she said, proceeding to paint several sheets of paper just whole blocks of purple. Since then she gradually gained more and more purple clothing until there was pretty much nothing she owned that doesn't have a bit of purple somewhere. I often wonder if she still feels like she's proving a point to Ally when she wears it, especially since after that fight she was the only one to actually end up colour-coding herself.

*

It took most of a day to bear facing each other again. When we finally crawled from our holes, the result was rather pathetic. Huddled under a vast sun umbrella on one of the outdoor tables of a café in the high street, I was still the only one with any degree of energy.

Teb was wearing sunglasses despite having bagged a chair on the shady side of the table. They hid half her face, as vast as the rings around owl's eyes.

Despite the hot summery day, Ally was wearing the Piper's coat again, a habit we'd almost made her kick when the first real heatwave struck and she'd passed out on the bus. She huddled under it, pouting dismally. The mostly black side was in the shade, the white side in the sun, glaring painfully bright.

Alana was dressed down, wearing a t-shirt and shorts, her hair still damp from the shower, hanging limply around her ears and beginning to curl at the back. The black dye she'd put in it at the prom had begun to wash out, leaving patches of speckled reddish-brown from her previous bleachings showing through like dappled sunlight falling on her through trees. Her deliberately scruffy fashion sense this time just looked scruffy.

"I don't get why people drink," Ally said, sipping her banana smoothie and looking at the world with accusing eyes.

"You weren't even that drunk," Teb pointed out. I got a hint of embarrassment in her voice for how drunk she'd got. None of us had made a joke about it yet, but getting to the point of standing up and singing has to be a memory to cringe about. If you can even remember doing it.

Sitting next to each other at the little round table, Ally and Alana exchanged a look which I easily understood to mean that after Teb and I had fallen asleep they'd stayed awake, probably drunk a lot more and definitely talked some.

Funny that they didn't seem to have moved from that hug the whole time I was asleep, because they had definitely had to untangle from each other when the cultists came.

I left them to their private moment and scanned the high street, because only Teb's insensitive comments could rescue us from that awkwardness. Today was about as crowded as Troutespond ever got. As much as we felt like the middle of nowhere, it was more like we were on the way to the middle of nowhere; the motorway scythed through the valley right next to our town, and the train line to Severstrong Abbey had once had a station less than a mile out from the village. People making the same journey by car on the old main road still got to drive right through the middle of the town. A slow line of cars crawled sporadically past, and the street was wide enough to admit the occasional tractor too. Tourists on foot numbered at least half a dozen: I'd been tracking one family in and out of shops and their pauses for ice cream. They had stood for a long moment looking dismally at the church, the little boy wailing and tugging on his dad's arm. In the end the mother popped in, but was back out again moments later, bored and unimpressed with our almost thousand year old walls.

One of the other men on the street with a camera was local; he'd been at the results day and we had him to thank for why we'd dragged ourselves out to face each other. The newspaper had arrived this morning and we had a copy on the table, open on the pages with all the photos of results day. The largest photo by far, taking up the middle of the spread, was Alana and I in our manic gleeful dance. I was going to have to buy my own copy to frame it. It was a really nice photo, and Teb and Ally were grinning in the background.

If we wanted to make a habit of showing up in the middle pages of the newspaper maybe there was going to be a feature about the sunny weather next week we could slip into if we played our cards right. Just like how the A Levels sold on the pretty girls bouncing up and down outside schools, a sunny day feature was never complete without those same girls enjoying the sun in some way.

I stretched out a little, showing off my tanned arms and legs, brushing the ends of my long blonde pigtails back. I glanced around. The photographer was taking a photo of a cat. I slumped down in my seat, pushing it back out into the middle of pavement with the strength of my disappointment.

"What are you doing?" Teb asked, I think looking at me incredulously, although her massive sunglasses obscured a great deal of her face.

"Nothing," I sighed, stretching for my drink again.

"Excuse me," a warm American voice said, blocked in his touristing activities by my chair.

"Sorry," I said, making a series of little hops to drag it back into line with the others. I flopped forwards over the table.

He kept hovering by us, though.

I noted, out of the corner of my eye, Alana leaning forward and self-consciously closing the newspaper.

"Do you girls know where the stone circle is?"

"The stone circle?" Ally repeated dumbly, looking around at the rest of us with a hugely significant stare, like, *it's happening all over again.* Trust her to be the first to break the "we're really not friggin' talking about it, okay?" rule. Alana had implemented it for the sake of *her* sanity.

As we all sat around not knowing what to do, I realised a rather awkward silence had sprung up. The man was about to back away, thinking we didn't speak English or were too stupid to tell him the way. I had to act fast—purely out of politeness. "Ooh, yes! It's up there!" I pointed over the roofs of the small collection of houses to the east that comprised Ally's neighbourhood. The hills rose up pretty sharply over them, a line of fields on the lower slopes to the west, but solid tree-cover right to the top after that. "There's a footpath you can follow all the way up if you walk out of town that way and keep your eyes out for the sign, or if you go up that road there, there's a gate you climb over, and—"

"Tanya, you can stop being helpful now," Teb said, putting a hand on my arm. "We're not sending this man out to be eaten by mountain lions."

I looked around. He was a presumably African-American gentleman, to guess his ethnicity from a first glance and accent. Though he was a little stocky, he wasn't carrying excess weight and he defied my mental image from before I turned by not being dressed in tourist fare—I'd had him in cargo shorts and big trainers, a t-shirt with his hometown's name on it, the hat his wife never let him wear around their friends. Instead he was wearing smart beige slacks, a short-sleeved button-up shirt with a crisp collar and a rather nice pair of sunglasses. Altogether more hip and hit the gym kind of dad bod and style. Wealth clung to him in a way his mostly plain style couldn't hide.

"Are you a reporter?" I asked, noting the camera hanging at his side, chunky and black with a long lens.

He laughed. "Not quite. An amateur photographer. I do love the English countryside. I'm thinking of setting something here. I'm a producer from a studio out in sunny California. You might have heard of—"

"Are you making a film here?" Teb blurted at once, and I think Hollywood actually might have temporarily blinded her to the oddness of yet another stranger with an interest in the same place. Never mind all the other issues in her life. You could be a film star and mysteriously tied to your home village at the same time, right? As long as the ritual never got in the way of your filming schedule...

Ally was still on oversuspicious mode, perhaps to compensate for Teb's lapse. "Why are you so curious about it?" she asked. "It's not exactly Stonehenge. You want to film old stuff that Americans recognise, you go to the famous places."

"I'm scouting out some lesser-known places, getting a feel for the spirit of the unknown. Off the edge of the map and all that," he said with a winning smile.

I looked around for a missing opinion from Ally's suspicion and Teb's starry eyes. Alana had gone paler than even the pallor of her hangover, sinking down so hard in her chair it was almost feasible that she had been forgotten out of choice. Maybe the man hadn't even spotted her.

I cleared my throat. "Of course you should probably get going now while the light's still good," I said.

He nodded. "Listen, girls, if you know your way around the countryside as well as you seem to, perhaps if you have anything good to show me, drop me a line. I'd love an insider's view of this pretty little town. My name's Mr Lane..." He produced a business card from his pocket and held it out to Ally, but Teb snatched it first.

"Thank you, Mr Lane," she said, still sparkling at him with a kind of enthusiasm I rarely saw from her. "I'm Teb Nandi, by the way."

"Indeed, and you are?"

"Ally," she replied grumpily, refusing to give in an inch further by providing him with a full name. Wise girl.

He turned his gaze to me and didn't even have to ask: "Tanya Pomphrey. I know a lot about the local area! I did my history project on all sorts of things around here." Hrm. I maybe was a little more susceptible to his easy smile than I'd anticipated.

He nodded. I gave him a look which he was already pointing my way: a sort of, *this isn't the last time we'll talk* look. Sometimes you just *know* the people you will encounter again, and he clearly had the same sense of frisson about me.

"Well, have a good afternoon, girls," he said, and with a moment to hoik his camera securely back up his shoulder, he turned and set off in the direction I'd pointed him.

Ally turned boggling eyes around the table: I could see Alana visibly drawing herself back into the scene. "Oh my *god*," Ally said. "Did you... Do you think he was..."

"Calm *down*," Alana said. "It's not like no one ever goes there except for... *purposes*. Think of all the dog walkers we've bumped into on our trips there. Whatever he says, we're far from off the edge of the map: we're right off the motorway and he's not the first tourist we've seen today. I think maybe we should go home now."

Teb was scowling. The business card had mysteriously vanished from sight. "We should have gone with him. Maybe if we showed him around he might offer us a part."

"I doubt anyone will make a film here," I said.

"That's enough!" Alana snapped, making us all jump. She violently sucked up the last of her drink and put the glass down heavily. "I'm going home now."

"Yeah, me too," Ally said, looking weirdly unperturbed by Alana's shouting. She gathered herself together and stood up, glancing down the road again. "I'd better get moving. Things to do..." She waved vaguely and headed off towards one of the alleyways that led back in the direction of her house.

Teb glanced around the table. "Yeah, me too." She scooted back her chair and headed off down the road in the opposite direction to Ally, cutting short Alana's attempt to leave: she had no desire to talk with Teb, who lived in the same corner of town as her, and had to give her at least a minute so it wouldn't be weird to trail three steps behind her without exchanging a word.

With Ally and Teb gone, it struck us at the same time that we were spending unaccustomed time alone together. I finished the last of my lemonade with slurpy straw noises while Alana stood awkwardly by the table, and with little dialogue but silent agreement that the party was over we picked up our bags and set off home. Since we lived at the same end of town at least, there was some more of the unintentional following going on, but we at least were less awkward than Alana and Teb alone together.

I stopped by the little newsagents tucked into a corner where it wouldn't offend anyone by not looking like it fell out of the eighteenth century, and I picked up my own copy of the local paper.

Alana was waiting outside when I came out, tucking the newspaper into my bag. I was half-surprised she'd waited for me when I'd already said "Okay, see you tomorrow probably!" and dived off the street with a wave over my shoulder like that was our goodbye. She didn't normally need anything more formal than that.

"Are we walking home together?" I asked brightly.

She frowned, looked back up the street towards the hills, then shook her head. "Bye," she said, crossing the road towards home.

I went my way, but before I passed the church I also looked up towards the stone circle. Alana was *extremely* troubled by this happening. And wasn't going to talk about it, however much she had wanted to and maybe had even tried to before what she took for common sense had stopped her. She had made the rules, and she was going to have to be the one to break them first.

*

I waited about two hours, spent quietly marinating chicken and chopping onions. I could hear Daddy in his office, talking on the phone and being lawyer-y. He worked from home quite often: more when he was worried about me, I felt.

When dinner was slow-cooking, I headed upstairs and took out my phone. I felt the time was about right, so I dialled Ally's number.

"Guardian newspaper, how can I help?" Hester sang down the phone.

"Is Ally back yet?"

"Hi Tanya! No, she's still out... Oh! I can hear her key in the door. I'll go put the kettle on..." I heard a click as the phone was placed down: I had a weird sideways feeling, like I too was lying on the hall table, looking in a fixed camera angle at the wall. I heard shuffling steps and Ally calling. "Hey Mum, I'm back!"

"Hi Ally! Do you want tea?"

"Always!"

"What have you been up to?" Hester's voice was further off, accompanied by clinking kitchen sounds and the kettle becoming more audible.

"Not much… Mum, the phone's off the hook. Did you take it down because you thought the government was trying to call you again?"

"Oh, you'd better check the line in case they're listening! I'm trying to catch them at it…"

I heard rustling noises and then the loud rattle as Ally picked up the phone.

"WAIT, don't hang up!" I yelled.

There was a cry of alarm and a huge clatter as the phone fell to the table again. A second later it was picked up again. "Hello?"

"Jesus, you're gullible sometimes," I complained.

"Tanya!" Ally sounded way too relieved.

"Yes, silly. It's me. So what happened up at the stone circle?"

There was a second fumbled phone noise, and I winced. My head had cleared up but loud bangs right in your ear are never pleasant. "How did you *know?*"

"I don't need to be psychic to tell when you're desperate to investigate. Alana tailed me home so I had no chance to go, *and* I needed to make dinner anyway, *and* I knew you were about to go up there yourself. I didn't want to sneak after *you* and frighten you because you'd probably scream and let Mr Lane know that you were sneaking after *him.*"

Ally said nothing for a moment, but then I heard a mumbled thank you and the sound of tea being put on a coaster: okay, she wasn't doing a deliberate dramatic silence, which was well out of her normal character anyway.

"Fine. I went up there. *Please* don't tell Alana."

"Pfft. What did you see?" I demanded.

"Well I think he went to his car first: I lost him and then he kind of came up behind me. I mean, he didn't see me, I heard him coming so I slipped off the path about the storm drain area and waited for him to go on up, then I carried on. He really looked like he knew where he was going. He had all sorts of measuring implements with him: those wheels that click every meter and have the measuring tape in them or something, and there were poles ending in spikes he put in the ground which measured something else. He paced all around the stone circle making notes and measuring stuff, and he took a ton of photos. I hid behind one of the trees at the edge."

"Hope your elbow doesn't show up in any of his shots."

"Oh no—I didn't think —"

"Anyway, I think we can agree that this is so freakin' suspicious, right?!" I pushed, hoping she'd crack and start spewing all her theories at me. She could talk through so many variables, she'd have to find the right answer just by sheer attrition.

"It sounds like someone trying to work out if he can fit a full film crew and cameras in there and still get a wide-angle shot of a heroine lying dramatically on the stone table."

"You believe him then?"

"I dunno. It sounded so sketchy when he approached us, but I didn't see him do anything weird. No mumbo, no jumbo."

"Are you sure?"

"Tanya, I pride myself on stupidly blundering into weird situations. I'm getting to be an expert. There was nothing odd about it."

I shook my head. I'd felt something… Maybe just the slightest tingling in my thumbs, but her frantic attempts at communication when he'd approached us had been saying everything going through my head too, and I didn't want to let it drop as easily as she was suggesting. "So nothing strange is happening after all," I said, very clearly and firmly.

"Exactly!" There was a pause. I'd heard the waver in her voice, and I let it come out, waiting for her to speak instead of suggesting anything myself. She started again, laughing uncertainly. "I mean, come on, how odd is it that someone will come here asking about it so soon after… Oh!" I could hear the hollow slap as she plastered a hand over her mouth.

"Ally. If you want to talk about it, talk about it. Come on, if something's up it's not *my* fault. Alana just didn't want me…"

"No. We shouldn't talk about it."

A moment later the line went dead.

I just hoped she wouldn't report my behaviour to Alana.

I opened my laptop and found the personal website for the Brothers of the Old Moon, where they unthinkingly had a public forum: after all, whatever they did, they probably assumed no one would care enough to look except for their own members. I found a comment thread where they were complaining grievously about being chased out of their own ritual site the night before. They didn't comment on the details: it seemed they had all been there and weren't recapping events for anyone, but there were some follow-up complaints, such as members discussing the identity of the group who had been hogging the stone circle with wild guesses and references to old grudges and a slightly off-topic debate about regulation and communication between the groups. I gave up by the time they got to infighting, it being clear they hadn't the faintest idea who the red-cloaked cultists who'd driven them off were, and closed the browser.

I went downstairs to make dinner.

When I had two plates of delicious-smelling lemon chicken dished out of the slow cooker, a neat pile of steamed beans and broccoli next to the dripping wings, I called my dad out of his office. He sat down and twitched his moustache in amusement that I'd found another dish that would be irritating to eat with the thick line of hair he grew above his lips, but just like the other stuff me and my friends weren't talking about, he could make no comment or he would have to admit defeat and shave it off.

"Daddy," I started once he had taken some of the microwaved wild rice I'd cheated with (it *looked* fancy, so what did it matter it cost a pound and could be heated up in two minutes flat? We were just getting it covered in lemon sauce anyway) and made a few comments on how nice everything was.

"Yes, pumpkin?" he said, wincing. He spat out a lemon seed. Oops. The key to my cooking may be *enthusiasm* rather than *skill*.

"You're pretty much the bestest solicitor lawyer thing in town, right?"

"That depends. I think I'm the only one who *lives* here, but the guys at the office are probably..."

"Yes, okay, but... Say someone was going to film something here?"

"Like the news crews we saw at results day?"

"No, like a TV series or film or something. They have to get permission to film, don't they?" I pulled a very long blonde hair out of my sauce.

"Yes. Are you going to make another film? I did enjoy the last one... *Inspired*. I wouldn't worry about the paperwork though... Just ask nicely if you're going on someone's property."

"No, there was a man we saw in town. He said he was from Hollywood and was going to make a film here. Has anyone applied to do that?"

"Not that I know of. Of course a lot of the paperwork they have is drawn up by their own lawyers."

"No paper trail?"

He gave me this very, very long look which contained all the weariness of knowing me on a soul-deep level in some very specific ways. Mostly weighing up how much trouble I'd get in trying to work things out for myself versus him just lending his advice and hoping it would be enough to calm me down and leave other less willing public servants alone. "If he was only scouting I would think there would be no paper trail at all: you don't have to ask permission to look at things, except for private property. I could ask..." He looked thoughtfully out of the window and pushed a few beans which appeared to still be half-frozen onto his place mat and under his plate. I pretended not to see.

"Well, I suppose if he's still just scouting things out he might not have made any formal arrangements yet. He's called Mr Lane, if you want to know."

"This is how you tell me to go look him up for you, isn't it, sweetie?"

"Yep!" I said cheerfully. "Thank you Daddy!"

We finished off our chicken pretty quickly, and I stood up to clear the plates. "Do you want pudding? I made jelly!"

He considered it for long enough to be polite and said, "No thanks, honey. I'll just make a coffee..."

Old Roads

Here's something you don't know.

I'm not always just moderately good at spotting cultists from a dozen feet away or feeling how my friends are doing without asking them. I sort of take it for granted I can tell how many fingers you're holding up without looking (go on), but occasionally, just occasionally, I can see so much more than that. I think it's been a lifelong gift: I've always had vivid and surprisingly true dreams ("imagination", as the child psychiatrist had called it), but just rarely the odd flash comes to me whenever it feels like it.

The first time *that* happened was when we were eight and I collapsed in Maths because I thought I'd been struck by lightning, which the rest of the class found hilarious. In my head I could see the sky opening up, the black clouds parting with a white glow, then the sudden sharp line down to the ground via the church, fast even in this weird slow motion in my head. I could see sparks coursing down the side of the steeple, along the copper strip of the lightning rod, deep into the ground, as rain ran in a river down the High Street. What was weirder was feeling it as if I *was* the church, like I could feel it searing through me.

When I managed to shake myself back to sensibility after all the screaming and writhing on the floor, I was sitting in the nurse's office and it was still sunny. I pretended that I'd been up all night reading and they sent me home to sleep it off, with one of the hundreds of notes to my father asking him to take better notice of what I was getting up to and to moderate me a bit if he possibly could, please?

Later that day it poured. I slipped out of the house as it began thundering and stood at a safe distance away in the awning of a shop so I could get a close-up sight of a lightning strike. I hadn't seen it wrong, and from then on I never doubted that the odd images in my head would eventually turn up in one way or another. Many I'm still waiting on.

(It was four, right?)

(I'm always right.)

*

The evening was warm and too lovely to waste sitting inside. It would be light for a couple more hours, I knew, and once I'd done the dishes I decided I just had to go out for a walk. I supposed this was the first real day of my summer holiday, the time between getting into university and actually going. A time where the stress of waiting for the news was over, where I had no summer homework, no reading lists or anything to do for the first time since pretty much primary school. Even back then they gave us "fun" workbooks to do if we felt like it, and I did because I am geeky about school sometimes. But not right then.

I was going to enjoy this freedom.

As a sign of good faith to Alana, I turned right out of my front door and went in a Bilsworth-ish direction down the main road for a little while. About as far from the stone circle as you could possibly go, right? It was still hot, the sun not even really getting to the point where you'd say it was evening yet, let alone sunset. The air was clearer in the village, but dusty and hard to breathe at the side of the road. It wasn't exactly busy, but tractors were the most common vehicle to pass and at the moment they were shifting a lot of dirt and grain. I was relieved to cut off the road and onto a footpath lined with leafy trees.

It was the path that went up to the local station. "What local station?" I hear you ask. Well indeed. It was completely disused to the point of massive trees growing on it. I remembered back in May how Teb had spent quite some time here. Alana had made it sort of her project to get her back to normal, so they had come here to talk stuff out. It felt sort of like intruding on Teb's spot when I clambered over the broken down fence which was meant to keep curious teenagers away. For a minute I wavered about exploring, but it just felt psychically complicated in a way I didn't want to deal with.

Instead I backtracked to the footbridge and made my way along the path. It was leading me right back to the fields above Teb and Alana's neighbourhood, though, having gone in a massive loop, so I took the first turning to the left and went up into the hills. These lay way well out of the way of our past adventures. There was nothing here that could possibly trigger thoughts that Alana wouldn't want me to be thinking. These hills rolled the length of Ransley Valley. The river ran between them in the middle of the valley, lost in the thickly-wooded, rolling hills. Here, there were trees so formidable and ancient I felt like the forests were untouched since ever.

Maybe I had once got that information from the noticeboard beside the bench I stopped at to down a quarter of my large bottle of water in one go. I read a little more about the Bronze Age hill fort at Ransley and the old road that ran across the top of the hills from that ancient settlement to the stone circle above Troutespond, the barrows we had by the river. I knew most of it all anyway, and I think I may have even come to this very spot some other time. But one detail struck me this time:

"The old road," it carried on, *"now Hill Road, still winds across the hills above the Valley as it has always done, as a part of the B road to Waitington. Though now a modern road, the edge is still lined with marker stones which have been dated somewhere between the Stone Age and the early Bronze Age. Further down towards Severstrong Abbey, an old, possibly Roman, road joins..."*

With no other plan, I consulted the map and decided that I would go have a look at these apparent stones that were the same age as our stone circle, seeing as I was something of a local history nerd and the thought of some small fact escaping me this long actually had me quite miffed. I wanted to see some of these stones, touch one, try to imagine the old road as it had once been and generally see if the stones here had escaped the fate of the mostly tumbled stones at the circle. It would be interesting, I thought, to find the place where the modern road curved up north to Waitington, but to keep walking straight, to try and imagine the rest of the road, the final part that would take me through the woods to the stone circle. Maybe some old rocks remained lining that final part.

Had anyone bothered to look before? I hadn't yet published an article in an archaeology magazine, despite my pretensions towards being some sort of amazing teenage polymath. Frankly, I was behind in a dozen of my chosen fields; with my eighteenth birthday past, any claims of being a child prodigy had been wrenched from me. There were kids half my age who already had degrees.

I put my water bottle back into my bag and stood up again.

"Right then," I said, a smile stretched across my face.

*

The footpaths took me up to the old hill road, where the sound of traffic broke in through the stillness of the trees and modern metal fences drew into sight, putting a line between my wilderness and the road.

This one was busier than the valley road that included, in part, our high street, because it linked to Waitington, the main town in the county. Until the motorway was built it had been traffic getting lost from the north of us rather than the south that had brought the largest number of confused motorists to our village. The new motorway, on its journey to link London and the North via a surprisingly convoluted route, had done nothing to stop local traffic following the only previous road out of here (someone hadn't thought about what Waitingshire would do in the case of a zombie attack). Ransley, not the largest but definitely the most interesting place on the map, was definitely better reached this way than the roundabout route of following the river past Troutespond, Bilsworth and a host of other small map dots on the way.

I was sure I was getting plenty of raised eyebrows from motorists every time I bent over to examine a stone, but I was in my element and no odd looks had stopped me before. The stones did indeed pop up as promised, squatting like short, fat trolls every hundred yards or so a few feet in from the road. They were about to my waist, the same mossy grey as the stones in the standing circle. One on its own might not make you think it was deliberate, but they were so accurately spaced and similarly sized that after three there was no doubt they had been intentionally placed. I followed along the treelined road for some time until it swung away to my left, and I had no choice but to climb over a fence and navigate by a vague remembrance of the map and my own sense of personal location.

The stone circle squatted at the top of one of the taller hills and since I wasn't too far from it I figured I'd be going uphill soon. And yes, my feet were being drawn with such a sense of inevitability I wasn't going to be able to turn around if I wanted to.

With those thoughts in mind, I began beating my way through the undergrowth. I was relying on two things, really, to ensure that the stones weren't just going to end up buried and make this fruitless: that until a lot more recently, say later than the seventeenth century, for example, people still used this road to get to Troutespond, before the new turning which had been cut and allowed Bilsworth to begin to appear, and that since then no one had tried to move the stones, say to put in another footpath. There must have been someone with chronic footpath syndrome in the local council because I did stumble across one within a minute—in fact crossroads. But at the signpost's foot was another squat stone. I smiled to myself. They were still used to mark the way, even today.

I carried on, following the branch of the footpath that went in the right general direction, and spotted one of the stones off in the undergrowth not long after. There were no fences, but there was a good solid mass of stinging nettles and brambles growing along the edge of the road. I've often wondered if someone came up with the idea of encouraging them to grow instead of spending money on barriers. Well, it couldn't be helped. I rarely covered my legs up, and today was no exception. On the other hand I wasn't squeamish about getting cut up and wandering around with odd rashes on my calves, so I took a sharp turn and plunged through the undergrowth.

I got up to the old stone and put a hand on its rough, mossy surface, either by fortuitous inspiration or just to say hello.

That's when everything spun around me and I found myself slumped over the stone, ears whining with white noise, head pounding, my heart likewise. I could taste fire in my mouth, more than just because I'd thrown up on a perfectly innocent patch of nettles who had been minding their own business and not stinging me. My mind was filled with scratchy dark thoughts of things I didn't dare mention to myself. I thought I could see eyes like hot coals looking at me from the undergrowth; for a moment I was convinced something was scuttling at great speed between the trees, a long tail swishing behind it...

"Tanya?"

I jumped violently as the rest of the images disappeared from my head. The whole forest seemed to shift. I felt like until a second before I had been looking at an entirely different patch of trees. As my eyes refocussed I saw a small figure approaching me from the undergrowth. Teb's friend, Jeremy. He had a huge bundle of dry bracken and dead nettles in his arms, though he set it down when he stopped a few feet away. "Are you okay, Tanya?"

"How do you know my name?" I demanded.

He flung up his hands, "I was at the prom! Teb named you by first name only. I wasn't... I don't..."

I relaxed. "Sorry. You startled me. I didn't think you would know us. I didn't think you *could* name us."

He shrugged. "Things have been different for me lately. I'm less bound by the old rules, if it serves Teb better not to be." He certainly looked more normal: he was wearing jeans and a baggy branded t-shirt, a purple cap and big trainers, but the whole look made sense and he seemed somehow bigger, fitting the clothes well.

"Were you following me?" I asked, trying to sound more conversational. I could hear my voice cracking, found my water and took a tentative sip. I felt better all over as it rolled down my throat.

"No! No no no... I was in the woods, collecting for a party." He gestured to the pile of dry brown plants he'd dropped at his feet. "I heard one of the big folk crashing through the woods, but when I came over to see, I recognised you! I saw..."

"You saw what?"

He shrugged. "Not what you saw, but I saw you seeing it. Tanya... You have a strange gift. I think... I think you're looking at something too big for you. The woods are less safe than they were. Things have changed here. Our protection feels weaker. You should not be poking at it."

"I'm not," I protested.

He gave me a long, searching look. I began to feel distinctly uncomfortable with his beady black eyes fixed on me. "Well, when you start poking at it, please... Can you leave Teb out of it?"

"What? I'm not going to! I have no idea what I even saw, and I'm not allowed to investigate it anyway. I shouldn't even be talking to you."

He pushed on, his voice becoming a series of distressed squeaks: "When you start looking and finding trouble, Teb should not go near it. As her friend, I'm asking you. Not just as her servant. Not as her champion. She is more fragile than you think. I don't want the forces you're looking at to become interested in her. If you care for her, you will leave her out of this. They can't know about her!"

"Jeremy!" I yelled. "Calm down."

He reacted by becoming even more panicked. "I shouldn't have talked to you! I can't!" He grabbed the huge bundle of dead plants and in a second he had fled into the undergrowth in the way only the fey can disappear completely.

The forest returned to quiet rustling and occasional chirps.

"I'm fine," I said out loud. "I didn't see anything. I'm still hungover and just had a dizzy moment." I was quite relieved to hear my voice was now completely normal and my own. "I really shouldn't have walked six miles in this condition. That's all." I had another good drink of water and then, feeling like my head had cleared a bit, walked back to the path, took the fastest, safest and most familiar route home and went to lie down for a bit.

Life Ban

Here's something you don't know.

You'd think Teb would be the sensible one, right? Because she seems all levelheaded and snarky. What you have got to understand about her is that she will follow me literally anywhere—on my maddest scheme—as long as there's the potential for something amusing to happen. She will hold open the hole in a fence for me to climb under, or give me a leg up over a wall. She'll hold the bag with the spare cans of spray paint or stand watch at the corner. She's totally bloody fearless, because even if she is terrified of being labelled a troublemaker, she's still got a criminal mind to match my own (I swear) and all it's tuned to do is look good, get A grades and then turn on the "but I would never do that! I'm going to be a doctor one day! You must have confused me with someone else! Is it because I'm Indian? Are you being racist? I bet you took one look at me and thought, 'oh look at that Paki, breaking and entering'. Well I'll have you know…" and so on. I've spent three separate occasions behind bars and Teb was there each time standing outside the police station waiting for her dad to come pick her up, with a great big smile on her face while I was waiting for mine to come collect me from custody and watch me get another caution.

I tend to get caught red-handed more often, because even when you're seeing someone coming it doesn't do much good when you're cornered in a room holding two halves of a broken mammoth tusk or something, and Teb's already backed off into the other room.

Nah, it's Ally who takes one look at a "DO NOT WALK ON THE GRASS" sign that she approached from the wrong side and runs away whimpering in fear that the Park Police will get her. I can't say she's the voice of reason, but if suggesting something makes her whimper, I'm probably on the wrong track. There are many cases in my life when I could probably have heeded her whine of horror at the thought of getting in trouble, but then she makes the same noise when I suggest a way to get two ice cream scoops for the price of one with just a bit of threatening a lawsuit on the way. "But isn't that perverting the court of justice?" she'd complain, and at that point I figure it's time to talk to Teb.

*

Now, every good superhero needs a supervillain to counter them, or there'd be no point being a hero. If I was anything it was probably not a superhero, but I still had a shadowy organisation that I liked to butt heads with.

Already on famously bad terms with the Bilsworth Museum after a certain incident on a school trip, I'd later accumulated a life ban for a piece of investigative journalism that I'd conducted on their premises after dark one day. But there were things that I had to know, and with no place to start but a strong hunch about who was making sure there was nowhere to start, I had no choice but to set out on an extracurricular field trip.

I phoned Teb first thing the next morning. "Hey, Tebster! Wanna come to the museum with me?"

"You remember the mammoth?" she asked.

"Yeah, but I can probably sneak in. I mean it is still a local museum, not a supervillain's lair. I think."

"I can't afford getting in trouble there with you."

"You remember we've graduated school and are responsible adults now? We're not going on a school trip and no one will give you a detention."

"I just mean I don't want my face showing up on security footage, as they drag the both of us out by the scruffs of our necks. Criminal records exist too, you know."

"I don't think the dear old ladies who sit on wobbly chairs in the corner knitting are quite burly enough to heave us out. They mostly just clear their throat at you."

"And call the police if you start *breaking the exhibits*."

"I won't, I swear."

"I'm sorry, Tanya. I don't want to be a part of your latest scheme. Alana said we weren't supposed to do anything else weird."

"You're not going to *report* me, are you?"

"Hell no; we both know Alana was trying to punish you and me specifically. I remember what you said about us being on a team together. I do... But I don't want to start anything up."

"Yeah, yeah, you have a lot of guilt and lingering desire to run off and never come back. I get it. But all I want is a friend to..." I realised I was talking to the dial tone. Okay, I'd known that saying that would annoy her, but the thing about seeing what's going to happen is that you still have to let it happen sometimes. I hoped she'd caught the bit about 'friend', but something told me Teb wasn't going to talk to me for a couple of weeks anyway. I sighed. *There you go, Jeremy. She was out of it.*

Well, I was going whether I had backup or not. Maybe she was just scared she was getting old and wouldn't be able to talk her way out of it yet again now it was clear that she should know better.

I tied my hair back in a high ponytail, the better for pulling through the opening at the back of my 'I ♥ London' baseball cap (a very worthwhile investment, however much I got mocked at the time. I actually bought it in Brighton as well). A pair of large sunglasses did the rest of the work, once I was wearing khaki three-quarter-lengths and a t-shirt with German writing on it that I'd bought in the winter market passing through Waitington a couple of years ago. I stuck on my comfortable walking shoes and to finish it off I accessorised with my pretty pink digital camera dangling from my wrist. I levered the cork out of my piggy bank and mixed in a handful of euros with my regular spare change before shaking my wallet up.

"*Ja, gut,*" I said to my reflection, tipped my hat up a bit for maximum foreign dorkiness, and Tourist Tanya™ was ready to roll.

"I'm just going to the museum!" I called, heading down the stairs.

From Daddy's office came a muffled, "Don't break anything!"

"I'll try!" I sang, letting myself out, umbrella in hand despite the glorious summer sun.

*

One sticky bus ride later (they really needed to wash the seat covers more often) I was in Bilsworth.

I meandered along, snapping photos of postboxes and a display of autobiographies of famous-ish Brits in a stationer's window. I paused for a long time at the signpost to the museum, to make sure I had my vocab exactly right and I wasn't going to accidentally direct myself to the sewage treatment plant due to poor language skills.

Then I took a photo of the signpost.

When I could play no longer with a straight face, I went up the steps to the looming red-brick museum, a monolith of turrets and crenulations even though it was built only two hundred years ago and the need for it to be fortified was completely absent. It was a power show: the building was sponsored by many of the richest people in the county and the building of Bilsworth in general had been an exercise in newly rich industrialists and the remains of local landed gentry showing off their toy town during a boom of money in the area. I rolled my eyes at the thought of it and went in.

There I accidentally paid two euros and fifty pence sterling for admission, babbled apologies in accented English and legged it before they asked for the right money in British pounds. The exchange rate was probably out of our favour anyway.

Once I was in, I was at the tricky part. I'd never heard of this road before yet it had triggered one of my rare incomprehensible flashes of Sight, and there was a strange tourist around who wanted to know about the stone circle as well. All things pointed to ancient history, so I took a left and went to visit my old friends and one-time roommates, the wax mannequins of the Neanderthal family. They stood right at the entrance of the human history section, looking longingly at the mammoths across the hall in the wing of giant lumbering monsters.

I had to admit that I had no idea what I was looking for: probably just holes in the logic somewhere, anything that contradicted facts I already knew or left obvious gaps in the supposed historical record. But for a place of learning, the museum's noticeboards said so little about anything. They described everything about the social history and daily chores cavemen children would have to do, but not one fact tying it to this land in particular. I drifted through the ages, and read about the hill fort above Ransley where Celtic warriors defended the land, but the fort seemed to have been about where the current station was, well, on the wrong side of the road. I glared at the little model of it made from lollipop sticks, daring it to tell me something useful.

The stone circle had its own little room, with a knee-high model and some druids I had a feeling were Christmas tree angels with the wings hacked off and cotton wool beards glued on. A couple of them had glittery snowflakes on their druidic gowns. I sighed. That wasn't even the right era for the stone circle to be used like that, never mind how accurate the druids were. I stopped to read the noticeboards again, in case anything caught my eye, but I found an exact repetition of the words on the noticeboard out in the woods, complete with the same pencil-drawn map with an emphasis on modern footpaths as if we were standing in the woods and needed guiding. They went into no further details, although they had a stone behind glass that they said came from the side of the road and looked pretty similar to the one I'd thrown up on.

I carried on drifting through the museum, although Troutespond was rarely mentioned again, Ransley taking centre stage in the exhibits about the Middle Ages, since a king had actually ridden through there once, and half the original houses were still standing. For some reason they used Victorian photos to highlight this fact. I wondered when the last time some of these exhibits had been updated was.

I had never realised it before, but the displays right up to those about Victorian times here didn't say an actual real thing about local history. There was the odd fact or date, but it was like a book saying, "In 1534 Henry VIII broke away from the Catholic church" then moving right on to his fourth marriage. There was no *narrative*. No hows or whys. I was sure *someone* at the museum had to have a degree in history and know about such things.

Well, twisty-turny as the museum was, this building was like an iceberg, only a small part of it on show. I needed to crash into the lower part.

I'd seen a security door back in the civil war room, the suit of armour angled so most people would be paying attention to how cool it was, an automatic minus five to Detect Hidden Doors.

I went back, sidled past the Cavalier and pushed down the bar on the door. Though the NO ENTRY sign glared at me no alarms went off. I let out a long breath and released the handle. The door swung open. I could see faded brown carpet beyond...

A hand clamped onto my shoulder.

"Miss Pomphrey. Welcome back."

The burly security guard (knew it) who'd caught me let go of my shoulder and I looked around to see him and the man who had spoken: a tall, thin man in a boring grey suit. Someone from middle management at the museum. I'd met him before. He'd phoned my dad before. I stuck my tongue out at him.

He did not seem too impressed with my childishness in the face of adversity. "My friend will escort you to the street. Please go along with him quietly."

"Where did I go wrong?" I demanded, reluctantly taking a step as the firm look of the guard intensified in the face of my immobility. I looked like a doll made of sticks compared to him. I couldn't fight. "At least tell me how you caught me."

Mr Suit blandly informed me, "I do not want you learning your way around your failings. You're preferable oblivious." If this man was able to show any emotion, he would have been smirking, but I didn't think he was capable of it. He stood still by the door, choosing not to follow me, not to gloat, not to give me a second more of his time than was required. Complete and utter disinterest and boredom was the perfect response to rile me up: they were pretending there was genuinely nothing going on, trying to make me feel like maybe I was the crazy one, imagining the things I came to investigate.

"Yeah, well screw you. I'll be back!" I called over my shoulder, aware that I was making a scene as a group of genuine German tourists turned their attention from the sword cabinet they'd been photographing to watch. "And next time I'll get past your security!"

I was frogmarched to the steps and the guard blocked the way back in, standing in front of the door with his arms folded. I considered standing opposite him with my own arms crossed, waiting to see who'd crack first. But I decided not to push my luck, really draw attention to the fact I wasn't just bothering them but turning it into a public protest, an issue they would have to resolve with the authorities... so I turned and trudged back onto the High

Street. What a big waste of a day.

The bus ride back felt shorter than normal, as I was lost in thought the whole way. Maybe this was meant to be a sign. I was clearly going about this wrong, and not getting anywhere was unusual for me. But really, if Alana knew that I'd been testing the Bilsworth Historical Society, if she knew I'd been conspiracy hunting again, then she'd blow her top. I really should just calm down and act normal like I was supposed to.

Besides, I had something much more important to freak out over tomorrow. I had a date.

Nosy

Here's something you don't know.

I actually liked Alana to begin with because her dad was dead. It sounds really horrible, but Ally and Teb have such perfect happy home lives, because even though Teb's parents argue sometimes, and Ally's Dad is so stressed about making sure Hester doesn't have another nervous breakdown, they still have complete families. Teb even got the chance to have a brother, which is brilliant, and we spoil him. I'm guessing Ally has no siblings because Hester probably didn't do so well with the pregnancy/baby thing the first time around.

When Ally started school we only ever saw her dad, and she was never allowed to invite us around her house. Ally's Mum became this great mystery, and for a few years me and Teb were always guessing about her, until one day Ally caught us talking about it (and making some rather wild speculations) and ran off crying. The next week we were invited around her house, pretty much without another word between events, and we found out, apparently, that all this time the big horrible secret was that Ally's mum was a hippie who liked painting. She made us cookies and told us funny stories, and we've all been madly in love with her since. It wasn't until we were about eleven or so and Hester had another little wobble, and Ally moved in with me and Teb for a couple of days each, that we found out Hester had deeper issues.

Anyway, I always felt closer to Ally because of that in a way, but Alana was in exactly the same boat as me, so I thought maybe we could talk about it, but it was something she never wanted to bring up. I tried to help her into talking about it, but she chose to distance herself from us. So I looked her up, and that was how I found out about what happened. I suppose she must be ashamed of him. He did, after all, use her to extort millions of dollars, then left her behind when he made his fatal escape attempt, leaving huge lasting scars on her life. Even so, there has to be a part of her, like me, that wants a full set of parents.

*

Taking fashion advice from Ally over the internet, I dressed in a short skirt, sandals of a contrasting colour to everything else I was wearing, and a baggy white t-shirt—with a dragon on it because dragons are awesome—that almost covered the ends of the skirt. I left my hair loose, the wispy blonde ends hanging about my elbows, but by the time I'd walked to the end of the street it was annoying me, hanging in my face and making my ears and cheeks hot. I swept it back into a ponytail and skipped up to the bus stop on the exact second the Bilsworth bus pulled in.

A few old women climbed out, and Warren followed them after a courteous pause to let the last one haul out her tartan trolley bag. He thanked the bus driver over his shoulder, then turned to me with his incredulously joyful smile.

"Morning," I said, leaning on the fence between me and the churchyard like I was the coolest thing ever. If I slipped I'd topple backwards and fall in the pond, but I was pretty confident I wouldn't. Because if I willed it, I *was* the coolest thing ever.

"Hi," he said rather breathlessly. He took off his big oval glasses and gave them a wipe on his t-shirt before restoring them to his face. He blinked at me again, as if unsure why clearing up his vision hadn't transformed me into a hag. I smiled and held out my hand. He didn't understand that just because I was pretty didn't mean I was stooping. Okay, so I ignored him in front of my friends a little, but that was a Teb problem and we'd talked about that. The rest of the time, though… He was cute, hug-sized and had springy curly hair that gave me an excuse to start flirting when we'd been sitting in the cramped yearbook office together because it was just so fun to pull on and watch it spring back. And he understood me when I talked, had a lot of the same interests and generally didn't think I was intimidating when I talked a hundred miles an hour about some wild plan I had.

Also we had a complete lack of shared baggage about fairy encounters.

I took him back to my house. I knew he was carrying a bag with video games and DVDs in it, things he'd been enthusiastically telling me about the last time I saw him. Most of our dates thus far had been hardly better than play dates, sitting in front of my TV, alternately competing with each other at classic games on my old Dreamcast or sitting a careful distance from each other on the sofa and making sarcastic comments about the film.

It wasn't too exciting a relationship, especially since the drama at the prom was long out of the way; at ten minutes to the last bus, around six o'clock so he couldn't stay for dinner (which was a relief in a way since I wasn't sure what he'd make of my cooking—if I could torment him into polite praise like my dad at all), I'd walk him back into town and kiss him on the cheek the moment before the bus pulled up. I kind of wished that we would do more, but locally there was little to do, and the buses were even less in my favour if we had the date in Bilsworth, as there was only one bus running the route. He was having driving lessons but hadn't mentioned them or the likelihood of him passing them for a long time.

Daddy was out at the office that day: there was a sort of unspoken agreement that he would be out working on the days I wanted to see Warren, mostly because I got quite shouty when I played racing games and a little because he respected our privacy.

Warren dropped his bag on the sofa and flopped down next to it, by now quite comfortable with my house. "Hey, so I brought that JRPG we were talking about last time…"

"Do you want a drink?" I interrupted, eyeing the spiky-haired kid with the huge sword on the box art he was waving at me.

"Uhhh… Sure?"

"We have, hmm… Wine, some old half-finished apple Schnapps—that's probably not safe—vodka…"

"Just water! Are you trying to get me drunk?" he said with a laugh.

"No, of course not. I just need a tactical edge if we do multiplayer."

"Aw, this one is supportive…"

"You mean you want me to play a healer class?"

He gave me this adorable puppy look.

"Hey, come on up to my room. I wanna show you my progress with my mage first!" I said. I had two computers: a pretty pink laptop, barely more than a glorified netbook, and a hulking black self-built machine with huge whirring fans and more RAM than a herd of sheep. The one that was any good to game on was an immobile monolith and therefore an excellent excuse to take Warren up to my room.

Clutching his glass of water he followed me upstairs, now beginning to look genuinely nervous. I'd taken him upstairs before, mostly to briefly prove to him that I was a girl gamer and not lying about being a geek, but that was early days: Daddy had been home, and I'd obsessively cleaned and tidied before he came anywhere near the house.

I felt a pang of embarrassment looking around my room: fortunately he was awkward enough not to dive right in and flop on the bed. I pushed a pile of clean laundry, including underwear, under the blanket and smoothed it over, throwing cushions from the floor into the corner, disguising it as a tidying action as he came through the door.

"The bed's basically a sofa during the day. Make yourself comfy," I said, flopping down in my swivelling desk chair and spinning to look at him as he goggled around. I caught his ankle between my feet and rotated: he hurriedly sat before I could knock him down. I giggled and bent over to boot up the computer, taking a second glance around the room. An untidy room says a lot more about the character of the person who lives in it than it does tidy: tidiness is an attempt to smooth out all the weird parts of your character. I saw the wardrobe hanging opening, showing off outfits which were much more theatrical than practical. Stacks of books were piled around, factual rather than niche nerdy fiction. I felt a little ashamed to my former self, but I was so busy researching these days part of my nerd cred was slipping away, though Warren and I had bonded over our choice of authors. There were maps and pamphlets of minutes of meetings from fifty years ago, things bought from local tourist information shops that no one in their right mind should have bought: books about prolific and profoundly dull turn of the century local letter writers, accounts from someone who had trialled every darts board in every pub in the county and written an essay on each. A book of 'poetic' descriptions of the cows pastured in the fields around Ransley year in and year out.

"What is all this?" Warren asked, picking up *A Journal Of Waitingshire Hedgerows.*

"World-building," I replied, shuffling papers on my desk to conceal some of the stranger ones at the bottom.

"What for?" His eyes goggled ever more.

"A story I'm working on," I half-lied.

"What about this?" he asked.

I felt my stomach flip with horror as he picked up something from my pillow with black straps, but the moment of insanity passed as I realised it wasn't a bra that I'd somehow misplaced and left in the weirdest location, but a walkie-talkie in a holster. And my bras were way thinner and lacier than the big heavy straps of the holster, which looked more like seatbelts.

"Oh, you know. Playing around with the girls. You know, send Ally to the bottom of a field and let her say 'Roger' a lot and her day is basically made."

"Oh…" He turned it over, saw the *Property of Bilsworth Historical Society* label and then I snatched it from his hands. Okay, taking him to my room had been a terrible idea. I dropped the walkie-talkie down the side of the bed and clambered onto it with him, leaning forwards until I was right in his face.

"We could play as well… Just say Roger?" I suggested, giggling.

"Uh… Uh…" I seemed to have broken him, or at least dampened his curiosity for the moment. I pressed a kiss on him, collapsing into him as gently as I could as the awkward perching became hard to sustain. But as soon as we were lying flat out on the bed he struggled to sit up again.

"Tanya, this is weird," he protested.

"What, us?"

"No! Well… I dunno. You said you stopped playing with all the dangerous fairy stuff. You said the prom was sobering and… and… You were going to be sensible. Look, you're stealing stuff from museums, you have all this weird business software on your shelves instead of computer games, your books are all about strange local things like you're looking for more patterns… You're clearly investigating something. And you didn't tell me!"

"Aw, no, Warren, it's not like that…"

"What is it then? You didn't think I was very helpful after all, or did you really only use me to get back at those girls at the prom? If you're done using me…"

"I'm not! I mean, I wasn't using you. I'm not done with you at all because all I want from you now is to be a normal boyfriend!"

"But I'm not, am I?" He gestured the stack of swiped security cards and identity badges my desperate paper shuffling had inadvertently exposed. "You're going to do stuff like this anyway, and you're leaving me out!"

I jumped up. "Come on, let's get out of here."

"What?"

I didn't want him poking through any more of my stuff if a cursory glance of my room exposed so much about me. "Let me get you some ice cream. We can do normal date stuff. I'll prove to you I'm not just playing with you. I mean, not just messing you around and also, I don't just want us to be all platonically sitting around playing games anymore. I *like* you."

I powered out of my room and relied on him being a little bit of a wet blanket so he didn't stand his ground or start dismantling my room looking for more spy stuff. He followed me meekly, grabbed his bag of games and continued to want to be in my presence after we left the house by not legging it as soon as I turned my back to lock the front door.

I took his arm again and leaned on him, smiling pointedly in his direction.

He didn't look particularly happy, but then he was perpetually worried about something or other. I suppose it was only a matter of time before he turned his anxiety on me. Apparently attempting to seduce him just made him more paranoid I *didn't* want to be doing it, though I suppose the room full of my own crazy stuff hadn't helped. We walked along in silence; I was thinking of my line of attack for the conversation we'd have to have at some point, and he was no doubt coming up with the rebuttals quietly in his own head. I was beginning to feel an extremely distracting but vague throbbing embarrassment that wouldn't go away and sounded rather a lot like *"JustsayRoger JustsayRoger JustsayRoger…"*

When we got to the town centre I nodded at the statue and took a left, taking us past the church and away from the village green.

"I thought we were getting ice cream?" he said, confused and suddenly terrified, like I was springing a trap: he was looking away down behind us at the rumbling Mr Whippy van parked on the grass.

"Nah, we're getting *quality* ice cream," I said. I lead us up to one of the first tea shops on the row: these were the tall, narrow three-storey houses of ancient lopsided timber and swinging signs in the front, olde worlde and beautiful in their own way. The shops were of a boutique level, offering less of just products and more the service or craftsmanship that came with them. Roberta's, the shop I took us into, had an ornate sign with a hand-painted teapot and scone on it, a shop window that looked like the back of an old ship with the curved frame of panels of distorted glass and a door that had a string of tinkling bells hanging in front of it. Inside was a long counter of dark wood, a shelf with not much more than an ornamental butter churn lying on its side and three tables for two with checked cloth over them and a currently unlit candle in the middle. The chairs were rickety wrought iron, the one-legged tables wobbly on the uneven flagged floor and even more overwrought iron. The whole lot was packed into a shop about three meters wide.

I made Warren sit, then went to the unmanned counter and pressed the large bell on it. A faint clang echoed from the back of the shop, and soon enough a middle-aged woman in a chocolate-streaked apron came out.

"Good morning, Tanya!" she sang.

"Heya, Bobbie. Two house specials, please."

Bobbie chuckled appreciatively, told me "Right away!" and bustled away into the back again.

I sat myself down with Warren.

"What is—"

"Shh. Shh-shh-shh," I chided.

He fiddled with a napkin, and I, having the seat facing the window, craned around him to look at the street. Another busy-ish summer day, but no sign of any snooping friends. Now that we were out in public I felt like at any moment I'd have Ally's goofy face pressed up against the window or Teb's phone stealthily wandering through the cracked-open door to grab a picture of me and Warren together. I had incurably nosy friends.

Roberta came back with a small tray, two tall glasses balanced on it. She plopped them down in front of us, winked at me and went around to the counter again.

Warren looked at his glass with wide eyes, taking in the five generous scoops of homemade local ice cream, the layer of brownie and the layer of M&Ms slowly leaking their colour against the side of the glass as the ice cream above them melted in the warm café…

"Go on," I said.

He picked up one of the extremely long spoons provided and took a tiny amount of chocolate ice cream from the top, the thinnest scraping of clotted cream… He popped it into his mouth.

"Okay, now we can talk," I said.

He swallowed. "Dammit, Tanya, I forgive you."

I grinned smugly, and we got to work polishing off the ice cream, cake, cookie dough, glacé cherries and who knows what else layered in the glass.

"How did you know about this place?" he asked once he'd got past the first stage of devouring and we were savouring the flavour and eating slower to save our stomachs.

"Spoooooky local knowledge… Pfft, it's Troutespond. If you can't name every shop in the town limits in under twenty seconds you're clearly not a real local."

"I'm from Bilsworth."

"This is literally opposite your bus stop."

"It's tiny!"

I giggled. "Well, I had to explore everything obvious first before setting off into the unknown. It's a bit out of our normal price range… I mean, if we had ice cream here every day we lurked in town, we'd be out of pocket." I glanced over at Bobbie, who was wiping down the counter, clearly making an effort to stay in the same room as her customers. "But it's an amazing treat. Perfect for dates." I nudged his foot under the table and he looked shyly down at his ice cream. I withdrew my foot, kicked the table with an embarrassing clang, then devoted my attention to the ice cream again for a minute.

All the little door bells went off at once, and I looked up to see another guest: this place would be at maximum capacity soon.

"Hallo, Bobbie," said the man: he had a camera around his neck and the sort of lean, hungry look of someone who did not eat ice cream. The photographer from results day and then later in the town.

"Hiya, love," she said. "What can I get for you?"

"Just a black coffee," he said, eyeing us on the middle table: it was dreadfully impolite of us. The great social awkwardness of Brits dictated that normally one always took the furthest potential table/bench/seat on the train from anyone else, even when no one was around, so the next person along would not have to pick somewhere right next to anyone else. He settled for sitting next to the door, his chair turned to face the ice cream lady rather than look directly at me.

Bobbie left again to brew up some coffee, and I directed my attention back to Warren.

"You can't turn it off, can you?" he asked in a low voice.

"What?"

"What what?" he hissed. "As soon as anyone does anything you act like someone's switched on *Eastenders* and you can't rip your eyes from the screen. I'm right here. You said you wanted this to be a proper date."

"Maybe I'm just terrible at eye contact?" I suggested.

He snorted. "*I'm* terrible at eye contact. I can still listen to what people are saying while I'm too nervous to look them right in the eye. I could have said anything to you right then, but the conversation at the next table is so much more fascinating. Are you actually obsessed with those history people, or is it just pathological? Do you listen to your neighbours with your ear against the wall? Miss a bus stop if someone's having a juicy phone call in the seat in front? Wander along at dusk when everyone has their curtains open and watch a whole TV show through other people's windows?"

Bobbie came back with a coffee pot and jug of cream, and I tried not to make my eyes follow her across the room, but she walked right through my line of sight. I forced my eyes back to the table in front of me before I could wonder if the photographer took sugar.

"Hey, this is progress! You're talking about things that bother you instead of bottling them up!" I said with forced happiness, against the sick feeling in my stomach at our first real fight (and wondering how much of this was Warren having to help Chris deal with the blows Teb had dealt him at the prom).

"Talking of bottling things up!" he cried, winced, and almost sunk right down under the table. He was not the loud sort. He continued in a murmur addressed to his half-empty ice cream glass. "We never said a thing about the prom afterwards. You just acted like it was totally normal. I heard from Chris what Teb did. I'm worried he was right. There's something weird about you girls, and..."

"It's Alana!" I blurted.

"What?"

"I wanted to tell you everything. I was going to have so much fun with you this summer... If you want a real date, I was going to try and sneak you into fairyland! But no, she put a lid on the whole thing. We're as worried about Teb as Chris was... Although obviously we like her better despite it. Alana thinks the best thing to do is to pretend that magic never came into our lives, and I can't be a good friend to Teb by playing with it... And I can't be a good girlfriend to you if I don't! How is it fair? We could be spying and being nosy *together* and you would understand, and we'd be able to share it all. And instead she says *no Tanya*, and so we've been sitting frigidly on that sofa watching characters on the computer screen have big magic adventures all summer while we do *nothing*!" I angrily shoved a scoop of ice cream in my mouth to try and chase away the hot tears that were welling up in my eyes. No one could cry while eating Bobbie's delicious ice cream.

Warren looked horrified that I was crying and ventured to reach out a hand and touch mine. "I'm sorry, Tanya, I..."

I shrugged. "No, it's fine. No one else can handle all this weirdness. I thought you could, but you still need to feel a *bit* normal. Maybe no one would know what to say to me right now."

"How about... I pay for the ice creams, then we go for a walk and look at stuff? Nosily?"

"Aw, but I was going to buy these. You took the bus over here already..."

"Don't be silly, Tanya. We're on a date. I'll get this."

I snivelled appreciatively and hastily ate the last bits of ice cream before they'd completely melted. Like his goodwill towards me.

It's a clue!

Here's something you don't know.

The first time I ever met any of the girls who would end up being better than sisters was not entirely by chance. We'd been at school for maybe three or four days, and I was sort of aware of Ally and Teb being in the same class as me, but I'd never really *talked* to them. Well, no one talked to Teb. She didn't speak much English and always took over the playhouse and snapped with her sharp milk teeth at people who tried to come in.

In playtime Jess Standerwick had dragged me off to sit with the other blonde girls in pretty pink and had thought me a perfect, if quiet, friend because I had Barbie crayons and didn't disagree with her when she wanted to use them in colouring time even though she broke the yellow one. It wasn't the last time she tried to make me her friend. Basically every year from then on there would be an initiative: any time I cut my hair or got a cool new thing, Jess would pop up. I think she wanted her own stuff like mine, but if I wasn't her friend, she was just copying, and when you're a kid, copying is awful. Unless you copy a friend with their explicit permission.

Anyway, I felt trapped in this circle, looking out, and the second week of school Ally had toughed up and made a move and she and Teb had gone into the playhouse and they were laughing and laughing. I couldn't see them but it was driving me crazy. I got more and more jealous every day because they were having fun without me, having more fun than the entire class by the sounds of it, and it looked a lot better than letting the other girls take my Barbie crayons.

So the next day in reading time before break I quietly worm-crawled away, an inch at a time, while everyone was listening to the story, and I got into the house and hid there. At break Teb came roaring into it with Ally chasing her, and I was hidden in the next partition. They took all the foam kitchen implements and began to hit each other with them: apparently when Teb bit Ally, she'd just whacked her with the foam frying pan in retaliation, and the fight had started and been so much fun they had carried it on for a week. In the boring side of the playhouse there was just a small chair. I wanted to play so I grabbed it and came out and hit Teb with it, and she turned around and *floored* me with the play oven. Then Ally, in typical fashion as I would later learn, ripped off the window because apparently we were destroying things and then the whole house fell down. The three of us got into a ton of trouble for wrecking it, and I had a black eye from the oven. Jess didn't want to sit with me for a while because I was *naughty*. But Ally and Teb adopted me, and that was that.

I've never undervalued curiosity and being a total moron because I wouldn't have two of the best friends in the world without it.

*

On the way out the door I nodded to the photographer. "Thanks for the awesome double page spread this week!" I said.

He looked up from his coffee with alarm and focussed on me as if he was seeing me for the first time... Maybe other people *weren't* as nosy as I was. Warren gave my hand a little tug, and we set the bells ringing again as we left the shop.

I'd tried this walking tactic before: when I'd first started *properly* going out with Warren I'd held an emergency panic meeting with my friends to try and figure out what options there possibly were for dates in the local area when neither of us drove. Alana had lamely suggested "go for a walk", and I'd laughed at it, but within a week been desperate enough to try, when I went to visit him in Bilsworth. It had amused me to think of her walking Ally in endless circles waiting for a result, but once the same set in with me, I lost my amusement at the charade. He showed me everything worth seeing in Bilsworth (next to nothing), and when we went in the museum I was too scared about getting kicked out and making a bad impression in front of him to do any of the research I wanted, so I just kept my head low, nodded at displays I'd seen a dozen times before and held his hand where no one else was following us around and making him embarrassed.

But as we walked down the road towards the village green that day I felt unusual shyness welling up. We were back out in public and since our conversation I had become acutely aware about how the policy of not talking about it extended to Warren. We'd remained very quiet about the prom, but he'd been a part of it—more so than Ally and Alana, even. The movies and games had been a great way of diverting him, and his awkwardness had done the rest. But Troutespond was... well, the sort of place where one would talk about it. It was where everything happened. He was blatantly trying to walk me around in circles maybe not until kisses happened, but until magic did. Hadn't I won him over in the first place by proving it could?

"So..." he started, looking away at a row of parked cars when I glanced down at him. He was more than usually shorter than me since I had on sandals with a slight heel, and when we talked he looked at my throat in a way that was very unsettling once I started thinking about vampires, because he was too scared to look up and meet my eyes and definitely too scared to look any further down, no matter how much shoulder my extra extra large t-shirt showed. This time, though, I could sense what made him worried about what he wanted to talk about. He'd been looking at the church, remembering some of the things that I'd said about it. Which meant if he wanted to take things to the next level and start snooping on magic stuff...

"Let's go down this way," I said, hastily diverting him before he could stop and ask any questions.

I stole a few glances at him as we went through the wide gates in the hedge around the green and crossed the grass. It was sort of horrible of me to admit, but I hadn't really looked at him as boyfriend material for a while. He'd been co-conspirator before the prom, but we'd really been on stasis for the last month until today's events had finally shaken me up and made me remember the sorts of things I used to think about him when we sat around in the computer room together not making eye contact. Warren all on his own was still a bit of a trial, even after all the gaming and sharing of nerdy movies we'd done. Neither of us was good at social interaction and, as I was finding out, with no school talk to occupy us we had quickly fallen into bickering and uptight paranoia and even fear of each other. I couldn't exactly go to Teb for advice on this when she'd nuked her own relationship from orbit when it hit this same point.

We strolled through the green in thoughtful silence, which I was only a little bit thankful for: I was so busy worrying about what he was thinking I wasn't sparing any thought left to my own actions. I'd made the mistake of heading down towards the skate park. He pointed to a clump of trees by the river. "Hey, is that where..."

"Yes," I said shortly. He recoiled, hurt.

I winced. "Yeah," I repeated, a little more softly. I glanced around. I was always half-afraid one of my friends would be around. As the only one of us with a boyfriend I was a novelty to the group, and the fact it was Warren had driven both Alana and Teb into partnership, planning to drift by to smirk at us whenever I unwittingly gave away that we would be appearing anywhere in public. I had only communicated my desire to get some proper date time with him with Ally, but it wasn't a dire secret, so I could imagine she'd have probably accidentally told Alana or Teb by now, and either of them would kill me if some innocent following for bored small-town entertainment turned into a witch hunt for breaking the silence and trying to rekindle the spark with my boyfriend via local lore.

"Do you want to go down for a look?" I said, deciding that we weren't in any danger from a sneak attack from Alana. We left the road and started cutting across the scruffy wild grass that grew where the land had been abandoned. I squeezed his hand tighter.

As we reached the trees, I reflected that I might accidentally have been extremely smooth with the handling of this date. The Green Man's grove was a miniature blip of forest, as deep and dark as if we'd walked for hours through trees to the oldest part of the woods. A huge oak grew in the middle, perhaps shorter than it seemed from a distance, but as girthy as it could be. The roots tangled darkly for some way at its base, and low-hanging branches reached almost to the floor, weighted with leaves and pale green acorns, ripening up as summer did. The knobbly trunk was about as thick as a car was long and covered in whorls and knots, lumpy growths of bark where ancient branches had fallen off or been cut by people in the middle ages. Smaller oaks and other kinds of tree grew around it in a cluster. The miniature wood—no more than six or eight trees deep in any direction—was still thick enough to completely block the sound of the motorway a hundred feet away, most of the sunlight and apparently half the air as well. It was still, cool and breathless under the rustling green canopy.

I hopped up onto one of the thick roots that was worn almost flat on its top from the amount of people who had used it as a starting point to climb the Green Man, or had just sat there. I had spent probably days of my life in total reading here. I swung my legs, the soles of my sandals scuffing on the dry dusty ground at his feet. I thought of Teb spending two whole months here in the fairy world and shivered. It was a lot cooler under the trees, the shade taking away the warmth that had soaked into my skin, but the Green Man felt almost like the sun had been falling on him all morning. I touched his trunk gently and felt a stirring run through me. How much time did she spend down here with her hard-won fairy husband?

Warren was still gaping at the tree, his mouth hanging open. Not being a native of Troutespond, I doubted he had ever really explored beyond the school or the paths to his friends' houses. I jumped down again, walked right up to him and put a finger under his chin to push it back up. He transferred his stare to me, terrified. I put my hands on his shoulders and slid his bag off. It landed in the dirt next to his feet with a dull thump. He didn't get too flinchy about the stuff in there being unceremoniously dropped on the ground. Good sign. Then I rotated him, and pushed him back against the tree, hoping the old, sexy power in it would be enough to help poor Warren out. Maybe, I thought, as I lowered my lips to his, he had been the smooth one. He must know well enough what that local lore said of this place at the very least. It was such an obvious one. An abstract researcher he may have been, but most of my work had only been telling him of things he already knew, *yes, it's real.*

I have no idea how long we kissed, but we ended up lying on a mossy, well… bed, under the Green Man's branches, the other side of his trunk to the one we'd approached by. There was plenty said about this moss mattress in local lore as well, but we'd only kissed a lot, so I wasn't too worried. Anyway, it was a warm day and I suppose we were getting quite sleepy and in danger of drifting off outdoors for the second time this week. Under the Green Man you didn't need alcohol.

Warren's cheeks had gone very pink, and he was smiling vaguely off into the branches of the trees. I watched him, enjoying seeing him close-up, sans glasses. It made him look a lot less pinched and small without them, and I was just wondering how to bring up the subject of contacts without making him think I found him unattractive but rather would like to see more of him looking especially extra sexy.

But he squinted, a frown coming to his face, and rolled over and picked up his glasses from where I'd dropped them to stop them getting too smudged up as I pressed my face against his.

"What's that in the branches?" he asked, pointing upwards.

"I have no idea," I said, following his finger to something red quite high in amongst the leaves. It was wobbling in and out of sight with the noisy breeze, huge clumps of leaves obscuring it in their gentle back and forth motions. I sat up, then stood. It looked like a small red bag, maybe. I wasn't one to interfere in other people's methods of worship, but I was curious.

"I'm going to climb up and have a look," I decided. Clues were clues, and a childhood of reading detective kid novels had made me rather excited about the possibility of finding them. Who knew what the clue was for, but for now it was enough that it might be one. I remembered that feeling that had made my stomach clench the night we'd seen the cultists, that feeling of, once again, being a *part* of something.

"Are you sure?" Warren asked, even as I hopped back up onto the seat-like root and grabbed the low branch next to it.

"Mm-hm," I replied, concentrating on selecting my next step. Maybe this spirit of adventure was what I needed to make things work well with Warren again: weird though it sounded, I had a feeling he was at heart a man of action, and the month of gaming and not much more had chafed on him as much as me. This would show him.

The Green Man was well-endowed with branches, enough that I could climb one to the other without stretching or worrying about missing a footing right up until I was getting to the springy, newer branches, with hundreds of leafy offshoots. They were rather livelier as well. As I inched my way along a branch a thin twig somehow snapped around and caught me across the behind.

"Hey, watch it!" I complained to the tree. "What would Teb think?"

The breeze through the leaves seemed to snigger at me.

I rolled my eyes and, judging myself to be high enough, twisted and leaned out to where, just a few feet above me, a branch had a small red bag hanging from it by long leather ties. My fingers swept by underneath it, too far off. I paused to breathe, counted branches and climbed a little higher. Finally I could shimmy along the branch next to the bag, so it hung just by my head. I reached up and touched it, my fingers brushing the smooth velvet, and with that touch I felt a much more definite swirl in my gut of excitement. And fear.

There was something that worried me about this bag, not in a psychic flash that could knock me out of the tree but something nonetheless. It made me remember Alana's concern yesterday, staring off at the hill with a frown creasing up her forehead. But it was with this fear that I made my decision to interfere in that instant. Weird stuff happened around me, and to me, whether I wanted it to or not. All I could really do was try to be as aware of it happening as possible, so I would be prepared when the weird turned around to face me, as it invariably did. And if there really was something so truly troubling about this, I would be at fault myself for backing away now I had begun to follow the thread.

It was hard to untie the two knots that held the bag, my fingers fumbling on leather that had sat through at least one rainstorm and gone tight and hard as it dried. In the end I loosened it up with much picking and red, pinched fingers from slipping, my other hand white-knuckling the adjacent branch I leaned from. I was so caught up on getting the knots undone I forgot about the bag for a moment.

"Watch out below!" I yelled as it slipped from my grasp.

There was a thump, then an "Ow!" from below.

"I said watch out," I chided, beginning my descent.

Five minutes later I was back on the ground, and Warren seemed to have recovered. We sat next to each other on the moss again to open the bag. Inside were the fractured remains of a bird skull, a lot of fancy rune stones, the symbols painted in fine green paint on golden tiger's-eye. There was dirt and a chip of old stone, some leaves, all brown and crinkled, and some bits of polished wood that had probably been whole before I'd dropped the bag on Warren's head. I sorted these out, curious about their shape, and put them together. The ends were freshly sawn, each piece a little rounded. There were specks of gold paint on the polished wood—it was shiny on the wider side of the curve, raw on the inner. I had an idea what this might be the moment I saw that some of the pieces had small round holes taken out of them, and I only had to fit half of them together to be sure—it was the pieces of an antique wooden recorder.

"What does that mean?" Warren asked, his eyes wide.

I stroked the red velvet of the bag thoughtfully. We'd seen an awful lot of fabric just like this very recently.

"It means," I said, very carefully since I was aware of the weight of what this meant, "that Alana starts talking about it again... And I have a lot of questions to ask."

Graveyards and Gunge

Here's something you don't know.

When I was three, my Daddy told me that there was a monster living inside my mummy. A dragon, eating her up from the inside. I asked why they couldn't get a knight to slay it for us, and he said they had one that was also going to fight inside her, and that was why she was going to be strange for a few months, but she should get better. He said she had to learn to slay the dragon herself, and the knight would only help her. He said to leave Mummy alone while she was fighting, so she could keep all her strength.

I might have been a bit of a trial to raise.

A couple of months later Daddy and I moved to Troutespond. Just the two of us.

I always thought I should be scared of literal dragons. They can be defeated. Just maybe not by one woman all on her own with an imaginary knight.

*

I went to the church first, since it was closest. We walked past the graveyard a million times a day and ignored the whole thing—church, graves, pond. They just became part of the background, like a blurry painting that rolled by behind us just to save us from walking against empty white space. I don't think I'd ever been in the graveyard. I don't think I'd ever been in any graveyards, really. I was left with my aunt at my mum's funeral, and since then I'd never had cause to go in one. I'd been ill the day our Religious Education class took a little tour around it. It may have been psychological. I'd had nightmares for weeks before the trip after they told us it was part of the syllabus.

I edged around the building and didn't let my eye linger very long on any one stone. *Someone's dead down there*, I thought. Then I remembered something Ally had told me when she went on that archaeology summer school. *The grave markers are all modern, comparatively. They don't show you how many people are buried in a churchyard. An old one like Troutespond would have hundreds of thousands of bodies in it, in every square inch of the soil. All jumbled together and forgotten, bits of people who'd once lived now just piled together in the mushy earth beside the pond.*

I baulked, backing away. I could taste acid in the back of my throat and my stomach was churning. I regretted a five-scoop luxury ice cream for lunch.

Warren put a hand on my shoulder, and only that stopped me running right out of the churchyard. "Hey, are you okay?"

"Go get on a bus," I snapped at him. "I'm fine."

"A-are you sure?"

"I can do this by myself!" I yelled.

He fled. There was a bus in less than five minutes—I could feel it coming without having to look up at the massive clock that hung from the top floor of the tea shop in the square. These things become instinctive in a small village with one bus an hour.

I took a few deep breaths and looked up at the single window the church had pointing down at the corner of the graveyard between the front gate and the road. I hadn't made it more than six feet in, not even past the church into the main graveyard.

And they buried the babies on the south side of the graveyard, right up against the wall of the church, I heard Ally's ghastly voice telling me with vivid enjoyment. It had taken her far too long to notice how pale and stiff I'd gone. I suppose I should talk more so my deliberate silences have meaning against my weird thoughtful ones.

I closed my eyes and staggered across the horrible uneven ground for several paces, opened my eyes for a flash of bright sunlight to check that I was still walking the right way and not about to collide with a massive stone angel or something, then carried on blindly, like it somehow made it better. I was as blind as the people beneath my feet, I thought, feeling the land around me open up in a yawning mass of people's lives lived. *And the church is on an old barrow as well; there's some Anglo-Saxon king down there and I bet there's a ton of treasure too. It's amazing no one ever dug it up with all these graves... Imagine digging away down there and instead of a skull you come across like a great big gold goblet or something!*

I slipped as I went down the slope and felt myself roll to a stop on the damp ground by the pond. I could hear the bus rumble by, and I lay low, hoping clumps of weeds and the thin iron railings would somehow hide me from view, hoping that Warren wasn't looking.

The pond was a lot better. I'd been here before—ignoring the fact it was in a graveyard was easy when you climbed right over the fence instead of going the long way around—because it had its own special significance. The nearest graves were a way away (and I was ignoring the probability of random bones that had sneaked out this far), and this was the sunny side of the church now that it was afternoon. I sat up and looked into the murky brown waters. It was said there was a monster that lived in the pond, but then, all the medieval people had been tripping out on some wheat fungus thing, and everything had been monsters and demons and witches back in the day. A newt raised its head above the water and blinked at me in a slimy way. I was guessing that was as big as monsters got in this pond. Usually.

"Hey, are you alright?" a soothing American voice floated across the graveyard. The newt freaked out and slid back into the murky water with a plop. I looked up to see Mr Lane, so-called Hollywood producer, standing in the middle of the graveyard with a surveyor's wheel. "You took quite a tumble there."

"I'm fine," I said, standing up and brushing the mud off my bare knees. There was no way to clean up my white t-shirt, which had dusty brown smudges on it already from making out with Warren, green mossy marks from the ground and yellow smears of lichen from the Green Man's bark. Now I had a few streaks of darker brown from the mud near the pond.

"You're Tanya's friend, aren't you? Alana?"

"I am Tanya. Alana was..." Not introduced to you.

"Right," he said, looking down at his surveyor's wheel. For a moment he was completely unreadable, even to me. He looked up again. "I saw you in the newspaper. You were dancing."

"We both got into the university we wanted that day. It was pretty exciting."

"Ah. Congratulations." There was a long silence where I didn't thank him, just stared at him, trying to force him to play more cards he ought not to have shown me in particular. He caved and changed the subject, sadly. "So what are you doing here? A picnic to celebrate perhaps? I find graveyards very peaceful and spiritual, and this one is fantastic. It's so old compared to any out in the States... So many lives connected through the years beneath our feet, and maybe one day we can be connected with them too..." He looked away, preoccupied with his morbid thoughts, but weirdly they did actually made me feel better. I never thought of skeletons having *motivation*. It made them easier to relate to.

"No, I'm on my own." I glanced back at the road: the bus was long gone, and this was the uncool side of the church. After only a row of houses, including mine, the road ended and became out of town stuff. No one was walking anywhere in sight.

"So what are you doing here?" I asked, clambering up from the dip in which the pond wallowed. I approached him feeling rather less frightened of the very ground I walked on, caught up in this new mystery. I knew he was lying. I just knew it. The Alana comment proved it. But I couldn't work out what else he'd said that could be a lie as he'd mostly voiced opinions. If anything else of what he'd said so far *was* a lie, why he would lie about it?

He gestured the wheel. "Still scouting. You do make things awful cramped here, you know."

"England's only small."

"You sure fit a lot in it for one small place!" He chuckled heartily.

"So why Troutespond?"

"Why not?" he grinned. "I have some family ties here, so I know what the town is like." He gestured around. "I mean, look. This place... It never grew up into the modern world. You have your old church, and the old houses..." I could see what he meant. Ignoring the roads, here in front of us was a church from the dark ages, untampered with since St Troute had finished building it, aside from attempts to stop the stumpy little steeple collapsing on itself. On the streets going both ways there were thatched roofs, little cottage gardens bordering the graveyard or timber-framed houses with wonky slate roofs, none of which lined up perfectly with any of the others. Ignoring satellite dishes, the laundry lines and play forts and swings in back gardens and that one woman who had a horrible modern glass extension on the back of her house, it was a street that weighed in between two and six hundred years old. To an American, even the newest houses were antiques. Mr Lane was smiling fondly when I looked back at him, his arms crossed as he leaned on the surveyor's wheel. I couldn't fault him for breathing in deeply and enjoying the same town I loved to bits.

"I just need to make absolutely certain it's perfect, and we'll get the go ahead. Would you be so kind as to hold this for me?" He handed me the surveyor's wheel and took his camera out of its case, which had been slung over his shoulder. "Want to do some measurements for me? It's pretty simple: I guess the boneyard is roughly round, and maybe fifty foot by fifty foot? I need to make sure."

I nodded. "We used these in Geography," I said. I looked down and saw he'd measured thirty feet of the current walk and set off as he began yakking good-naturedly, some anecdote about how strange it was being back in England, the nightmare he'd had getting across London and renting a car, like he may as well have been speaking a completely foreign language. Listening to him, I wasn't scared to walk around between the graves, focussing on the task at hand.

Four back-and-forth crossings of the graveyard later on his directions, and I had an odd feeling I might have marked out a pentagram. I looked at the grass I'd trodden over on his orders and didn't see any markings I'd left behind. I bent and checked the wheel and it didn't feel like it had been leaving a line of any sort. Maybe he'd just told me to check from one side to the other in a peculiarly neat four-sides-of-a-star way. I could imagine he'd done the other side before I arrived.

"Done, Mr Lane," I said cheerfully.

"Ah, you'll make a good assistant. Feel like helping out on set if I come here to film?"

"That would be great, sir," I said, grinning.

If I had wormed my into his good books, he wasn't letting on about anything suspicious he might have been doing. We wrapped up the encounter with a smile and shaken hands, and he packed up the surveyor's wheel and put away his camera. We stood for a moment, waiting to see who would be the one to watch the other leave, but I leaned into being a sulky teen with a phone in hand looking ready to stand there for a thousand years, so he cracked first, waved a cheery goodbye and went back around the church and vanished from sight.

I wandered over to the window that I'd been staring at when I had my freak out and frowned at it. If I hadn't started thinking about the dead babies… (I swallowed hard.) Yes, something had caught my eye: a thin leather strap hanging down from the indented sill. I backed up, took a running jump, caught the high window sill by the tips of my fingers and scrambled to climb the side of the ancient church, probably committing all sorts of sins. I found footholds in between the stones where the cement had washed away years ago and pulled myself up bit by bit, leaving new streaks of ancient grey church grit up my front. Finally I managed to get both elbows up onto the stone ledge, folding my arms under me. My shoulders shook from the effort, and I knew I couldn't stay up long.

The sill hadn't been cleaned in, like, ever, if the moss, small plants, dead bugs and slime were anything to go by. I could also see one very out-of-place thing: though crusted with a thin layer of dirt, looking rather flat and soggy after so much time out in the open, was a red velvet drawstring bag nestled behind a patch of yellow flowers. I grabbed it and fell back to earth, grazing up my arms so streaks of pink and red showed up between the black and green mossy gunge I'd picked up.

I reckoned it'd be probably best to go home and wash to prevent infections before I went to check the stone circle. I was already pretty sure that I'd find one of these bags there too.

Social Circles

Here's something no one knows and I just speculate about based on what I do know.

Once upon a time, there was no music. There was no chaos... No order. Just things happening and growing and dying, leaving massive fossils in the bottom of lakes.

Then one day there was a girl. There's always a girl. She sat with the man under a tree, and he wasn't attractive, or tall and strong like her mate. He didn't know what to do to gesture to her that she should be his mate instead, and so he did what most baffled people do and searched about in desperation for some inspiration. Above him the birds were singing, so he pursed his lips and imitated the call, not whistling like the hunters did out on the savannah. Just doing it because it was something to do and he was bored and nervous and frustrated. She was surprised, and laughed, and in his first notes of the first song, and her first laughter, the first fey spirits were born, and so was imagination. From her laugh there came the lineage of elves and goblins and shadows and helpful lights in the dark, monsters and dragons and demons and angels and even gods. From his song there came cave paintings and pottery and language and machines and medicine and war and religion and apathy, boredom and excitement, cinema and rock & roll and the internet. Maybe he was the one who invented music. Maybe he was just born in that moment, along with the potential for everything else in this world. I don't know if that first whistler became the Piper, the spirit rushing into him from the power of the inspiration, or if he took his cue from there: the moment human imagination blossomed, before it even spread to daubed ashes on cave walls, before most tools. That's a moment I think many entities would want to claim as their own, but the Piper is definitely very old.

*

Washed and patched up, and wearing rather more resilient clothing, I headed up to the stone circle. I had two red pouches in my bag already, and I was determined to get a third. I would take them to Hester, and whether the rest of my friends wanted to talk about it or not, I would get to the bottom of all of this. If I had Ally's Mum's seal of approval, I could get Alana to sit down and pay attention.

The walk up to the stone circle was easy enough, though I kept my eyes open for cultists or Mr Lane, half certain that I'd see him running around up here with his surveyor's wheel. But maybe he'd gone to sample the cream teas available in town, because there was no sign of him as I took confident steps up the hill. Now that there weren't terrifying psychological horrors to overcome I did sort of wish that I hadn't sent Warren away, or that one of my friends was with me. Ally in particular would keep up a nice reassuring babble of conversation and theories and confused questions that would help me think.

Well, it wasn't to be helped. They'd chosen this, after all. I just felt vaguely annoyed that I had a *really* good reason to be investigating this, and yet it would still look like I was stirring up trouble if I was caught by Alana. Then again, what was new?

The stone circle looked much the same as ever: three stones standing in odd places around the edge, five more tumbled over where they stood, or vanished down the hill. The air was still, sunny, silent. The day was hot but the woods absorbed some of that, the stones more. They were warm to the touch on their sunny side, but cold as deep underground in the shade.

I skirted around the perimeter and looked up into the branches of the trees that surrounded the stone circle; I crouched under the altar stone and rooted around in the dry grass at its base; I climbed atop the massive slab and saw a little corner of red peeking out from on top of one of the still-standing stones.

I retreated back into the woods and hunted around for a nice long fallen branch, preferably with a hooky bit, and soon found one that would do. Once I had that it took just a few seconds of poking around and stretching next to the tall stone before I had a third grubby bag in my possession. I opened it up and took a rather more whole section of wooden recorder out, so all three bags were now empty of that particular relic, which, I felt, was about the same as disarming them.

"Tanya."

I pride myself on not being easy to make jump, and this is one of those cases where I had seen it coming. I knew exactly what my actions would do and therefore knew exactly who was behind me and that the bastard liked a jump scare. I turned. The Piper was sitting on the altar stone. His big black and white boots stuck out awkwardly from beneath folded legs in battered grey jeans. His ugly face was long, as was his dark hair, curling untamed and messy. He looked grim.

"I should have known it would be you," he continued. There was no "Well met" in his greeting.

"Good afternoon," I said, backing away just a step. I had never given him a reason to be happy to see me. I was sure his foul appearance was reflecting our lack of desire to be bestest best friends.

Also probably because someone had been putting curses on him.

"I ought to thank you."

"You're welcome!" I said, trying to sound bright and cheerful. In a sunny yellow jacket of light canvas I'd thought to put on to protect my arms from further scratches, I thought I looked rather his opposite. Though he was usually seen wearing a fair mix of black and white, today aside from the one boot it was all black and stormy shades of grey. His eyes, however, were empty and white, like blank pieces of paper that someone had forgotten to pencil in the iris and pupil. The one caught in the shade definitely glowed a little.

"Or was it just that you were only meddling again where you should not be and found the curse bags only by chance?"

"The first one, actually, my boyfriend found," I said. "I recognised the piece of recorder in it and thought it had to be something to do with you. I went to look for others in the more magical places around town. There are these cultists in red doing strange things. We first encountered them a couple of days ago right here... Why don't they want you interfering? It was a spell to banish you, wasn't it? The bags looked rather old. It hasn't even rained for a couple of weeks. How long have you been gone?"

He rubbed his forehead, though I assumed he couldn't get a headache. But he did actually answer, which I think made this the most words we'd ever exchanged. "Since Midsummer. I thought it was you at first, or the Huntress's power growing, since I heard from Alana that you were working Teb to your side for some plan that no longer matters in the grand scheme. But when I still could not return the following day I began to suspect a different power was at work. However I could not get close to the village, or send a message; it was a very thorough spell."

I had waited for the lecture about what happened on the night of the prom. *Months* of anticipation, and that was literally all he had to say on the subject. Instead, he abruptly jumped down from the altar stone and walked up to me. I cringed away, backing into the standing stone behind me, but he stopped a safe distance short of me and held out his hand. "The curse bags."

I handed him the one that I was already holding, then took the other two from my shoulder bag a little more reluctantly. I loved keeping souvenirs of the adventures we had, and one of these would have been a great little memento.

"And the pipe parts," he said.

I sighed and took them out of my pocket. "So Alana's not been doing anything magic-y for the past month because you haven't been around to tell her what to do, not because we agreed not to?"

"She hasn't done anything? Why would *you* agree to that? Why would you agree to that?"

"Ally was getting a bit freaked out." A slight misrepresentation of her emotions, I suppose. But her name was the magic word with him.

He nodded, resigned to the fact that he wasn't allowed to argue if he did, in fact, care for Ally's well-being as suggested by his overdramatic farewell to her. "I suppose there is a lot of work for me to do here, if you girls have stopped interfering with the magical balance of things."

"Doesn't that mean it stops you having extra work to do?"

He fixed me with a rather belittling glare. "There is a lot more happening here at any given minute than what you and your friends are up to. And at the same time you are all becoming significant to the magical landscape. The Huntress going about her duties will keep the fairies in line, and Alana should be working in my stead." For a moment he seemed to almost flinch with his anger and frustration, like once again he was schooling himself back to the placid neutrality he was supposed to exude. "She should have found that I was missing and stopped this a month ago. She can't let her feelings for Ally stop her from doing her job, not when something this big is happening. The land is unbalanced at the moment—there are some huge gnarls in the tapestry that I can hardly understand on first glance. I will need some time to set it right. To even understand what has happened in my absence. I never got to set right the tangles you put in the Ritual at Midsummer. The star boar alone will be a day's work, but I will have to put it far down my list of priorities..." He was pacing back and forth by the time he reached the end of his speech. I really ought to have told him to run along, but I loved being able to talk to him, to grill him for answers. To hear him talk about his own work to me almost as if I were an equal in understanding. (I think I almost got what he was on about, at least.) It was an extremely rare opportunity, maybe for anyone in human history.

"I can imagine whoever blocked you out the first time won't be making things easy for you either now you're back."

He scowled. "No." Even the Piper I could read, at least on the same human level that I could read you or anyone else. He was ashamed for saying so much, for revealing the very human way he thought about his problems, the people in his life, his job. He knew it was a weakness he was exposing to me—someone who considered herself his rival. And he was shedding answers to questions I'd never have dared ask him out loud.

"Would you like some help?"

"I already have Alana working for me."

"Tactful, but that doesn't stop me offering to help."

"And by offering you mean that you will follow Alana or me until you fall into trouble and become a hindrance and a part of the problem, forcing one or the other of us to take you under our wing and involve you in the process. Fine. But talk to her first."

"I will, I will," I said.

He nodded, turning away from me, ready to make his mysterious disappearance.

"Oh, one more thing," I blurted.

His look was so dark even the brilliant white of his eyes seemed clouded and dim in the shadows as he turned. "What?" He knew what I was going to ask.

"Why *do* you leave all those old pipes around?"

He took his time replying, and I knew it wasn't his whole story. "You understand my nature. I cannot exist without a way to temper my power, or perhaps then I would be tempted to become an absolute. None of us exist wholly unaccountable to humanity."

I nodded. "To create order first there has to be a chaos to make it out of?" I could see why I had come across one of his pipes so early in this whole saga. I'd caused rather a lot of the chaos lately.

"No." He thought through what I'd said some more and winced. "Also, please don't take what you said to heart. Just... Don't. You're bad enough as it is."

And then he vanished.

"Yeah, and you're boring," I grumbled.

*

When I got home I took out my laptop, sat on my bed and opened my favourite mindless game on the internet. However, my brain was thinking hard about Other things.

The Piper was a clever one—he had be able to read me and everyone I knew a million times better than I could, which to me was only ever just a vague impression of feelings and intentions and some hints of their pasts. He *knew* now that Alana was enforcing this rule on us. Telling me that I could work with Alana was the same as forbidding me to investigate, but in a much politer way. I could not even bring up the subject with her and it was going to become really obvious really quickly if I was running after cultists all day. I was at his mercy to allow Alana back into the game. Perhaps he would appreciate her help, I thought, but then he was pretty much a man with the powers of a god, so it wasn't like he was going to find it too hard to cope on his own. He had for thousands of years.

Although... Those cultists had stopped him once already in the last months.

In any case, even if he did tell her and recruit her to stop the cultists, it was up to her to invite me to join in. If she didn't want to tell me, which was quite likely considering how things had gone in the past, then I could not break the silence to ask her to let me in. If she caught me following or investigating, even if she went back to her job, which he had pretty much told me to my face she only stopped doing because *he* stopped doing his, then I would probably wreck the friendship between all four of us. I was considered the loose cannon: the one that everyone else was watching, and even though they were almost daring me to slip up after how excited Ally had got, even going off to investigate Mr Lane herself, I would be accused of ruining something *nice* just for trying to save them all.

I had to admit, it seemed like he'd got me.

I played three games in a row, sorting out all the different possibilities, all the ways I might walk up to Alana and tell her what I had discovered while emphasising how it had all just happened to me completely in the normal course of my day.

I decided that there was just no honest way to tell her.

Fortunately, my reputation as a schemer was well-earned, and I turned my mind to a variety of ways that I could trick Alana into falling into the adventure, hopefully without Alana realising that I'd been the one guiding her. She just had to see Mr Lane again, and hopefully at a great time for making him Alana's problem. If he did something odd and suspicious in front of both of us, then Alana would be duty-bound to investigate it. We'd have to break the silence about it just to say "Oh my god" to each other, and three words of recognition would be enough.

I mean, come on, we'd all seen the cultists and she least of us would like Mr Lane; she had sensed something about him that she was not sharing. Something so awful she'd completely befuddled him about who was at the table.

Despite apparently offering me a job, Mr Lane hadn't left any contact information that wasn't held by Teb.

I tried phoning her, and she didn't answer. I doubted she ever let her phone more than a foot out of reach, so I had to conclude she was ignoring me.

Because of *Jeremy*.

How on earth did I track down a goblin? I suddenly knew what I had to do. I couldn't ask Ally for help: she was too eager to break the silence, but that eagerness would have her accidentally tear the whole thing open and send it tumbling down. She was all elbows where she should have had subtlety. And that immediately exhausted the list of available friends when I was seeking help to get to Alana via information locked up in Fort Teb. Friends of friends, however…

I played two more games just biting my lip and thinking about that. By the end of them I was pretty relaxed, my mind focussing more on the hypnotic clicking of my mouse than my problems. I knew what I was supposed to do;

the only thing worrying me was that I had forgotten to put dinner on, but after some internal debate I had to accept that there was only really one way to deal with that. I got up, put my jacket on and called to my dad that he had to order pizza tonight: I was going out.

*

The day was a little cooler as evening came in, but that had caused an odd summer mist to drift about between the hills and it had settled along the high street. Now the town was at least trying to look the part of a place where sinister cultists could lurk. Well, okay, it smelled of flowers and the green smell of the fields and trees, and the sky was a gentle powdery blue, the sun low and heavy and gold. But the mist could be sinister... If it wasn't draped like gauze over the town like lines of lace. You know what, it was a terrible night to be hunting cultists. It was a terrible town full stop for cultists, looking like a postcard at any given moment. The most Gothic thing here was the font the greengrocers used.

I made my way to Ally's road and dived past her house. Safe on the other side, I glanced into her garden and saw the curtains were closed in the front room and my theatrics had been for nothing.

I strolled up her neighbour's drive and rapped smartly on the door.

The bad-ness of the idea struck me when the door opened and my former teacher looked down at me with bewilderment. "Tanya? What do you want?"

"I... Er... Is Cathy with you?" I asked Mr Brooke, our youthful, pretty former history teacher. I wouldn't say I was jealous of Cathy, but he had made the subject easier on the eyes at least.

"Ye-e-es... Are you friends with her? I never saw you together before." Well, we had briefly been in the same room once when she came to the school and we had both been at the prom together, but under Alana's watchful eye I had never been too friendly with his fairy girlfriend, because he had no idea and Alana didn't want me saying anything that would give him one.

"Oh yeah, we go way back," I said cheerfully. "Can I see her for a bit?" On my end of the friendship, away from Mr Brooke's eyes, I had met Cathy in the fairy world where she had been recently banished by the Piper and was pretty upset about being pulled away from her mortal lover. I'd made it my mission to cheer her up for the couple of days I spent there with her. It was a much more solid base to our friendship, but I had literally no way to tell him that without also letting him know his girlfriend was a fairy.

"Of course. Come in."

"Oh, um... Thanks." Escorted by him, I was taken to a heavily-perfumed front room with a TV playing. Cathy sat on the sofa with her knees drawn up, staring at *Masterchef* with utter fascination.

"Hey... Cathy."

She looked up. "Oh! Tanya! Hello!" She turned the volume right down on the TV, but I notice didn't mute it, let alone turn it off.

Mr Brooke gestured a chair to me and sat himself on the squashy floral sofa beside his fiancée. She beamed at me, sparkling and clean, her hair shimmery red, her pyjamas a white that would make a detergent salesman cry with joy. Her human disguise was sort of lousy because she hadn't realised that zits, imperfections, split-ends and the like made you rather more realistic. Aside from that, though, she looked about as normal as I'd ever seen her, her aura of sparkly fairy-ness almost aggressively beaten down by her surroundings.

I stared at Mr Brooke instead, willing him to go away so I could talk shop with Cathy, but he seemed a little bemused at having a former student in his house and felt he couldn't leave us to talk without first quizzing me on my exams, my university acceptance and what had happened on results day, then the sort of history I would be studying on my strange course. Cathy's eyes drifted back to *Masterchef* and I felt like my own would do the same soon. She seemed way too polite to butt in and ask why I was here, and Mr Brooke, as someone who talked for a living, seemed happy to provide all the conversation.

Eventually he paused after I managed to wean him off that conversation by getting more and more monosyllabic, and I got a chance to turn to Cathy. "How have you been lately?"

She shrugged. "You know. Keeping busy. I'm getting very good at making omelettes! It takes a lot of practice, but the trick is beating the eggs well before you put them in the pan."

"Uhuh. Oh, thinking of eggs, have you heard anything from our friend Jeremy lately?"

She gave me this utterly blank look. She knew Jeremy, but fairies were very literal and Jeremy was absolutely nothing to do with eggs as far as she was concerned. I kicked myself mentally: worst thing you can possibly do is confuse a fairy.

"That is to say, I would like to catch up with him, if you know where he is."

"I know how to find him," she said, still looking very wary of my motivation, not because I was on some sort of blacklist, for once, but just because I really wasn't stating my purpose very well.

"Well, if you could give me some advice on how to do that?" I was getting quite desperate and frustrated. I'd forgotten how annoying it could be talking to fairies. Half the time I thought they were only winding you up because they could tell you had an agenda, but their fanaticism about honest talk and being upfront was far too well-known: they did seem genuinely bound to this custom.

"He watches over her, as he should," Cathy said.

I caught myself from blurting out an instinctive "Who?" because... *duh*.

"Thank you," I said. "I should get going."

"Wait, do you want to stay for a cup of tea?" Cathy asked. "I didn't even offer you anything!"

"No, no, I have a lot I have to do. It's not compulsory."

She pouted like she thought it really was.

Mr Brooke stood up as I did, to show me to the door. My compulsive movement to prove I was leaving seemed to say clearly enough to Cathy I was done: she turned the volume back up and her eyes towards the TV. I don't think she was insulted, just that her standards of politeness were very different and she thought more than enough had been said considering I'd declined the tea ritual. Mr Brooke, being human, felt the need to babble small talk goodbyes to me, telling me to drop by if I wanted, to bring my other friends, to tell him about my course some more, maybe there were some books that he could lend me and so on. I nodded and thanked him repeatedly, even though he hadn't given me anything except more trouble than I needed by sitting in the room while I was trying to wrangle information from Cathy.

It was a relief when their front door shut and I was on the other side. I turned my feet to walking and headed back across town.

My First Goblin

Here's something you don't know.

I think we all have our 'first goblin', that moment you realised something was not quite right with the general population, that something stranger than imagining was moving beneath the surface.

Teb's, of course, was the goblin on the bus who inoffensively sat there while she freaked out at the horror of seeing an almost alien creature quietly wandering about in human skin to get its shopping done. Ally first really became aware of it when she started interacting with the skateboarding goblins down by the river: something wrong about them crept up on her, and even before she saw their chosen goblin forms, she knew what they were. Alana just wandered into the world, as she'd have us believe it, knowing everything, and makes it quite clear with her folded arms and narrowed eyes that there isn't a story to tell there.

I was on the London Underground, aged about sixteen. I got split up from the others because they wanted to go to Highgate Cemetery and I got on the wrong tube somehow in the crowd of people and just surfed around using up my Oyster card, people-watching, being very calm about the whole ordeal, possibly because I wasn't being dragged around a field full of dead people. Since Ally's Mum was leading the expedition, she pretty much just said, "It's Tanya, she'll find us," and took them to a McDonalds near a big station to wait for me and to pump Ally full of McFlurry until she stopped fretting.

Anyway, after I'd made a loop of the Circle line I felt I ought to head back to our appointed meeting place: the signal wasn't great underground, but I had a sense Hester had taken them to the station we'd come into London by. The only trouble was, I couldn't find it on the Underground map, and every time I tried to stand in front of it another huge group of people came by and jostled me and I got dragged a dozen paces away. It wasn't scary being lost, but trying to become found again began to get kind of worrying.

So I looked around for a station attendant, and then I saw her. She was standing by the ticket barrier, but that gate was out of order, and something about her seemed *wrong*. She had a DayGlo waistcoat, but it somehow made her less visible; her uniform looked old and like it had been made by someone imitating the Underground uniform, not by the Underground company itself. She wore stockings and sensible black shoes with a tiny heel. She had an old-fashioned cap on her head and her hair was in a perfect neat roll at the back of her neck with finger waves visible underneath the cap. Yet as presentable as she seemed to be, she was *wrong*. She didn't fit the time, or the place. Even the way she stood seemed to be out of line with everyone else. No one looked at her, no one bumped or jostled her. No one stood beside her to fish their ticket out of their bag…

And her shape was wrong too. I could see a slim, pretty woman, but I could see her arms bending wrong as she moved, her weight held wrong like she was resting unfamiliar feet on the ground. Her head turned sharply but her eyes stayed still. And there was a sense of a pointed nose, wicked teeth, like when she wasn't paying attention to looking nice, when her attention slipped, something monstrous lurked beneath.

The one or two people who passed by her and showed her a ticket looked *wrong* as well, in their own ways, though they hurried by before I could look too closely. She opened the barrier for them and my thumbs tingled, like something strange had happened, but of course it was just a mechanical process: people commuting, gates opening, tickets flashing… Where had I seen that the gate was out of order, though? The harder I looked the more it seemed bizarre that idea had leapt into my head upon looking at it. It was a perfectly functioning gate: perhaps more so because so fewer people were using it.

So of course I hurried over to her and began babbling my problems as fast as I could between sobs, waving my Oyster card at her like that would fix everything.

Her alarm was evident: she boggled down at me, as surprised as I had been staring at her from across the busy station. She seemed horrified that I had even seen her, let alone dared talk to her. She didn't know how to reply at first, but then she took my card from my hand and held it a second, before handing it back. "You should know where to go," she said.

And weirdly, when I was holding the card again, I *did*.

*

The sun had pretty much gone by the time I got to Teb's cul-de-sac: the houses were lit up and most front rooms had a blue square of TV light visible through the net curtains (I forced my eyes away: I was not here to prove Warren right), but there was a thankful lack of kids running around on the driveways. This was the young family area, since the primary school's multicoloured fence was just visible around the corner, and the utter lack of traffic meant the road acted as a safe playground any time the kids were out of school.

The street was guarded by more than neighbourhood watch. I got to the streetlamp in front of Teb's house and glanced up at her window to make sure that her curtains were closed, then I said, in a perfectly reasonable tone, "Jeremy."

"What are you *doing* here?" his voice hissed at me from the shadows. The goblin stepped out from behind Teb's wheelie bin. He wasn't dressed as a modern human, like when I'd seen him in the woods: he wore a tunic of neutral pattern but purple cloth and had on some rudimentary armour, gold-edged plate strapped to his shoulder and elbows. He had no weapon as far as I could see, but then Teb also never looked like she was carrying a weapon. "I told you to keep Teb out of it!"

I stood my ground. "And I am. This is me doing just that: you think it would be at all strange for me to walk into her house? I even have a spare key! That is how much her family doesn't flinch to see me wandering into their house and helping myself to a drink from their fridge. I need your help, Jeremy."

"Why would I give it to you?" he asked, looking extremely resentful that I would ask. His dark eyes were deep and distrustful, glittering with intelligence that even the sharpest rodent eyes should never have had. His characteristics as a ferret were less pronounced than when I had seen him at the prom: I'd seen his siblings scrabble on all fours in tough moments during the fight. But right now his basic body structure was undeniably human, the needlelike claws and sharp teeth an accent, not a defining feature.

"Because I *can* go into the house with my spare key and grab some leftovers from dinner, head up to Teb's room, sit on her bed and casually explain everything, and she'll hear me out, forgive me for insulting her on your orders, and in ten minutes flat I can have her helping me investigate things and blow the whole scheme wide open. This is *Teb*. Her help will get things done twice as fast as if I was acting on my own. She'd still be faster than Ally and Alana combined. I have a good motivation to do that. Oh, and I imagine she'll be pretty pissed off that you told me to fall out with her 'for her own safety'. She doesn't like being looked after."

"Why do you think I came to you instead of telling her to stay out of it?" Jeremy said miserably.

"And that's why I'm talking to you first."

We stood in an uneasy impasse.

"She doesn't know I'm here either," Jeremy finally confessed.

"She doesn't? I thought you were at her beck and call."

"Yes, but I could be on an errand to the South Pole and hear her call and still be at her side in a second. There is no reason for me to be outside her house all night."

"Nor in armour. You're worried about her!"

"I'm… Uneasy. I'd rather be here and bored than not certain what was happening and elsewhere."

"It would definitely liven things up for you if you decided to help me. If you don't want me getting involved, I can't go in there and ask her for a phone number she has on a business card for a Mr Lane. She took it the other day in a fit of Hollywood starry eyes, and I need it now for my investigation. I'm certain he's behind the trouble you're sensing."

Jeremy frowned, perhaps weighing up how difficult the task sounded. It might be as easy as going through the handbag Teb had that day, and I was about to open my mouth to reassure him about how hard it wasn't.

The front door opened and Mahesh came out with a big black bin bag in his hand. He stopped just beyond the doorway, framed with the hall light and blinking at the sudden darkness outside. "Is that Tanya?" he asked, surprised.

I glanced around: Jeremy had melted away completely.

"It is," I confessed. What was I going to do, leg it and have him go in and tell Teb that he'd spotted me loitering around outside talking to their bins?

"Well what are you doing out here? Come on in!"

"I just walked over," I said, putting on a big smile. Teb's dad returned it warmly and stepped aside so I could go to the door without brushing past the bin bag.

I stood blinking in Teb's hall; it was really just a corner of the front room, the entrance compactly leading to the stairs which lurked in the background of their living room. Teb wasn't downstairs, but Sarika was, her feet up, toes wiggling in relief at not being in tight work shoes anymore. Teb's mum greeted me warmly, as I found myself kindly shunted further into the room by Mahesh.

"Have you had dinner?" he pressed me.

"Um… No, but…"

"Ah, we have loads left over! If you don't have it Avi will, and I worry he'll grow up fat like me!" Mahesh patted his stomach, which to be fair was not much bigger than the average middle-aged man's paunch, making him, I felt, by far the cuddliest of our combined parents, if we put him at the top of the scale and Alana's mum at the bottom. He headed into the kitchen, but not before yelling "Teb!" up the stairs with all his lung power.

"What?" came an irritable teenage voice, several seconds later.

Mahesh came back out with a huge slice of pie on a plate and winked at me, gesturing the sofa. I plopped myself down and tucked in, waiting for Teb. I thanked him in the meantime, and we got started on my tenth "That was so unfair of Mr Westcott" conversation of the week, though I only found it funnier as time went by and the relief of getting into university sank in.

"*What?*" Teb's voice came down the stairs again, but she still didn't. I was beginning to crack up. I may have lost my opportunity to talk to Jeremy but the entertainment was worth it.

"She can be really prickly, can't she?" I murmured to her parents, keeping my voice low so Teb wouldn't hear and catch on too soon.

"She gets it from her mother."

"She does *not!*" Sarika squawked in a very Teb-like way and threw one of her shoes at Mahesh. "She's just upset she didn't get her grades for university. I said we should send her to summer school to make up the points, you know, but she's just looking for jobs! I said, what can you get with just GCSEs these days, not even A Levels since you failed them all, and…"

I could see why Teb had been avoiding downstairs; Sarika's playful mood vanished the moment she remembered that her prize-student daughter had suddenly become an unwelcome lodger. Mahesh glanced at me while his wife continued to rant. He knew the truth of Teb's grades, though not the truth behind why she had publicly renounced them. To be honest, *I* didn't really, except that maybe if Teb really was now such a powerful goddess tied to these lands, would she actually be able to leave them? The Piper had said that she should be doing stuff for the ritual, the source of all her power. Even merely existing here helped stabilize things and cement her into the landscape. Perhaps she was wary to leave in case the powers stayed behind when she didn't.

Teb's door opened and she came thudding down the hall, stomping down the first few stairs, until she stopped short on seeing me sitting there with a plate on my knees and a grin on my face.

"Heya, Tebster!"

"What are *you* doing here?"

"I dropped by for a chat and ended up being fed dinner to save your mum having to buy Avi a new pair of school trousers when he gets too fat for his old ones."

A different childish voice echoed from upstairs, "*I'm not fat!*"

"Not yet you're not!" Teb called over her shoulder and came the rest of the way downstairs. She sat on the arm of the sofa and regarded me critically. "What's up, Tan-tan?"

"I, er, thought I should drop by to apologise for being a brat the other day." I put down my cleared plate on the coffee table and stood up, offering her an impromptu hug. She looked at me like I was insane, but didn't resist when I gave her a squeeze. I quickly ducked out of it to grab my plate and take it through to the kitchen: Teb followed me.

"Did you go to the museum?" she asked as I dumped the plate in the sink, where there was still-warm soapy water. I got to work scrubbing.

"Huh? Oh! Yeah, I did, but nothing happened. Have you been out and about at all the last couple of days?"

"Not really. I went to Ally's but she was being weird, all her stuff everywhere. I mean, literally, you had to jump across her room to get to the bed there are so many books on the floor. I think she's purging for going away to uni, but from the looks of it she's just getting nostalgic and deciding to keep everything that she owns after all. Good thing Danny's got a big car, huh?"

"We've got like a month and a half before we go!" I exclaimed.

"Well, have you thought about what you're taking?"

"Not really. I assume a laptop and a case full of clothes; the kitchen stuff Daddy says I should buy there so we don't have to carry it and I'd need to get a full set of my own plates and pans anyway because there's not enough to spare at home."

"Oh Tanya… You're going to end up taking *so* much more once you get down to it. I think Ally might be onto something, having a clear out. I'm not even going anywhere and I have started looking at my stuff, seeing what kiddy things I still have…"

"Chucking it all out? Oh, Teb. Teb Teb Teb… I came at just the right time to save a load of old nostalgia, didn't I?"

"You want to keep all my old junk?"

"Nah, I wanna save it so I can give it to Ally so she takes it to uni! Let's see if between us we can force her to take a whole extra suitcase of Friend Rubbish, huh?"

Teb was laughing too at that point. "Come on upstairs, we'll have a look at what I've got!"

I got myself a glass of juice from their fridge and followed her to her room.

To my surprise Teb, of all people, didn't start up a conversation about anything strange. She had taken the "don't talk about it" to heart remarkably well. I assumed that she still *had* to meet her goblins about some things, but the summer was a pretty clear schedule for her, goddess-wise, with the Hunt being the most important thing she would ever have to do in her whole life, and even the repeats in later years would probably be the highlight event. She'd got pretty shaken up about the changes she had gone through since becoming the Huntress. Perhaps these normal moments with her friends were a deliberate attempt to reconnect with her old self.

I went to her window and glanced out: I couldn't see any sign of Jeremy lurking in the driveway, but then if he wanted to remain hidden to Teb he would be doubly hidden to me. I had no special affiliation with him: my only power was knowing that he existed, as well as an ability to call him out of the shadows by using his assumed name.

For a while we just pulled boxes out of Teb's meticulously stacked cupboard and went through the contents, our conversation turned to whatever we found and the memories brought up by it. Teb's room made Ally's look spacious, but her extreme neat-freak ways were possibly because of this, and definitely helped. With her habit of tidying everything away the room felt airy and comfortable, like you could lean on any given surface without knocking something over, unlike Ally's room, which was a disaster in slow motion. I felt guilty stacking things on the small square of floor by the door, but Teb was in a good mood. Like I'd said to Jeremy, we were friends, deep down and all the way back into our pasts. A few squabbles couldn't put a real dent in that.

Remembering my conversation with Jeremy, I had a subtle glance around but there was no sign even of Teb's handbag, let alone a business card lying around cluttering up her desk. She'd probably grabbed it on a whim, but as with many of her mad career aspirations I didn't think she'd ever be brave enough to phone up and ask to be in a film. I, on the other hand, would have been booking plane tickets to Hollywood yesterday, if that was really as deep as Mr Lane's story went.

Teb had hefted down another box from the top shelf of the closet by then and she levered it open. We looked into it with curiosity: a bundle of rainbow-coloured skipping ropes, knotted neatly together, lay on top. I pulled them out and sighed. "So this is where they went to!"

"What do you mean?"

"Don't you remember when the skipping ropes all got stolen, and we were all so upset? We ran around for days looking for them, and in the end we got so distraught your mum sat us down and told us things were things and we shouldn't get so attached? Ally's Mum was going to buy us more, but your mum said we had to learn."

"Oh! I remember! I was skipping inside and smashed a pot plant... She took them all away, but she didn't know they were yours and Ally's as well!" Teb laughed. "I never told you two because I was terrified you wouldn't come around anymore in case she took more of your things. I found them a few years later, but I thought we were a bit too old for skipping ropes by then."

"I was going to ask how they came to be in one of your boxes. You think we're too old for them now?"

"Tanya, don't you dare try skipping in my room!"

I laughed, but it sank into a sort of sigh as I looked around at all our shared memories spread out on the floor. "It's going to be strange being away from you all."

"Hey, you're the ones leaving *me* behind."

"Yeah, but it's like... I have to go right down south. Ally's going much further north. Alana's going to be well on the other side of London from here. None of us are an easy journey to anyone else's university, *or* to Troutespond. We're basically not going to see each other much, if at all, except for the big holidays."

"Are you saying you want to take a skipping rope all the way to university?"

I took the one she offered me without saying a word.

We shuffled through the boxes in front of us a little longer, but my heart was suddenly aching too much to make this fun. I stood up. "Yeah, I should probably get home. I ran out on Daddy without telling him where I was going and it's getting late."

"You always do that," Teb observed.

"Maybe I feel a bit guilty about it, even so," I said, with an ashamed little smile.

"Hey, are we doing anything else this week? I got the sense it had all been a bit too much excitement for Alana. I was waiting to see if you would put together any expedition, but Ally said you were seeing Warren and..." she shrugged. "I don't like spending the summer cooped up in my room, unlike Ally."

I smiled. "I'll let you know if I find anything fun to do."

"That's why I keep you around!" Teb said, I felt with a rather artificial cheerfulness. She shooed me on out of her house like she had been the one to decide I should leave, and I headed back home, skipping and feeling surprisingly not disappointed with the way my evening had gone.

Bookstore

Here's something you don't know:

About a month ago, not long after we agreed to stop talking about it, I realised Ally had stopped talking... entirely. At least to me. Sometimes just around me. It was a horrible realisation, because I couldn't actually say when it had happened or when was the last time we had a real conversation. I had a hunch that made me feel kind of ill that we hadn't had a real talk since she met the Piper, but being frozen out entirely had to be a result of the prom.

Being desperate makes me kind of crazy, so I went out one day when I knew she had arranged to meet Teb and I had told Teb I couldn't come when she checked with me.

I trailed them down the high street and when they went onto the green I knew they would go sit in our favourite spot in the grass, so I crept along the other side of the hedge to get to the place behind them.

When I got there I found Alana already lurking behind the hedge.

She, also, was listening in as Teb obliviously put down a picnic blanket just beyond the shade. Alana and I stared at each other and said nothing, aware that we were both in the wrong and the last thing we wanted to do was let Teb and Ally know.

I sneaked off one way, she the other, and well clear of the site I collapsed into the only fit of hysterical giggles I've ever had all by myself, though to be honest I was imagining Alana laughing her bum off somewhere on the other side of town. Maybe she genuinely was.

I learned two things that day: I'm probably not the most messed up a person can be, and even if I am there are others down here with me, and secondly, that I am ridiculous. The next day I phoned Ally to propose we all go to Ransley for high tea and trying on posh hats in the boutiques, and when I actually made an effort to be normal and friendly, engaging her and remembering to include her, she unfroze and instantly went back to normal.

On the other hand I think Alana came to a silent agreement with me that we would never ever talk about the catalyst for the turning point in our summer friendship.

*

I awoke the next morning and it was then that I began to feel some regret that all the walking had been for basically nothing. I'd found Jeremy, but that ended up going nowhere. As I enjoyed a lie-in where no responsibilities awaited me I wondered what else I could do.

Each day that passed I felt more and more certain that there was work we seriously needed to be doing. The Piper needed our assistance: that little extra something that having dumb humans blundering into supposedly well-kept secrets gave to a situation. What I needed, then, was to do some blundering of my own, and the caveat I'd been given only said to keep Teb out of it. I had others to call on. And a big gamble I could take.

I found my phone and, still lying in bed, dialled Alana.

The sound of her mobile trilling on the other end went on for some time: I was convinced it was about to go to messages, or cut off entirely, so I almost hung up reflexively when the dialling cut out: "Hello?" She sounded groggier than me.

"Heeey, Alana!"

"Oh, it's *you*." Yeah, fair enough, we didn't often phone each other up to chat.

"Thanks a lot. I heard from Teb yesterday that Ally's got in a weird manic state about university. We should go save her from herself, take her out, get some fresh air, that sort of thing."

"Oh no. What did she do?" Alana was *very* monosyllabic first thing in the morning (first thing to a lazy teenager: it was nearing eleven).

"Apparently started packing already. We should really go stop her before she loads up Danny's car like they're leaving tomorrow."

"Maybe she's about to leave town anyway?"

"Well in that case we definitely need to get over to hers, right away. Meet you by the statue at twelve?"

"What *is* it with you and that statue?"

"He's a good meeting place! And kinda dishy for cast bronze."

"You're *mental*."

"Will you be there?"

"Yeah, yeah. Whatever. I'm going crazy home alone with my mom anyway." She hung up on me.

Properly motivated, I dragged myself up and began assembling an outfit for the day. I didn't know what today would bring, but I was going to do everything in my power to make it interesting.

*

The day was fresher to match my mood. The sky was dotted with almost comically perfect clouds in between wide spaces of blue and a breeze was at least attempting to move the air about a bit.

Alana looked as summery as the day was when I found her sitting on one of the benches checking her phone. Though I'd clearly woken her up, we must have got out of bed at the same time; while I'd only managed to locate clothes and brush my hair before leaving, she appeared showered and neat with perfect make-up, generally putting across the impression of being a presentable human being.

She also seemed a lot more amiable than she had on the phone. The cloud that had been on her after we first met Mr Lane had dissipated and though the glow of the exam results couldn't last forever, her general mood had clearly improved. Maybe she always looked this good, but I never noticed because she was so busy scowling and walking about with a scratchy dark aura of misery all around her.

Already on her feet by the time I reached her, she greeted me with an understated little wave. "Ready to see Ally off then?"

I laughed. "You don't think we could scare her into thinking she actually has to leave today?"

"I haven't known her as long as you by like a decade and a half, but she does seem *awfully* suggestible."

I cackled and set off at a skipping pace towards Ally's, Alana walking behind me at a much more unconcerned pace. After the second time I had to stop at a corner and wait for her I tried to fall in line with her step. We strolled along together and for once it seemed almost normal to be together. Maybe this was a side effect of not talking about it: things *did* become easier with Alana. I wasn't sure she and I could have amiably walked along like this while we were still so busy worrying about the secrets the other was keeping. Except, well, she hadn't bloody told us the Piper was missing, and I certainly wasn't telling her that I was scheming on his behalf since she'd been so lax in her duties.

At Ally's Hester cheerfully let us in and informed us that Ally was "still hiding upstairs", leading me and Alana to glance nervously at each other. I put a finger to my lips and gestured up the stairs; we crept up as stealthily as we could. On the tiny landing I put my hand on Ally's door, took a deep breath and then threw it open, yelling, "ALLY, ARE YOU READY TO GO TO UNI?! WE'RE LEAVING NOW!"

The door bounced off her desk and almost slammed itself shut on me again, but I got a good glimpse of Ally leaping up from the floor and screaming before being lost to sight with a thump: several smaller bumps followed. I pushed the door open more gently to see she'd tumbled into her wardrobe and was now struggling to get up amid an avalanche of books falling from the space beneath her clothes. Her room was a complete tip: it was about the width of a cupboard and just long enough for a bed. The fact Ally had fitted a wardrobe, desk, chest of drawers and bookshelf into it as well baffled me: she was terrible at the actual game of Tetris. Currently clothes were stacked on her desk, burying her laptop (I supposed that was where her recent radio silence on the internet came from), and her bookcase was half emptied, the books stacked in the miniscule space of floor she had. Her bed was likewise covered. All the books were old, hardbacks bound in faded cloth that may once have been bright colours but now all clocked in somewhere between brown and grey. The room smelled of dust and foxed paper, like we'd wandered into the old wing of a library.

"Where did you get all these books?" I asked, amazed. I wanted to come in: Alana couldn't even see past me, but there was just nowhere to go.

"My legs have gone completely dead," Ally moaned from the wardrobe. "Help!"

I squeezed through the door (which had never opened fully because of the desk and created a sort of airlock where you had to squish past it and half close it to finish coming into the room if you were anyone but Ally, who was stick thin and therefore didn't realise the health and safety hazard she lived in). Alana peered curiously in and burst out laughing to see Ally reclining in her wardrobe, the folds of her prom dress's skirt artfully arranged over her head. I tiptoed between the stacks of books and hauled Ally up.

"Ow. Ow ow ow." She rotated on the spot and collapsed onto the bed, heedless of the old books spread across it.

"Seriously, what is going on?" I demanded, not wanting to let Ally get away with being exceptionally weird even for Ally. "And tell us *slowly*."

She winced and sat up, pulling dusty volumes from beneath her. "Um. Well you know I have that habit of buying all the twenty pence books from St Troute's shop?" She massaged her legs: judging by the tiny clear space on the floor she had been crouching or sitting on her feet to squeeze her lanky frame into such a tight space. I was amazed that she'd managed to grow so big while living in such cramped conditions, but then maybe it was just goldfish who only grew to accommodate the space you gave them.

I nodded. I'd seen her buy one at least once a month for years, sometimes several. It had never occurred to me that she *kept* them, mostly because there just hadn't seemed to be space in her room. Her little bookcase was full of Garth Nix, Rowling, Pullman, and all the authors from our Literature classes, classics, Shakespeare, some more modern works, all glossy bright covers printed in this quarter of the century. For all the evidence of her junk store buys she could have just been eating the books.

"You've been stashing them in the wardrobe?"

"And under my bed and in the desk and the bottom drawers of the cabinet since I don't actually own that many clothes…"

I pulled open a drawer and saw that it was currently empty of books, although there were some other finds from the junk shop I remembered Ally buying: a miniature set of brass teapot and cups, some tobacco barrels with ornate design she said she'd keep pencils in but clearly hadn't tidied her desk in three years in order to go through with that, a box of assorted buttons, badges and coins that she added to constantly with found and bought oddities… There was a weirdly familiar set of porcelain dolls lying haphazardly in the corner: a couple of dancing girls and a tacky, ridiculous Pied Piper ornament in bright yellow and red, comical dots of red painted on his cheeks, a manic grin on his face. "*Really?*"

"Hey! You made me buy them!"

I noticed that the antique wooden recorder of unknown origin that I'd made her buy at the same time wasn't stored in the same junk drawer.

"So what's with the books?" Alana asked, having made it into the room. She leaned on the door, since there was literally nowhere else to go while Ally had the bed and I had the middle of the room.

"Um…" Ally looked a bit panicked now. "I do actually read them, you know. It's just…" She gestured around at them all like that might explain. It was fascinating: tell the girl not to talk in a frantic babble and she loses the power of speech entirely.

"Come on," Alana said, getting impatient. "What the hell is this all about?"

"I think I read about the stone circle before!" Ally blurted, then slapped a hand over her mouth. We stared at her. She slowly lowered her hand. "Um… Well… *Come on*, I had to know! There is no way strange cultists show up and upset everyone and it's not weird! We're like the only people in the town who know magic is real, right? Or at least as far as we know. What if they do? What if they're going to do something awful? No one else would stop them, because no one else would care about all the early warning signs! We saw the cultists with our own eyes, and we *know* that they seem dodgy. Even if someone knew the stone circle was being used for rituals, apparently every coven of pagans in thirty miles comes here too and again as far as anyone is concerned they're not doing anything because the magic they do, if it works at all, clearly does not have any pronounced effect on anyone else's life! There are people like me who could literally *grow up in the same house as a witch* and not realise that magic was real, because if Mum is such a powerful witch, why aren't we rich, successful, attractive people in a big house *anywhere but here?*"

"I think those are all things Hester would actively ward you *against*," I commented, trying to calm her down as Ally got to the slightly bug-eyed stage of her own personal brand of mania.

"Well we know they're up to something. I um… I was going to check in on you and Warren on your date…"

"By check in you mean stalk?"

"You're *adorable* together. But I saw Mr Lane again getting out his car with all this equipment, more than he had at the stone circle. He took it into the church and I heard him arguing with the priest. He is definitely not making a film after all! I caught him saying stuff like 'You knew this was going to happen,' 'Give me the list, I know you kept it,' and, dun-dun *dun*, 'I can't be held up by your sentimental bullcrap—' to paraphrase '—the ritual is in just two nights!' Huh? How about that!"

"Did you see where he went after that?" I demanded. Curse having a boyfriend! I'd missed the most interesting part!

"Um… You and Warren came out the ice cream parlour and I legged it into the junk shop. But oh my god, he came in a minute later! And he remembered me! He said 'Oh, you're Alana's friend from the café,' and remembered you two were in the newspaper. He was being all friendly, like you couldn't tell he'd been shouting a few minutes before. He quizzed me on my interests, asked me if I had a boyfriend and if I was going to university and all that junk that adults ask when they're trying to make friendly conversation, and then he bought a box of old pennies and left. And then I didn't know what to do because you were busy on your date, so I went home."

"So how did all that lead you to looking through these old books?"

"I don't *know*! Most of these are really old and strange. There are all sorts of local history things and boring special interest books…" She picked up as an example a book where the cover was almost flaking off it was so old and knackered. I think she bought the books mostly because they were aesthetically pleasing: she clearly imagined herself in a house with a room she could just fill with old books one day.

To my surprise I recognised the title: Montgomery Berkley-Norton's *Severstrong Abbey: Flora, Fauna and Pondlife*, a title I had once chanced across and tried to trick Teb into reading while she unwittingly provided cover for me to sneak into the Bilsworth Museum's reference section. Of course that had been a copy of it on the Museum's intranet: I couldn't believe the original book still existed. I couldn't believe she had a copy of it mouldering away here when I could have been using it to try and triangulate the actions of my enemies via all my own weird book hoarding I absolutely wasn't judging myself against her for.

It made sense, in a weird way, how Ally ended up with all these. Local interest books would probably not tend to travel far out of Waitingshire, as a rule, because what interest did they have beyond our county's borders? And as time passed and old books became older, they passed out of even being relevant to the people who might have once owned them. And where did everything useless go when the oldest family member who might still care about a crate of old books passed on? You didn't throw books away. That was obscene. Even using something as bland as Berkley-Norton's book as firewood still felt weirdly sacrilegious, the inherent power of books only surviving because we were trained to treat all books with respect, to not just destroy our predecessors' knowledge wantonly. So you did the next best thing and left the crate of books outside the junk shop one early morning, and there they would be sorted and priced and picked up by someone like Ally who had a hipster interest in the covers looking nice when lined up on a shelf.

Except no one was like Ally. No one else collecting the books because they wanted an antique shelf would stop to *read* the things. And here was the reminder that somehow, knowledge always found a way to come back around and serve its purpose again.

Considering I mostly had modern guidebooks and the like, I was almost drooling at the thought of the treasure trove that had been concealed inside Ally's miniscule room all this time. She had been collecting these a lot longer than I had been investigating, and I think she got to the good books before me, because I had never seen books half as intriguing in the junk shop.

Ally dismissively dropped the old book, like she didn't even care what was in it. "It's stupid though. I read like one thing years ago and I can't remember what book… I have a feeling it was not even relevant to the subject of the rest of the book. So I've been going through them all trying to find out! Except I keep getting distracted and reading big chunks of the books and my brain feels all mushy now and I can hardly remember why I was looking in the first place…"

She trailed off, then picked up a rather less fragile book and lobbed it away from her, gently enough that it only bounced to the foot of the bed. Either she was being jokingly symbolic about how fed up she was, or she really was that bad at throwing.

Behind me, Alana cleared her throat. I nearly died: I'd forgotten she was in the room.

"So you were really going to investigate this whole thing all on your own?"

"Um… Yes. If you won't help me."

I turned to watch Alana's reaction, but in the end there almost wasn't much to see: she had a reserved smile on her face, tempered by exasperation that came to everyone who tried to deal with Ally for long. "Of course we will. Do you have *any* idea what sort of book it was?"

Ally shrugged morosely, not even seeming to realise the significance of Alana just giving in and agreeing to help. Perhaps she had cracked so easily because this still didn't involve Teb. She hadn't even asked me if Teb was going to show up. Maybe she knew or trusted that I was on top of things and understood that I was keeping Teb away. "I was sort of hoping that getting them all out and looking at the covers might help me."

"Okay, let's do this logically," I said, shifting things from the desk chair and sitting down. "Let's at least sort the books out so we have a pile we can say definitely *won't* mention anything because they're not even about the local area and the like, and maybe this won't all look so intimidating."

Ally nodded and began to shift books to make room for Alana to sit down. She crossed the room and plonked herself down next to Ally, and now I could see the resignation on her face: she didn't like this, but she also knew that if she wasn't in the room me and Ally would rampage off and start to do this all by ourselves. The least she could do was oversee us and make sure we didn't do anything untoward. A third pair of eyes to turn on these pages would help us a great deal, so I certainly wasn't going to make a scene reminding her that we had agreed not to talk about it and challenge her to a duel of principles.

We fell silent for a bit, turning our minds to the task at hand. We started a towering pile of books that really weren't relevant: reference books from far afield, some collections of essays and poems from various olde timey academics, old editions of classics we instantly recognised: it was obvious *Jane Eyre* wasn't going to tell us any more about goblins than Mr Rochester's odd choice of pet names. I began to find I was having the same problem as Ally though when it came to the local books. As soon as I saw a title I thought might have something to do with any local lore I found it next to impossible to skip through when my eyes glued themselves to a paragraph, refusing to skim while there was knowledge I was genuinely interested in and had possibly never read before.

I read about a spurious theory on Waitingshire's name in a book of county maps (if I remember correctly it's something to do with old English *waet* for "swampy hellhole that we're determined to live on even though all our early history will just be reports of flood and typhoid") about a maiden left in the hills, wandering them and *waiting* for her boyfriend to come back for her when he had died far away. I read part of a guidebook that tried to explain a remote ruin of a church along the river road with a myth about a red dog that used to prowl the lowlands, chasing travellers up to thirteen miles until they could find shelter in a church, and the terrible luck that was visited on them after (though the beast apparently never mauled anyone). There was a shrine in this church with Latin for 'dog' engraved on it and that was, as far as I know, the full and only source for this myth. I read in an archaeologist's field guide to the county how Waitington had Roman ruins under it, how the shape of the city centre (circa 1910) still reflected the two thousand year old street plan and how that suggested a lost world of ruins beneath the financial district.

"Aha!" Alana cried, and when Ally and I looked up, in a reading daze, we found her trying desperately to smother her enthusiasm and go back to being dry and unaffected by the quest for knowledge.

"What is it?" we chorused together, both of us totally enthralled and with no shame about our curiosity.

"I have an amateur local historian here who decided witch trials were fascinating, and wasn't put off at all by the fact that the county literally has one recorded witch ever from that time. They wrote a full treatise throwing together a load of general knowledge on witches and witch trials, plus a ton of local history to pad out all the parts of the book that aren't about this one witch. There's a chapter here about the world she would have lived in… Literally a description of Troutespond from *our* point of view: what sort of 'magical' stuff she might have encountered."

"Well go on then, read it and tell us something we didn't know!" I cried. Ally put down her book at once.

There were a few minutes of unbearable agony as Alana leafed back and forth through the book. She was beginning to look rather awkward about reading this to us, like she had just realised she was absolutely breaking all the rules we'd set down after the prom. But like Ally said, something awful may happen if we didn't do anything about it, and like the Piper said, it was Alana's job more than anyone else to make sure that bad thing didn't happen.

"It says that the area has always had an association with magic… Goes on about the stone circle and possible connections to the druids, which is bollocks…" Alana flicked over a page. "In more recent times, that is, between 'druids', whenever the hell they were supposed to be, and the time when everyone was burnin' witches, the land became Christianised but 'native beliefs were allowed to continue', including 'strong folkloric traditions' of monsters and witches, and then there are pages of stories about goblins stealing babies and all that. There's talk of a beast that haunted the hills and all sorts but nothing particular about the stone circle. She seems to think mentioning the druids was enough about that… Like no one else was going to use it again. Pfft, we know that's not true." She flipped ahead.

"What did she say about the beast in the hills?" I asked, thinking of a rustling in the undergrowth under trees that were not our trees.

"Why?" Alana rounded on me, suspicious immediately.

"I mean the stone circle is in the hills, right? We've got to look for any links. Call yourself an investigator?"

Alana shrugged. "Well…" She flicked back a page. "It says there was a beast that terrorised the town. She doesn't say what it was, but it came out from the hills and took 'many brave knights' to set it to rest. Apparently it was hunted in the hills where it made its lair, and it would come down and steal children, devour livestock, etc etc. It was probably a wolf or a bear or something wild that we don't have any more, and the 'brave knights' were pretty stupid too if it took so many to catch it."

I shifted uncomfortably. "Well, even if it was just a wolf, back then there's a sort of… power that these stories have. You tell them too many times and if they really do survive to the modern age then there could well be enough power for the actual monster from the story to now exist."

"So you're saying the cultists are summoning a monster?"

"I'm saying that if we're taking the cultists seriously, we can't be really cynical about anything else we might read or hear.”

“Tanya,” Ally interrupted, “do you have a weird feeling about this or are you just being stubborn and pedantic?”

“What do you mean?” I asked, trying not to sound too alarmed by her random beam of perception. She actually managed to see things clearly more often than not, but her permanently furrowed brow yet vacant stare could make you forget she was even looking in the first place.

“Well if you argue a point this long it often turns out you’re totally onto something and you just don’t want to tell us yet, and then it turns out you’re right and we get annoyed with you for not telling us. Did you ask about this because you *know* something?”

“No!” I complained, sounding maybe a bit too wronged by this true accusation. “Have you ever considered that if I started telling you all the weird things I thought that they would never come true? Or that even when they do, there are a million things which never did? Sharing feels like a great way to kill any chance I’m right, and that means I’ll have *no* idea what I’m looking for any more.”

“So you are asking questions about this because you have an idea of what you’re looking for!”

“No! Argh, stop... asking questions!”

“Tanya’s right,” Alana said, abruptly closing the book. “We shouldn’t question what she sees, or doesn’t see. If all we’ve got to go on is Tanya’s gut instinct, then we go on that and don’t ask why.”

Ally pulled an exaggerated face of scrunch-nosed horror. “Isn’t that a *terrible* idea and probably a direct cause of three of the biggest messes in our lives?”

“Three?” I asked.

Ally ticked them off her fingers: “You deciding living with fairies would be fun, you deciding setting a monster on the prom would be fun, you deciding that unleashing an evil clone of Teb on the town would be fun.”

“That last one was not my fault!”

Alana waded in before Ally and I could fully revive an old argument. “Look, everything that happened those times happened because I dropped the ball. But Tanya’s sitting here with us trying to help, is *clearly* as worried and in the dark about the cultists as you and I, and this time I’m keeping an eye on her anyway. This is different. Now are you going to come help us investigate the cultists or are you going to sit around sulking?”

Ally groaned and heaved herself to her feet. “*Fine*, but I’m putting shoes on.”

“I never said you shouldn’t.”

Our venture made it to the bottom of the stairs before the Fellowship broke: looming up from the sofa like a wrathful Balrog clad in shawls instead of shadows, Hester put herself between us and the door.

“And where do you think you’re going, young lady?”

“Um... Out with friends?” I’d never seen Ally look so alarmed in my life, although admittedly I'd missed her hasty exit from the dance floor when the star boar showed up. Hester was usually as strict as damp bread when it came to parenting.

"I've seen your room! You're going *nowhere* until you've put those books away! What if you tripped and broke your neck in there!?"

I was scared of her too.

"I'll tidy them when I get in!"

"And when might that be? In the middle of the night when it's dark and you're tired and forget an entire bookshop is spread across the floor? Get up there right now and sort it out!"

"But *Mum!*"

"Go!" Hester shrieked.

Ally fled back up the stairs, shouting a wounded, "*This is why I don't wear shoes!*" Her door slammed.

A little shell-shocked, I grabbed Alana's sleeve and began sidling for the door.

Hester rounded on us. I froze.

"Girls... Be *careful*, okay?" Ally's Mum sighed, deflating a little. She was giving us this sad, sad look, her eyes practically brimming up, maybe as a result of shouting at Ally. But I could feel her concern: there was this weird moment, where it was me, Alana and Hester and none of us said anything, but I think all of us felt a little more understanding of the others after that moment just from three conflicting psychic energies filling the air between us.

"We will," I said, quickly letting myself out before the scene got any more intense.

Talking About It

Here's something you don't know.

I saw a castle in the woods behind Troutespond. I was three years old and stupid and you might want to tell me I was addled with grief and exhaustion. I'd screamed for a whole week, and my aunt said to take her house, get me out of the old one where everything reminded me of my Mummy. I'd only stopped screaming because no sound was coming out when I tried, so I sat upright in the back seat of the car, ignoring all the books and toys my dad had helplessly piled in with me. I watched the motorway roll away underneath the car, wondering with every rectangle of yellow that flicked by what it would be like to be one of the lines in the road, cars driving over you all day until you were just a flat stripe.

Finally my dad said, "Look Tanya! It's our new home!" I think he'd forgotten to be sad about Mummy in his attempts to stop me going crazy. I still don't know if he ever got a chance to really mourn for her. We never went home. Aunt sold the house and that was that.

I looked up, and I saw the castle. It was sitting on the hill, looming over the town, guarding it. Full of knights to keep the dragons back. The towers stretched up as far as the clouds and the keep had walls a mile long. There were banners flying and guards marching on the battlements, and the sun shone through the pale mist of that horrible day and lit up the shining tiles on the roofs. Smoke rose from a dozen courtyards and kitchens beyond the walls and mingled with the mist, darkening it. I watched it all the way off the motorway until we were in the village and houses on the high street stopped me from seeing up the hill.

I slept for a day and a half and when I came down for breakfast, in the poky little house that smelled like my aunt, I asked in a scratchy unused voice, "Can we go to the castle?"

And my dad had smiled at me and said, "There isn't a castle in the village. Did you mean the church?" because three year olds aren't known for having amazing vocabularies or a good understanding of the world around them.

When he proudly walked me down the street and gestured the church, the little one-room building on a titchy hill in the middle of town has always been the biggest disappointment in the universe for me. Aside from the related complete lack of castle on the hill.

*

"This is bad," I announced when Alana and I were well clear of Ally's house.

"It is," she agreed. "*Why?*"

"Did you talk to the Piper yet?"

She visibly jumped before turning to me, grabbing my shoulders. "You've *talked* to him? When?!"

"Yesterday afternoon. He said he had a lot of work to do. I have a feeling he was just waiting for me to bring you up to speed to save him the trip. He was pretty pissed off about… Well, everything." I quickly summarised the curse bags, the highlights of my conversation with the Piper. "He said I could work with you, and he said whatever was going on was *big*. Hester knows it; she doesn't want Ally anywhere near it. Cathy and Jeremy sense something too. One's practically in witness protection, the other has set himself up as a full-time bodyguard for our not exactly helpless Huntress. The fey are *freaked out*."

"Tanya…"

"Yeah?"

Alana sort of grimaced and I think deleted the first words meant to come out of her mouth. After a hesitation she said, "Thank you for finding this all out. I should have said that if things were in dire need, we could start talking about all this again."

"Well were you ever going to tell us the Piper had disappeared?"

"I thought he was giving me some space! Like we said, a summer to be normal. Those cultists on results day were the first time I realised anything was wrong."

"And Mr Lane? I felt you hide from him."

"I didn't like him. Something felt *wrong*."

"He's measuring places in the town. He marked out the circle when Ally was spying on him after he talked to us at the table… And after my date I helped him measure the graveyard."

"Wait, *what?*"

"Oh my god, you did not even need to be psychic to know she was going to do that, Alana."

"I mean you! Why did you help him?"

"Er, to get closer and see if I could figure out what he was doing. Don't be mad at me for investigating: Ally clearly started it this time."

"Tanya... I seriously, *seriously* do not like the vibe he gives off. He feels predatory. And you and Ally are merrily chatting to him and helping him? He's luring you in! Whatever he wants from you, it's not good... And I can tell he wants it badly. Just because you think you're in control and aware he's up to something does not protect you from him."

"Why not Teb then?"

"Huh?"

"Well you went all invisible and whatever when he talked to us, Teb made huge sparkly eyes when he said he was from Hollywood. If there was one of us he was going to trap, Teb would be easiest of all!"

We looked at each other for a moment, clearly thinking the same thing (and between the two of us it was very easy to tell when our thoughts joined up). "Teb's house?" I asked. Alana nodded. We broke into a run.

*

We arrived at Teb's close a minute later. I was a hundred yards ahead of Alana and hadn't been saving myself for the sprint: my legs were killing me. In fact it felt like I was walking in gravy... Treacle... *Cement*. I froze solid a whole three houses down, barely around the corner.

"Alana!" I yelled. "Stop!"

She barrelled around the corner, huffing like the goblins' ghost train, and pretty much just collapsed into the barrier of energy around the eerily deserted close, like she was more relieved than upset to stop moving.

"Is it... the... cultists?" she gasped.

I was looking wildly around, my eyes still free to move while my limbs were all dead. I couldn't see anything. "It feels wrong," I said. "I mean it *doesn't* feel wrong. This is neutral magic... Not evil at all."

"Then who..."

"I *told* you to stay away!"

Jeremy appeared, striding right down the middle of the cul-de-sac. The goblin was at least five foot tall, armoured like a knight, gold from head to foot. There was a purple plume in his helmet, a purple owl in flight marked out in gems that glittered on the breastplate. All he lacked was the sword. Now I recognised the power. Teb's magic poured off him: the same I'd felt around her on the Hunt. But I had a feeling she was an unwitting power source right now.

"Come on, we're just going to see our friend," I complained.

"You *can't* bring her into this!" he insisted, stopping just ahead of us, confident that we couldn't exactly grab him right now. "I have to protect her. That is my job, and you will not stop me."

"We were just going to ask her if she had any contact with the cultists!"

"She hasn't and she won't. Goodbye."

"No, Jeremy, wait! What's going on?"

He gave me a long, searching look with his dark beady eyes, the only part of him visible behind his golden helmet. Again I got the sense that he was looking for something in me: something he expected to find and couldn't. Sometimes being psychic is just finding out a new annoyingly vague level of intention under people's already opaque top layer.

"It's the men from the grey castle. If you know what I mean by that, you'll understand who they are, Tanya. The grey castle. Please don't try to contact the Huntress again. I will do anything to protect her."

He vanished, and our limbs all came back to life.

"What in the *Hell*?" Alana asked, staggering a few steps and clutching her ribs, still out of breath from the run.

"Um, you haven't seen Jeremy since the prom, have you?" I took her shoulder and guided her out of Teb's close. I didn't fancy seeing him again either.

"No! Was that the little rodent goblin that she named her champion?"

"Yeah. He seems to be taking the role quite seriously."

"He's way too powerful!"

"Teb's the most powerful thing in the whole valley. If she gives him free rein to protect her, he's got about one percent less power than her. All his spells felt like she was the one casting them." I set off walking back towards the town centre. Alana followed, very much not done with this conversation.

"And she doesn't *know* this? We are having *words* later."

"I dunno. Like I said, he's panicked. And he's a goblin. They're pretty single-minded. He's using that power to look after Teb. Surely that is about the most desirable situation out of all the potential issues having a goblin that powerful in town might bring."

"Well I'm keeping a close eye to make sure he doesn't hurt anyone in this so-called defence. The Piper would be pissed off if he had a rogue goblin to deal with on top of everything else." She took out her phone. "I wonder what he's doing? He must know something?"

"Ooh, can you call us up a deus ex machina? I'm stumped."

"I can try." She tapped through her contacts and pressed her phone to her ear. We walked for twenty seconds in silence, Alana's brow getting more and more furrowed. By the time we were back in the town centre I thought we'd had it, and Alana was just about to hang up when she jumped and pressed the phone hard against her ear. "Hey, Piper... I am..." she looked at me. "We are... Oh... Right, you too." She lowered her phone and stabbed the end call button with a shaking finger. "Apparently we've got this." Her voice was bitter and dry, full of disappointment in the Piper for letting us down. I was inclined to agree: I'd never been left this confused by a mystery before.

"We have not! If Jeremy thought he was giving me a huge clue, he absolutely was not. Can you think of anything that might be the 'grey castle'?"

"Around here there's Ransley Castle, and Severstrong is sort of fortified at the top of the hill. But it's more than that. We both know the fey talk in riddles; the likelihood of it being a literal castle is tiny. What's grey?"

Standing in the centre of town I had a clear view up the hill. For a second my eyes drifted up to the empty-but-for-trees skyline. No. Not that.

I led the way over to the benches and plonked myself down, deliberately facing away from the hills. "I think maybe the 'grey' part might be more symbolic anyway. They seriously colour code everything. No wonder Teb fell in with them so easily. You've seen what she's like with purple." I was sat on the bench right underneath the statue of our single war hero. He died in both wars. No, no one's ever explained it to me in a way that makes sense either, but then… sometimes there are mysteries in life you don't bother asking questions about. Maybe he brought the rest of the boys home safely again, so I wouldn't question it. I had to admit, I had a bit of a crush on him, sideburns and epic moustache and all.

I tipped my head right back to admire him, hoping he might give me some inspiration.

Alana, still loitering nearby, sighed, clearly as fed up as I was. Now we were free to talk, suddenly we didn't want to discuss magical happenings anymore. "You'll get a crick in your neck doing that," she said.

"Already have one," I said and sharply tipped my head side to side to make my neck crack.

"Ew! Don't do that," she complained.

"Sit down or I'll start popping my knuckles as well," I warned.

She sat down. I reached into my bag. "Twix?"

"Who are you calling a Twix?"

"This delicious chocolate bar," I replied, waving it at her. She caught it, and in a second she had it opened and a bite taken off the end. I will not admit to carrying chocolate just to solve all the little problems in life, but I did get through several multipacks a month without eating any of them myself.

"You're not so bad," she told me rather thickly through a mouthful of caramel and shortbread.

"You totally are though." I grinned at her, but she didn't seem amused. "Okay, the swimming pool does swing it in your favour, but you lose points whenever you get too self-important."

"Could say the same about you. It's actually a relief to have you on my side and as dumb as the rest of us for once."

I shrugged, not sure how to answer that either.

She munched the rest of the chocolate loudly, swallowed, then got up to put the wrapper in the bin. As she crossed the square I watched her for a moment, but then ended up with my attention drifting around the little town centre. We'd made it to late afternoon: the roads were clearing a bit as people headed back for dinner. The air was still, misty again, though much fainter than the day before. It had been a cooler day, and the weekend was over: day-trippers were fewer in number and not many people stayed in the town. Even in this busy period the nights were almost as quiet as winter ones.

And there was a man running down the street. He wasn't a jogger, clad in tracksuit and trainers, and those were rare enough as it was when we had all those footpaths to run on. He wore smart-casual office clothes, but in the warm evening had sprouted two deep blue circles under his arms, dark patches on his chest. A heavy-looking duffel bag was thumping at his side as he ran. I recognised him even without the camera, having crossed paths with him so often over the last week: the photographer from the local paper.

"What's with him?" I asked.

"Huh?" Alana said, but didn't have to follow my gaze because at that moment the strap on his bag broke, tripping the photographer, and he fell down with a yelled profanity that was hilariously out of place in our peaceful town centre. The overstuffed bag split as it landed, the buckles bursting open, and folds of heavy red velvet spilled out.

Alana and I looked at each other, then back at the cultist, struggling to push the fabric back in.

"He's another one!" I hissed.

Alana stood up. I grabbed her arm and yanked her back down, getting her back in a normal sitting position and facing me just as he glanced wildly around to check no one was watching. I gave a high laugh like Alana had said the funniest thing in the world, adding in a quieter voice, "Let him sort himself out first."

"I was going to go lend him a hand."

"He's almost got it. What good would it do except for him to know you saw his robes? He'll be even more suspicious after."

He wrestled the cloak back in and popped the buckles back over it. With another wary look around the street that I caught out of the corner of my eye, he tucked the bag under his arm, clinging tightly to the top of it in an effort to stop the straps bursting again, and set off at a fast walk. I waited for his gaze to pass over us, sitting and chatting. He moved on, reassured no one cared about his fall.

"Now we follow him," I said.

Alana didn't even start to argue.

Candidates

Here's something you don't know.

Real names are really important.

If demons learn them, they can possess you or lie about you to angels or something like that. Fairies can steal names completely or control you in a way that's just as bad as possession. You can also sell your true name in a way which is rather cheaper to the soul and much more flexible if you want to gain power. The name on your birth certificate doesn't have to be the true name you want to keep hidden. I think Teb's was anyway, which is why she got so powerful selling it since she never used it for anything until the day she sold it, and so few people in her life knew or remembered it anyway. Not like we had ever had a full set of teachers who could pronounce it or hadn't made a joke about it on the first day of term.

I think the rest of our names are a little better guarded, though the day we all had to bring our passports into school for a civics lesson and spent a lunch break giggling over them means we at least know each other's. I think Teb's passport probably changed itself to Teb Nandi when she lost the rest of her name. Someone was working overtime to fix the hole she left in the world. Some lesser cousin of the Piper that's an entity dedicated to annoying paperwork. Do *not* get on their bad side if you don't like him.

Alana treats her name as the first sign her parents hated her from birth. Alana Susanna Larbie isn't exactly an easy name, especially when she insists on rhyming Alana with banana and Susanna with savannah instead of leaning into the middle A. (I think it is okay to reveal names in this account, because the chance of fairies taking the time to read such a thing is quite low.)

Ally has a gorgeous name, and no one really realises it. I suppose being an Alex makes it easy to pretend you have a normal name, but Alexandria Thebes Guardian is totally the daughter of an excitable hippie in the middle of an antiquity obsession. I'm sure Hester would have kept on tacking more ancient cities to the end if she hadn't been stopped by Danny or ran out of room on the birth certificate.

In comparison the boring set of family names I carry, Tatiana Anastasia Pomphrey, is quite a lucky escape. Same for my great-grandmother who escaped for England around 1918 with the remains of her family. I take my middle name from her, but hours of internet research have rather disappointingly revealed it's not *that* Anastasia. In any case, whatever else was Russian in our family was lost: language, songs, everything but a photo album and some books and letters I can't read because my mum died before she could teach me about my family. All I have left are the names from my mother, hidden under the blanket of a stuffy English surname.

Names are important.

*

I had a weird flashback feeling to tailing Ally and Teb down past the playground, though this time Alana was on my side. We followed at a safe distance as the photographer hurried down the road past the green. We had to hope it was a safe distance anyway: apparently neither of us had trailed a man in a life-or-death situation before, and moving stealthily and keeping him in sight at the speed he was going at made it a hard chase. I had my practice playing secret agents with Ally, and Alana I suppose had all her work with the Piper hopefully preparing her a little for this. At least we didn't have Ally with us, so her flip-flops weren't pounding the ground with a noise equivalent to gunshots with every step.

Now that I was focussing so hard on the man ahead of us I could feel his panic almost like a visible trail he left behind——the feeling was too overwhelming to say what had caused it, or if there was something in his mind about watching out for being followed. But he only glanced around once after he had stumbled, and he broadcast it enough to give us plenty of time to dive out of sight behind some hedges. He might not be watching out for it, but he definitely still didn't *want* to be followed.

We were rubbing scratches on our arms from our trip into the hedgerow when he decided to leave the road. If you hadn't guessed where he was heading, you're as easily surprised as Ally—or not paying attention. It was the Green Man's grove.

"What's going on *there*?" Alana asked incredulously. "Are we really sure we want to go eavesdrop on them?"

"I'm sure it's nothing dirty," I said, blushing a little as I remembered rolling around on the moss at the base of the tree. "At least we have them cornered, as it is... I mean, they're clearly going to be doing something at that ritual site, it's safe to assume. We can slow down now and sneak up on them a bit more stealthily."

"Are you sure we should? I'm not saying you're not sneaky, I'm just saying they probably massively outnumber us, and we have no idea what they're here for."

"Well, only one way to find that out!"

"Were you just, like, born without a fear gland or something?"

"I used up my life's allotment of it early, that's all. Come on!" I beckoned her to follow and, trying to keep a low profile, set off across the meadow.

Alana cursed quietly and followed me.

Under the tree line the deeper shadows of twilight had already gathered themselves up, as if massing for their attack on the land at large at night's command. Though the copse had only a dozen trees across, they were densely packed and it was hard to see to the centre even in good light.

Stepping into the darkness gave us a better sense of the seriousness of what we were doing: we didn't speak again as we approached the vast tree in the centre of the little grove with caution. Fortunately all the deep magical ritual spots in the village provided plenty of cover around themselves, so we got to pick our ancient gnarled chestnut to hide behind with some ease. We cautiously peered around it.

The cultists seemed to be out in full force in the space around the Green Man, because I could not imagine more than seven of them existing completely unheard of. I mean, if we'd lived in a village where almost every resident regularly dressed up in sinister hooded cloaks and met in public, you'd think someone would have found out a lot sooner and gone *Hot Fuzz* on them.

A few of our red-cloaked cultists stood to one side, preparing for their ritual. One of them stood talking to another in the most casual way despite having a four foot long sword at his side. He rested a hand on the hilt and stood with the point down in the dirt at his feet, slowly rotating it and tearing up clumps of moss as if not realising that he was doing it, inadvertently revealing the very real sharpness of the blade (which he was probably blunting, to the benefit of anyone on the wrong end of the thing).

Two more talked together near the edge of the grove, near us. One of them was clearly panting and still adjusting his robes as they had their pre-ritual catch-up.

"—so that's all my preparation done," he gasped as he stuck a hand deep inside the hood, clasping a handkerchief to wipe his sweaty face. "All that's left is your part now, so maybe we don't have to miss another phase of the moon." Perhaps that was why the curse bags that had been keeping the Piper out of the town were so old and manky by the time I found them? Really it was a miracle he hadn't found a way to get through to Alana and started us off investigating a month ago: perhaps the spell really had been that strong.

"Don't worry, I'm working on it. I have a couple of possible candidates ready." This new speaker had a gentle, reassuring American accent. Called it. Well I mean, *Ally* called it, but I did too before consulting her. It still counts! Perhaps the photographer's wariness about him was just because Mr Lane was an outsider, somehow drawn into this web. There was something mistrustful there, as well as the obvious resentment. Troutespond folk weren't good at trusting Bilsworth, never mind someone from another continent.

The main huddle of cultists had a breakaway: he headed to the centre of the grove, right up against Teb's husband, and there he cleared his throat with an impressive roar. "*Hrrumhmmhmm!*"

I grabbed Alana's arm so hard she squeaked involuntarily.

"*No way*," I breathed. It was almost too good to be true, certainly one of the most chilling moments to have struck me in my life.

"Calm down!" she hissed. "You knew they might be people close to us!"

She might have been more excited if it had been someone *she* had been routinely seeing and been hounded by from a young age.

As in the school corridors, Mr Westcott's impressive baritone cough caused order to descend on the cultists. Mr Lane and the photographer filed in to join the rest of the group, and they made a loose circle together. The cultist with the sword stepped forward and spoke, thankfully a voice I didn't recognise at once: "Brothers, the time we have long awaited is nearly upon us, the preparations well underway. We have gathered seven righteous men to complete our ancient ritual, which we are bound to by blood and by our duty as Christian men..."

"Well that was unexpected," I whispered. "I thought they'd be pagan."

"Ally said they were threatening the priest," Alana reminded me. "Why would they even go near him if they weren't connected in some way? Now shh. Trying to listen."

"I knew that," I muttered. Honestly, even for me there had been a bit too much to take in lately. I had a feeling Alana was enjoying seeing me surprised.

The sword cultist was carrying on: "Each has done his part and made his sacrifice... Soon it will be time for the town to make its own. Let us pray to purify this land, so that it may be ready for our blessing..."

"Are they the good guys?" I whispered to Alana.

She was frowning intently at the scene before us. "I don't know. They think they are. It might be the only way to get a group of people together to do something horrible. They think they're *righteous*."

"Well right now they're not doing anything objectionable. Maybe they really are just a group of people who didn't find church hands-on enough? I mean it's not like we're short of rich evangelical Conservatives around these parts who think society as a whole is going to hell and no one's doing anything about it. Can't be hard to find people interested."

"They said the town was going to give its sacrifice too. And he said *candidates*. And he's been grooming you and Ally. Excuse me if I don't let them carry on unobserved until I know more."

"So what do we do?"

"Keep observing them. We'll find out what their ritual might actually be about. Then, when we know all the facts, we stop it."

"You know for certain that we have to?"

"Tanya, look at that sword."

"Swords are used for loads of ritual things and no one ever gets hurt. They're powerfully symbolic items, particularly for a male coven at a phallic shrine. You'd have heard about it if witches were going around stabbing people on a regular basis."

"Yeah, but these apparently aren't witches."

"Hm. Point."

I looked back at the cultists, hoping to immediately catch them doing something mysterious that would tell me exactly what their end game was. Instead I saw that there were six of them still in the circle. A sick feeling of being watched hit me.

"Um, Alana?" I turned around. There was a red-cloaked figure right behind her, and he was reaching out…

"RUN!" I yelled, grabbing Alana's arm and jerking her forwards. She stumbled, hit the floor with both knees, and I thought we were going to be killed then and there, but she heaved herself up with a strength I'd never seen her use before: she normally looked and acted and *ran* like the kid who always had a note to get out of PE. But now she surged up, twisting out of a second attempt by the cultist to grab her, and she set off running with a hug tug on *my* arm while I was still standing there horrified that I'd pulled her over and watching the man lunge her way again.

Fortunately, however much we slack off during our gym classes, teenage girls will usually have the jump on a middle-aged man when it comes to energy. Once we broke from the tree line I looked over my shoulder and saw them close behind, but a few seconds later I risked another glance and saw we were dropping them: only three were following and they were not close enough to try grabbing us. I turned and focussed on running, staying upright and breathing properly because staying ahead of them rather depended on all three.

"Where should we go?" I gasped. "We can't go home!" We were aiming up at the town again, but I had no desire to lead the cultists to any of our doorsteps.

"I have an idea," Alana panted. She hadn't let go of my arm, but now I was hauling her along, and she was getting heavier by the second.

"The pub?" I managed, after a few more seconds concentrating on where my feet were (and then moving them very quickly to another place).

Alana made a huffing noise that I wasn't sure was an answer or a sign she was going to die soon. Every stride I yanked on her arm now, and I was getting worried I would pull her over again. The sheer panic of being almost grabbed had worn off, and she didn't seem to have the backup energy to keep running.

We staggered past the green: I turned and saw two red-cloaked figures struggling after us, a dozen meters behind. Of course they were wearing a ton of heavy fabric… One was holding up the bottom of his robes as he ran, revealing suit-trousers and shiny shoes that were again terrible for running in. The other was lagging further behind him. Cultist number three had clearly given up a while back.

"I think we can outrun them!" I gasped.

"No we can't!" Alana wailed. We were beginning to lose our head start: my legs were starting to tire from the misuse I'd put them through today, with two heavy sprints both lacking a warm-up beforehand. The dash from Ally to Teb's alone would have had my calves aching in the morning. Alana weighed me down like a ton weight attached to my wrist: she was clinging on for dear life and I could feel her slowing me down. "Left here!"

I realised what she was aiming us towards and put on one last burst of speed, taking us around the corner, across the square and to the gate of the church. We crashed through it, the rusting iron screeching open and clanging on the ancient stone pillar, then our slight uphill run turned to a steep three meter climb up the steps. I thought a tendon in my leg would really snap from this treatment.

As we slapped the huge wooden door, left ajar to catch the pleasant evening air by a priest who had no idea what chaos was going on outside (unless he absolutely did, which seemed to be Alana's plan), I glanced around again.

Only one cultist had made it to the end of the road and stood the other side of the square, hands on knees, apparently feeling as awful as we did. His hood had fallen back, and I recognised him: a plain man with a sort of ageless look that could have put him from mid-twenties to late thirties depending on how clean living he was, a bland sort of man with an unremarkable face and mousy hair in a short, neat cut, who wore boring suits to work every day. Where he curated Bilsworth Museum.

I saw it then, in my utter exhaustion, my brain flickering almost randomly gave me an image of something I had never seen in person but recognised at once because I had seen it a million times before: Bilsworth, in the fairy world, was just *boring*. All the light was dull, all the colours muted. The station had been tacky and washed out when we came through on the fairy train. A big red brick building with turrets on the corners and an imposing front façade would wash out in that aesthetic to become a grey castle.

Alana grabbed my other arm and hoiked me through the door, slamming it as soon as I was clear.

She let go and staggered to a pew, sat heavily and put her head between her legs, I think fighting the urge to throw up on consecrated ground. I leaned heavily on the seat behind her and tried to stop my head swimming. Jeremy's fear seemed a lot more grounded all of a sudden. Here was the explanation to all my questions about how these cultists knew so much and had the power they did. The only time I'd met people from this world doing Big Magic, albeit for petty reasons, they were traceable to the Museum. That and many other inconsistencies had led me to realise that they must know. Their display on St Troute missed out key facts that we honestly just knew from school, but somehow they didn't want to mention, like putting it in words was dangerous. There were gaps in their displays that missed the most interesting parts: why did Ransley Castle burn down? When did the family leave the Manor and why was Severstrong Abbey already empty just before the dissolution of the monasteries? Why was the Roman "room" permanently closed for renovations, actually just a staff room with a water cooler and vending machine when you broke into it, like they never planned to actually make the exhibit? All stupid questions, not important... But they all felt important and made me itch in my fingers when I came across these facts, or where they were supposed to be.

Whatever they were, they knew a lot, and apparently that was something to be seriously feared.

The priest came out of the little back room, drawn by the slamming door, and stopped short to see us there, with shiny red faces, still panting and trying to recover.

"Are you girls alright?" he asked, his voice cooing and soft like a pigeon. He had an inquisitive look like a bird, his head tipped to the side a bit: a habit from having one eye considerably more impaired than the other.

"We were chased here by men in red robes!" I blurted. "They had a sword!" I let a tear slide out of my eye: they weren't hard to summon when I was ready to cry just from exhaustion.

The priest's knobbly hands fumbled with his gold-rimmed glasses on the chain around his neck, and he took a harder look at us with improved vision: in particular his eyes raked over me. "Did they see you come in here?"

"Yes!" I squeaked.

"Quick, come here," he said, gesturing us.

I helped to haul Alana to her feet and we staggered after the priest. Either he was going to bag us and we had done a very impressive run for nothing, or he was our actual salvation.

He stopped at a screen of carved wood set into one of the alcoves and reached out to bop a carving of Mary Mother of God on the head. Before I could laugh at the absurdity of the action the screen swung open, revealing a narrow space behind, not much bigger than a closet and rather lower. "Get in here. I'll tell them you ran through."

I summoned one more use of my quickly solidifying legs and hauled myself in, then assisted Alana up. We crouched in the small space and the priest swung the heavy screen back into place. The wood was layered up: at the front there was a sort of frame, carved to look like many arches, and behind that a layer of much thicker wood, artfully shaped to have dozens of nearly fully three-dimensional figures, including the effigy that so kindly acted as a hidden switch. The back layer was thinner, shaped into trees and clouds and rather flatter weird cherub things: I was familiar with this screen, having once sketched it for school. What I had never noticed was that there was no black background behind this all; there were many small gaps where there was neither frame nor figure nor angels, little gaps never wider than a penny, through which the light of the church came and gave light and air to someone hidden behind.

"This isn't so bad," I muttered.

"My legs have cramps from my ankles to my thighs," Alana hissed through gritted teeth. "Shoot me."

The priest began a retreat through to his room, all the better to claim innocence when the cultist arrived, but he had barely left our tiny field of view when I heard the door being heavily forced. We hadn't locked it or anything: I think the curator just gave it too much of a shove in anticipation that we had.

I heard his shiny shoes pace menacingly along the stone floor, the echoes sharp and pointed. He had given himself a minute to recover, I guessed, because he didn't sound out of sorts at all. He probably jogged in the morning. There was a heavy *flump* like someone dropping half a ton of red velvet over the back of a pew (at an educated guess). "Father Walter!" His voice was almost amiable. "Where did the girls go?"

"Bartholomew." He seemed to be naming the curator almost in the way I named Jeremy to try and gain some control over the little goblin. Names had power over people as well. If these cultists were genuinely Catholic and local, this was their only church until Severstrong Abbey or Waitington and "Bartholomew" would have been coming here all his life under the supervision of this priest.

"They were spying on us. You are as responsible as we are for containing this. Where did they go?"

Father Walter tottered back into our field of view, not, I think for our benefit but because he didn't like being too far away and not able to see who he was talking too properly. "I saw them run through here; they went out the back. I don't imagine they would have stayed long in the graveyard."

The curator strode up to meet him. "Why didn't you *stop* them?" His voice stayed level, but something in it cut harder.

Doddering as he was, Father Walter seemed tougher than this verbal blade. "Local people can use this church however they see fit, even as part of a racecourse. I couldn't stop them: the word of God doesn't give me nets and traps."

The curator stared long and hard at the priest, not at all satisfied with that answer, mostly because it was all cheek. "If I find out you've been hiding them…"

"Even you wouldn't hurt me, Bartholomew."

"We are the foundations of this church! You like having your house? You like the roof being fixed on this crumbling old ruin?"

The priest snorted at that. "I've met the foundations of this church, and you're not him. If you're trying to control me with money, you have gone astray, my son. St Troute built this place stone by stone and if you take one down, he'll put two back up in its place."

"You have no idea what *St Troute* is. You're foolish if you think he…"

"He still walks among us?" the old priest prompted.

I glanced at Alana. She shrugged, like *old news*. Of course, in her dealings with the Piper, she must have come across other people in his address book locally. Since this used to be his neighbourhood he still had a disproportionate interest in our doings. And, I suppose, protecting his own indelible history. I'd tried using his musical instruments to draw his attention. It hadn't even occurred to me that relics of his could be enchanted to bind him. And we were feet away from his supposed tomb…

The revelation that the priest knew the Piper in person seemed to have stumped our cultist. He had only recently done a spell specifically to banish the Piper, never mind what else he knew. He was marked as an enemy of the guy. But apparently he was not allowed to betray that fact to the priest, no matter how much Father Walter knew himself. He didn't seem quite able to say "No! That's stupid!" though, perhaps fearing quite rightly it would make him sound childish and like he didn't have a grasp on the situation after all. Neither could just out and say they knew who the Piper was, as it would betray too much of all their other practices and reasons for knowing. I'd have to guess that whatever the priest did with him wasn't typical church stuff.

He settled for briskly turning. "Not helping us is punishment in itself. You know we do God's work, even if you can't stomach it yourself. You know what not helping us will bring upon this town." The curator strode from the church, hardly breaking stride to pick up his robes with a final dramatic rustle. The door slammed again.

*

Father Walter let us out of his hidey-hole, but we had to stay still and quiet in the church for a while. He had a kettle and a packet of biscuits in the back and we devoured half the custard creams each and washed them down with tea. By the time we had recovered a little from the leg cramps and exhaustion, he came back in from scouting around the graveyard and front gate.

"I can't see anyone that I know to be in that… *sect*. Whatever you know about them, I can assure you they are not upholding the teachings I preach." He looked especially hard at Alana. "What *do* you know?"

"Not much, to be honest. The Pi—St Troute hasn't been in contact lately. If he thinks he's testing me with this, it's actually just testing my patience."

Father Walter looked upset at Alana's scowl: he clearly took the Piper as St Troute a bit more seriously than she did, even if that was the actual truth behind his name. "There are reasons beyond the obvious for those such as himself to act the way they do."

"He was banished," I said helpfully. "They put a spell on him so he couldn't come in the town."

The priest looked somehow more unsettled by my suggestion that the Piper was governable by the actions of men.

"Anyway," Alana interrupted, "could you tell us anything about them? We don't even know why they are doing this 'ritual' of theirs."

"To protect the town," Father Walter replied on automatic. He engaged the critical part of his brain and at once his brow furrowed and he began kneading his fingers together again. "I'm not sure what from. Some ancient curse, they believe. They teach each other the old story. I'm afraid all I know is that they believe they have a very good reason to be doing it. The last time the ritual took place I was a little boy: I only found out about it ten years ago, in a warning my predecessor left me concealed in a replacement censer."

"A *warning*?" I cried with a bit too much excitement.

His response was stern: "Yes, Miss Pomphrey. You and your friends are in grave danger. The ritual requires a young virgin. I refused to hand over the names of my younger congregation: I believe in times past the priest worked in collusion, helping them select a girl. They seemed quite bemused that I hadn't picked one despite my knowledge that this day would come. I saw you talking to the American yesterday. I am now certain that he intends to use one of you girls instead. You do tend to hang around town making yourselves quite... *obvious*. Alana's work alone..."

"Well we're trying our hardest *not* to get caught by them."

He nodded. "I shall check again to make sure there is no one watching the church. I advise you to hurry home and stay indoors until this danger has passed. However strong you normally are, their methods leave you vulnerable like you never will be again in this town. Our paths may not cross often, but I feel a duty to protect all the people of this town, as our dear saint does."

Alana rolled her eyes a little as he turned away. Being stuck in a room with a beacon of Catholicism seemed to irk her more than cultists chasing us, or even the thought of more walking: she heaved herself up and gestured me to do the same. "Thank you for taking us in and hiding us, Father. We both know how much easier it would be for you to have handed us in then and there. I mean... Priests are sort of expected to be good and do the right thing, but it can still be a surprise to actually experience it."

I gave her a look to hopefully warn her to stop talking before she made him reconsider his help. I added my thanks, and after just a few more glances out the back door we were allowed to leave.

I didn't spare the graveyard a single thought as Alana took charge again and led the way across it, confidently picking her way through the graves and lumpy grass now that darkness had properly fallen.

"My house is back that way," I said, tottering along on the wobbly pins that were once my legs.

"I know," Alana said.

"So why are we going this way?" I paused to let her help me over the fence, and we were standing on School Road, way off course to mine, but...

"My place is better. Your dear old father shouldn't get involved. My mum though? Meh, what do I care if they threaten her? There's no shock value left in her finding out what dark stuff I get up to."

"Fair, if grim, point. I thought you weren't allowed guests overnight though?"

"I'll just have to sneak you in then, won't I?" She turned and gave me this look which I'm fairly certain was sort of jokey-flirty, but it was so unexpected to see the cheerful side of Alana that I didn't get a chance to realise she was being saucy before she was back to looking worried and paranoid, glancing around the road before setting off at the briskest pace we could manage towards home. I kicked myself for half the walk for not joking back.

Slumber Party

Here's something you don't know:

Our first 'brush with the supernatural' happened when we were about thirteen and decided (I decided) that being teenage witches would be amazing. I was going through a phase of collecting ankhs and spider earrings anyway, although I could never dress *just* in plain black. Teb and I play chicken a lot over things like "Is it appropriate to practice witchcraft in your bedroom?" This particular evening I liberated one of Hester's spellbooks from her secret altar in the cupboard in her and Danny's room, and when a suitably long time had gone by and she hadn't made a sign of missing it, I produced it at a sleepover at Teb's.

There was a moment when the two of us stared at each other. It was genuinely scary: no one, even Teb, knew for certain that magic didn't work. We'd done a Ouija board at school with about half the class one rainy breaktime, and some prankster (genuinely not me: I'd been curious if my natural talents would draw something in for real so I hadn't gamed the system) started sliding the upturned plastic cup around the table, trying to spell out "DIE" but fighting with the nine other hands resting on it to get out a coherently scary message. Most of the school had spent the rest of the week freaking out about being cursed until someone broke down and Mr Westcott held an angry and, I now see, hypocritical emergency assembly.

Anyway I was grinning my best "It would be so fun if we could work magic!" grin, and Teb was fixing me with this look like "It's not safe, we could die, we could end up haunted, what if something terrible happens." All the things she'd been saying post Ouija-gate a few months before.

Then Ally said, "Well it's not real, is it? I don't see the harm in it." Ally was my guide to see if I was stepping over the line into danger and that was about as cool as I'd ever seen her after a mad plan was announced. Ah, Ally's scepticism. You will be missed.

So we draped ourselves in bits of Teb's old Halloween costumes and tried to set up an altar in the middle of her floor, using mostly leftover party food as the reagents to the spell: since we had none of the essential oils or mysterious rocks and the like the spell book advertised, we decided to just set up something spooky looking. I got Teb, as the one with the better handwriting, to draw us up one of the magic circles on a big piece of paper, and Ally nipped to the bathroom and came back with baby oil ("It's pretty essential, right?") and a bulk bag of little tea light candles Sarika kept under the sink in the hope that she'd ever get some free time to have relaxing candlelit bubble baths.

Once it was all set up, I said, "What spell shall we do?" and we flicked through the book and fought about what was the right thing to try casting. Teb was still convinced we'd curse ourselves whatever we cast, and Ally kept sniggering and picking the most outlandish spells which had no relevance to us as kids like "A Spell To Bring Happiness and Fertility to your Marriage" and "A Spell to Cast for Guidance in Business". In the end I decided we should do a simple blessing: it had a nice poem to recite and we had to agree the likelihood of cursing ourselves whilst doing a spell meant to purify the room was much slimmer.

We propped the book up against the door, studiously chanted the words, and waited.

Somewhere out in the woods right near the back garden, a fox screamed.

We all screamed as well: Ally jumped up and kicked over several tea lights, which went out but spilled hot wax all over Teb's carpet, and Teb and I grabbed each other in fright. It took a long time for us to even wind down enough to dismantle the ritual and all night long we stayed awake, eyes wide, waiting any moment for the curse to come down and smite us.

I had a feeling Teb was going to uncover the hastily concealed evidence at some point in her clear out: all the stranger for her than me to think about it. I think in the long run it contributed such a healthy dose of scepticism to our group that even I caught it for a while, and that explained everything about Teb's behaviour to the world of the strange come our grand entry to it in the spring of this year. I wouldn't have believed Alana at all if we'd met her right then and there. Sometimes friends have to wait until you're ready for them.

*

We passed through a thin line of suburbia and soon we were traversing the leafy way between drawn-back gravel drives. Alana's house and the road to it were now very familiar after half a summer spent making use of her swimming pool, but we always came during the day, and were always sent away long before dinnertime. Approaching in the dark with the threat of lurking cultists high, the closeness of the looming trees that were planted between each house gave me the sense we were walking through haunted woods to a house of horrors.

The road thinned and became a glorified driveway, with large gates at irregular intervals. I spotted the big Cadillac that Alana's Mum drove (or perhaps didn't—I wasn't sure how she'd get it through all the twisty little roads around here) parked right near the front of the drive so the world could see the expensive American car in all its glory. I looked up at the house as it came into clear view and wondered how I had never felt like it qualified as a haunted house before: it was huge, with many dark windows blankly glaring down at us, somehow feeling unlived in though one of its residents barely left, the Mrs Haversham haunting its halls.

"How are you going to sneak me in?" I asked.

"Well I was just going to try the front door, to be honest. Sorry if you were expecting awesome spy moves, but I want to get out of the open as soon as possible. Besides, Mom's as bad as fifty cultists if she decides it's weird not to hear me come in the front door."

I shrugged. Whatever got us to safety. I had a feeling if the cultists were such upstanding members of the community, they wouldn't be breaking, entering and kidnapping, at least in person. It gave us a little time to prepare ourselves for what might come next.

Alana opened the door and peered through it, then drew her head back outside. "Yeah, I think she's up in her office. Only mood lighting downstairs. Come on in, and wait in the sitting room until I've defused the bomb. Then we can sneak up to my room."

"Ooh, daring."

"Shush." Alana glanced around once more up the drive, just in case a cultist was standing behind us (it had happened once already, after all) and then ushered me through. "In in in," she hissed, pushing me right through to their magazine-perfect posh living room.

Sure enough the sound of the door closing did its trick: Alana had barely put a toe on the bottom step when a much more accented voice than hers drifted down the stairs: "Is that you, Alana?"

"Of course it is, Mom. I don't give copies of my key to random strangers."

"There's no need for that tone." I heard a door opening further up the house. I fancied Alana brought on some of her parent troubles by talking back when a simple yes or no would have done. "And where have you been all day?" Her mother's voice came out clearer now without a door between them: I heard footsteps creaking along the hall above us. I was seized with panic that she would keep on coming down the stairs and I sank back into the shadows.

But Alana spoke again, and the footsteps thankfully stopped without reaching the stairs.

"Just out with my friends. We went to Ally's and read books. I lead a boring studious life now, like you wanted."

Thinking of boring lives, I looked around their darkened front room as quietly as I could, because my snooping instinct remained strong no matter what the situation. What struck me was that there was no attempt to make it look more like people lived there, rather than just the shiny people from adverts on TV: I almost expected to look around and see a false wall and studio lights. The picture on the wall was a generic abstract design that almost certainly came packaged with the rest of the room's furniture and details, matching it all down to the accents on the lamps. Never mind photos of the occupants, there wasn't so much as a TV guide sitting on the coffee table… Or even coasters, a telltale sign that even the neatest of neat freaks still used the room *sometimes*. I felt like I might be spending the most time in it that anyone had for years.

"You should phone if you're not going to be back in time for dinner. I made chicken. Now we have too many leftovers."

"You *always* make too many leftovers. Are you trying to make me fat or something?"

"I don't need to try! Do you eat nothing but candy while you're out with your friends?"

"I'm not—!" I could literally feel the tug on the conversation as Alana reined herself in, perhaps finally remembering that she had a witness to her little family feud hidden in the wings. Or that all she'd eaten today was a Twix. In a much calmer voice she said, "Ally's Mum is a vegetarian. Everything she makes is ethically and locally sourced and freshly made. You've seen how thin Ally is. Trust me when I say that Hester is not fattening me up."

Her moment of dry humour passed unnoticed by her mother, but shut off the argument before it spiralled out of control. "Just remember to call when you're going to be out late."

I heard feet shuffling back along the hall, and a door closed.

Alana came into the sitting room and carried on towards the kitchen. When we'd put a few walls between us and the hall she said, "Well, she'll want nothing to do with me for the next twelve hours or so. Let's grab some of those leftovers and head upstairs." The kitchen was about as uninspired as the front room, all sleek black counters with no novelty mugs or quirky magnets on the fridge.

"Won't she notice you eating enough for two people?" I asked, leaning on the kitchen island and trying to picture Alana sitting there in pyjamas with morning hair, eating a bowl of cereal, reading her phone with scrunched up sleepy eyes. I couldn't make it happen.

"Nah, you heard her. She is *expecting* me to gorge myself on a huge second dinner. Might as well not let her down for once."

"For what it's worth… I don't think you're fat."

"Well if we run about like that much more, I'll be as thin as Ally!"

"I hope not. You look good curvy."

Alana shrugged and dived into the fridge. A moment later I was being handed plates with clingfilm over them: chicken pieces on a bed of leafy salad, cold new potatoes with pieces of bacon and rock salt crystals large enough to make a blinging engagement ring, a bowl with a fancy silicone lid that possibly contained some sort of vegetable casserole judging by the tomato-covered courgette stuck to the underside of the translucent covering.

"Damn, your Mom needs to give me some cooking lessons!"

"Not happening." Alana didn't even look up from getting forks and plates.

Between the kitchen and Alana's room were four flights of stairs in freshly vacuumed cream carpet, with shiny mahogany bannisters and a total lack of photos on the walls. I was sensing a theme here: a house that had been bought with the money that couldn't purchase happiness. This was what it looked like: the saying come to life in front of me. Alana's mom wanted no reminders that her daughter existed, or her past life, and kept so much to herself that there was nothing new and interesting to put on the walls in the place of family moments.

Alana poked me to keep moving when I paused on the hall where one door had a faint halo of light coming from around the edges. I was madly curious to glance through one of the other darkened, slightly ajar doors that lined this hall: it was the floor Alana's mom seemed to live on. I could sense trails of bitterness and sadness dragged through the air around here day in and day out. Alana seemed to flinch at the touch of the dead air on this landing: she might not see things the way I did, but she sensed them. This was a black hole of negativity. I glanced around and she gave me a stern look to keep sneaking along. Well, I sneaked, and Alana clumped noisily behind me to disguise any stray squeaks which would betray there being a second person on the stairs. It was with a sigh of relief from her that we made it to the top landing, her private attic apartment. She leaned past me and pushed open the door. I shuffled after her, hampered by the bottle of lemonade she'd tucked under my arm.

With the door closed, the gloom from downstairs was cut off and Alana's room had as much warmth as any other one of our rooms; though not as familiar, a nice person spent time here and the very walls reflected it, though there were few pictures to show it (largely because most of her "wall" was roof).

As soon as Alana had unburdened me of all the food, I collapsed down on her huge bed, my feet dangling over the end while I kicked off my shoes. "I am never moving again," I announced, staring up at her wind chime-hung ceiling with weary eyes.

"If you want to eat on my bed you have another think coming," Alana chided me. She was being unnecessarily fussy by unwrapping food and laying out the plates nicely on her dresser, I guess so we could serve ourselves. I assumed she wanted me to move to her sofa in front of the TV. She was the only girl I knew who had a sofa in her bedroom. She was the only person I knew who had a bedroom *big* enough for a sofa.

"Now I'm here all I want to do is sleep."

"What, without discussing our cultist problem? Are you ill? I was relying on your analysis!"

I hopped upright again, crossing my legs; I leaned forwards enthusiastically, betraying the extra energy that always lived in my hyperactive limbs. "Okay, food then conspiracies. Then we put on pyjamas, braid each other's hair and stay up all night having giggly girl-talk. Proper sleepover stuff."

Alana snorted. "Girl talk? Are you serious?"

"Yeah! I haven't had a sleepover with you yet… You might say we're getting too old, but I say this might be the last chance we have before we *are* too old. Shame the others aren't here, but two's a party when it's us. Why not?"

"Well I'm sorry but I have no interest in your 'snogging' activities with Warren, and I'm sure you don't need to hear all about my utter lack of a love life."

I spoke almost before I could calculate the enormity of the casually spoken comment I ended up saying: "What I *need* to know depends… Are you and Ally dating?"

Alana spluttered and reddened, suddenly deeply interested in her mum's chicken. "What are you… Why…? I don't think…" I felt a pang of guilt that I'd sprung that on her. I suppose it had been weighing on my mind: I'd normally have tried to find a more casual way to subtly draw out the information, but the last time I'd been alone in Alana's room we'd been getting ready for the prom and I'd been subtly feeding *her* lines to make her incompetently hung up on Ally all evening so I could get my way. Perhaps I owed her some straightforwardness.

"Well, the way I see it, my job with my friends, if I have one, is I have to check the people apparently crushing on them, maybe going out with them, make sure they have honourable intentions… And I have to be a shoulder for any lovelorn friends who have spent too long crushing on someone they can't have. With you and Ally it's both! And I feel responsible… I said some things that were way out of line that day before the prom. I want to make that up to you, if I can."

Alana put down the chicken leg that she had been distractedly holding aloft and sank down on the end of the bed. "This is all on me, don't worry about 'making it up', Tanya."

"Really? I wasn't trying to absolve myself: I'm going to feel bad about being a brat at the prom for the rest of my life. I was just… concerned. I mean, you are my friend as well, and today I'm realising that more than normal."

She waved me away, trying to act all unconcerned when I leaned in to touch her shoulder. "Nah. I talked to Ally, a bit. I mean, I didn't say anything, but… We're not an item. She said she wanted to wait and see what happened with the

Piper. But, like, he said he will *never* see her again. And I believe him. He does not do being emotionally compromised. So she has to wait out her feelings for him, and, well, if it was a competition between me and him, he won already, if there was ever a chance I could have won even if he wasn't in the equation. The only thing that will shake Ally out of this is something new. Short of me getting a wig and fake French accent or something, I'm not going to get a chance to be her new thing. I've known this since March. She's *confirmed* this for me, in her own way. I just can't stand to tell myself that. My heart is as dumb as hers. I want to wait it out and see where the Ally thing goes; she's not helping by thinking because we talked there's nothing to worry about here so she's as snuggly and touchy-feely as ever, and only a shock to the system I'm not going to get staying here in the town will do to me what needs done to her to stop her pining over the Piper."

I managed to get past her attempts to push me away with an elbow and gave her an awkward sideways hug. "See, girl talk! It's good to get things like this off your chest, right?"

Alana gave a sort of sniffly laugh and shook her head. A moment later she leaped up. "What are we even doing talking about this?" she cried.

"I dunno, that was prime sleepover material..."

"Right now! I mean, half an hour ago, we were hiding cramped up in a secret hole in the church, being hunted by red-cloaked cultists. Are you really not going to talk about this? Isn't this the classic 'Tanya moment' that your friends are always warning me about? And now I see one of these wild adventures first-hand, and you don't even want to talk about it?"

"Rich of you to say, Mrs. Don't Talk About It."

Alana furiously turned away and began serving up cold leftovers with a vengeance. Leaving me one plate piled high, she flopped down on the sofa and took several angry bites before she could look at me again. "Eat," she ordered, already halfway through her dinner.

I didn't want to argue with her, so I took the plate she'd made and sat beside her. We devoured leftovers for a bit, and only when I was feeling much less hungry did I try to continue the conversation.

"I'll be honest with you, we spent so much time not discussing things like this, and I've never really been one for sharing what's on my mind when it comes to the truly weird, that I'm not actually sure what I should be saying."

Alana shook her head in disbelief. "Literally the first thing you said to me was 'nice aura'. Are you just trying to be contradictory?"

"Well it was. I don't mind talking about weird stuff in a nonsensical way. It's just... These cultists, all we've seen and heard of them together neatly sums up all that I know about them, and you were there for all of it. Is there anything you know that I don't?"

Alana was forced to shake her head.

"See," I continued, "Ally babbles on and on and on and she has this crazy paranoid imagination that will eventually suss it all out as she runs all the ways the scenario could kill her or us through her head. I just know, or I don't. I never guess if I can help it, because guessing muddies the neat piles of facts I have in my head. Shooting the breeze, or talking about other serious stuff that's completely unrelated, at least, will help me not think about the facts relating to the cultists, and maybe help a new idea sneak in. If I try and concentrate on it, all I'll be doing is running through the same ideas over and over. I have to do *research* to learn new things if no one tells me what I see means. It could be that there's nothing left for us to work out, and everything we need to know is totally out of our reach at the moment sitting here."

"This is just a fancy way to say you're stumped, isn't it?"

"I've been tracking, for *months*, the weird inconsistencies in local history which suggest there is a cult—or until this week I'd have just said a secret organisation—interfering in the knowledge we have available to us, but I've never got inside the museum, and never found anything outside of it to suggest they existed until this week. I'm explaining *why* I'm stumped."

"Wait, how do you know they're from the museum? Bilsworth?"

"Yeah. Um, that's the grey castle."

"What?! That would have been something useful for me to know earlier! You said you had no idea!"

"And now I do."

"But… it's red."

"Oh… Well in the fairy world it's not. I'd eat my shoes if it's not grey. How did Teb describe the town when she was telling us about riding through it on her hunt?"

"You can be so brilliant and so infuriating at the same time, you know?"

"I'm going to take the compliment and ignore the rest."

Alana chuckled. "So if they're from the museum… Well, I suppose they're a historically minded cult: the priest said nothing like it had happened for a good chunk of his life… It might be that there are magic-related historical secrets in there which directly relate to this: something which would make them able to convince themselves to do such a barbaric thing as prepare for human sacrifice."

"What bothers me is the way they say it's for the good of the town. You must know better than anyone else I could talk to about this that when you're doing magic it is exactly as important as you think it is. If they're convinced that something bad will happen if they don't do the ritual… What if we stop them and something bad immediately happens afterwards?"

"That something bad has to go through me first." She posed dramatically, like she was trying to be a brave warrior, but then she sank back into the sofa before the impression could stick, not confident enough to commit to the joke. She pushed aside her now empty plate. "I think you're right though. We have no way to find out what it is they're doing and why they believe it. At least not without getting into the museum or spending some more time around the cultists. But they must know it's the two of us eavesdropping on them now. Mr Westcott and Mr Lane would be able to name us. We can hardly sit around in the town square hoping to catch another one of them at it; they're more likely to wait for a quiet moment and kidnap us!"

"Well maybe we should."

"Should what?"

"Let them catch us. They must know we're holed up here by now. Mr Curator... Bartholomew knows me a little better than I know him: we've butted heads a few times before. He knows I'm persistent, if nothing else. He'll have them ready to bag us as soon as we're out wandering unaccompanied in town, because he knows I will not let this drop. He knows that this is what I was looking for: he won't have been at all surprised to see me there."

"Wait, wait wait wait. Why have you been butting heads with him?"

"Oh! Right! I've been making runs on the museum for ages. They're good for general research, and through totally innocent non-magical reasons, um, I may have broken an exhibit and got banned when I was small. It made me get all *Mission Impossible* about my research. Finding out there were layers of secrets underneath that was just the icing on the cake."

"And how did you find out about *those* secrets?"

"Gee Alana, you really are out of the loop!"

She gave me this long, unending glare, no blinking or anything, just a foul look that dragged on for minutes.

"Okay, so I've known they're bad guys for a while: the secretary at the front desk runs a coven and in their spare time a couple of years ago they were trying to destroy Troutespond's chances in the county flower show via black magic. I was tracking Ally's missing hamster, stumbled on them, thwarted their plans, brought the hamster home and later looked up, er, a leading clue that pointed to insider knowledge at the museum."

She carried on with the look.

"What?" I complained.

"What was the clue? I need to be in the loop! The time for your secrets is over, Tanya. This is life or death, and it's *your* life on the line. Or Ally's. I suppose we've drawn the cultists down on us, so in fact... Tell me, the one person who's qualified to help you, what's going on, or *die*."

I swallowed hard. When she put it like that... "They were using one of the Piper's pipes to do the spell. Just like the cultists did this time to banish him."

"*What?*"

"You don't have one?"

"No! What? Why would I *have* one? I'm just his assistant. Do you have one of them?"

"Er, yeah. That's where the star boar came from. Ally does too. And Teb."

"How do you know Teb has one?"

"The other day I was helping her sort of some of her stuff while she was on a cleaning rampage, and she had it in a box with her purple goddess dress and the mask."

"Why? Why do you three all have one?"

"Well you were there when Ally got hers. It was seventy pence in the junk shop."

"That was…" Alana trailed off, kneading her temples.

"I don't understand how you're so surprised by this."

"I guess I thought… I wanted to *believe* he wouldn't be so stupid as to leave actual *magical* artefacts all around our nice peaceful society where nearly the entire population thinks 'magic' as we know it is nothing more than children's stories and drunken tall tales. I thought the recorder Ally found was just a clue he planted while he was winding her up."

"How did you figure the star boar came about?"

"I thought you cast a spell! I don't know. It was a really stressful evening."

"I am sorry that… we didn't share all of this," I admitted, carefully shifting the blame onto the group as a whole. "You've had a right to know all along. You trust us way more than we've trusted you, and I know it seems like it should be the other way around…"

Alana shrugged. "I blamed that attitude on Teb and moved on a long time ago. I'm just staggered at the depth and complexity of this particular secret… And a little jealous that I don't have one of those pipes! I've always wanted to have a proper look at one to see how they work."

"I'm not sure if it means something, or they just start showing up in your life when you get to a certain level of secret inside information. Way too many of them exist: he seems to chuck out a pipe after every use. The cultists have been happy to smash them up as spell parts."

"Wow. Great. Next thing I know he's sending me out to scoop up all the missing ones in these parts."

"Anyway, you transcend all that since you work for him directly. I'm not entirely sure what the pipes are for, but I bet he can use them as a sort of… anchor. To find people again. And to help them find him. A business card maybe. But that's way too subtle for your working relationship. You have him in your contacts list on your phone."

"Well complaining about this won't get us anywhere on the current problem of my house possibly being surrounded by cultists who want to sacrifice you. What do you propose we do about them?"

"Get caught, learn information, make an informed decision on the spur of the moment, then leave it to Future Tanya and Alana to sort out?"

"You could get sacrificed. Do you *really* want to put yourself in a position where that might happen?"

"Eh, I'm canny: good at squeezing out of tight spots. We'll see what happens."

"It's not much of a plan."

"And how often do complex schemes with many steps and a big reliance on the actions of people beyond your control actually go as intended? Let's skip a step of panicking and despairing that it all went wrong and keep goals in our minds that can be adapted depending on what happens."

"Well…" Alana shrugged, I guessed because she didn't have much else to contribute. She had, from the sounds of things, been relying heavily on my input for this, and with me not giving much useful input (though saying all sorts of vaguely off-topic things to distract her from how lost I was) she clearly was too out of her depth to come up with a plan alone.

Tricksy and magical though they were, fairies had such a clearly defined rulebook that meant they were a million times easier to deal with than prominent human figures from our own society. I wasn't even a hundred percent sure how to worm my way around Mr Westcott, and I'd been butting heads with *him* for years in a totally non-culty setting. Everyone else in the cult was an utter stranger when it came to me knowing how to push their buttons.

Alana finally sighed and stretched, floating a plan. "We should definitely wait until morning. It will make things a bit more on the level: if we make it to the town centre, they can't violently abduct us where anyone might see it. My house has magical protections and an expensive normal security system. I suppose we can only really go to bed and face them in the morning."

I nodded silent agreement, which she didn't even pay attention to as she was hauling herself back to her feet, moving sluggishly from exhaustion. She still fussed with the plates, taking mine and stacking them all neatly by the door along with the empty containers. "You can borrow pyjamas. I'm guessing you don't have much stuff on you."

I patted my pockets. "Just my phone… Oh! I should call my dad and make sure he knows I'm sleeping over somewhere."

She nodded and headed off into her tiny bathroom to get ready.

*

One call turned into two. When I hung up on Daddy, who seemed totally cool with me sleeping over with friends, as I had done at least a full half of the nights in my life, I found a text from Warren checking up on me. While Alana was in the shower I sat on her bed in a borrowed pair of pyjamas and called my dear Warren, tugging on the drawstrings to get the pants down to a Tanya size.

"Hey sweetie, were you missing me?" I crooned as soon as he picked up.

He sounded vaguely insulted, like I was calling him clingy. "I didn't see you online all day: I thought we were going to play tonight."

I had to concede that I wasn't being the best girlfriend, even if my duties only went so far as online video games at that point. "Something came up. I've been with Alana all day. We accidentally found a hive of cultists based in

Bilsworth museum. We're laying low at the moment."

"You *what?*"

"Aw come on; you knew I was onto something, better than most people."

"I mean, why didn't you let me know sooner?"

"This is me letting you know as soon as I'm not being actively pursued by angry cultists. I'm sorry you weren't involved, but it sort of happened organically: one minute me and Alana were chatting in town, the next this guy with a big red cloak came running past! You'd never have made the last bus to come join us, and he was there in that instant." I felt pretty guilty for not thinking of him at all—that excuse was partly a justification to myself about why it hadn't occurred to me to ask him for help; of course, he was unable to offer it at that point.

"Wait, when you say they're based in the museum… Does that mean you're in Bilsworth right now?"

"No, no no no. At Alana's."

"Oh." He definitely sounded disappointed. "Well I'd have offered you a place to stay…"

"Aw, sweetie, that's very kind of you. You know, we might be going to Bilsworth tomorrow. Maybe you ought to keep just half an eye out for me? Things might be about to get very strange."

"As strange as at the prom?"

"For all I know, stranger. After all, when it boiled down to it that was a perfectly natural event, with Teb's Hunt and all. It just happened to take place in an unusually noticeable way."

"Is there anything I need to do?" he asked, sounding very alarmed.

"I don't know. I'll have my phone on me, hopefully. For now, let's just agree, if you hear or see anything from now on… Just roll with it and hope it all plays out in our favour." I heard the bathroom door opening. "Oops, Alana's coming back."

"Oops? Did she say not to talk to me?"

"I don't know. I don't want her to get unduly stressed. Well, keep sharp. Hugs and kisses!"

I hung up on him before I caused more problems with Alana. We'd just about come to an agreement.

She came back in vigorously towelling her hair. She carefully closed the door before she spoke to me: "I'd offer you the use of the shower but, you know, noisy pipes. Curious Mom."

"Are you going to sleep with you hair wet?"

"Sure. I always straighten it in the morning anyway."

"Isn't it wildly unhealthy to sleep with wet hair?"

"Pfft, old wives' tales. I'm not going to die of damp hair."

"Fate gets weird ideas for people sometimes."

Alana shrugged. "I think it was more of a concern for people who didn't have antibiotics or basic hygiene helping them stay healthy."

"Isn't washing your hair basic hygiene?"

Alana gave me a long stare, which she ended by snatching a pile of pillows from her bed.

"Are you so pissed off with me about that comment that you're going to go sleep downstairs? After everything, *wet hair?*"

Her fed up look just amped up to looking at me like I had a screw loose. "No, I'm going to sleep on the sofa here so you can have the bed."

"Your bed is literally the biggest bed I've ever seen. There's room for the two of us and then some!"

"I don't know…"

Something in her hesitance made me realise this was more than just the sort of petty teasing and bickering my other friends got into: it always did run deeper with Alana.

"Oh my god, I don't think you're going to, like, *rape* me in the night. Would you chill out and get into bed?"

"I guess… I guess I had a few too many sleepovers with people who did. Being treated like a leper leaves its scars."

"Well we're loads better than your old friends, so get comfy. We can top and tail if it makes you feel better."

She threw her armful of pillows down at the foot of the bed, rather relieved at having that option. "Maybe baby steps before I get into your slumber party mentality."

Only a few minutes later the lights were out and we were lying there, Alana's feet by my shoulder. She was clearly desperate to sleep, but whether it was the heavy weight of food I'd just eaten sitting in my stomach or the calm, dark quiet of a room where finally no one was trying to talk to me, my brain zoomed into overdrive, begging me to pay attention to all sorts of thoughts that had been too frail to bloom when we'd been sitting around talking.

Would the cultists really *kill* me tomorrow? That seemed ridiculous. I was not going to go into the day assuming that I was going to die. We were going into it assuming that we'd win somehow, that we were gathering information, not even caring about the possibility of ritual sacrifice. Maybe it was all just a step too far: the fantastical existing was easy. Ask anyone and a good proportion of them would own up to ghosts or aliens existing, at least in ineffable far-off ways that we might never know about but it was as hard to disprove as it was to prove. Most would have a tale of the unexplained. Horror movies only worked in the first place because people could be made to think that ghosts might be a real-life threat, and you'd only go back and see another if you still believed it in some subconscious way even after the ridiculousness of seeing the monster at the end, because in the moment when a door was creaking open though no one was supposed to be home you had to believe that a malevolent force was pushing it. Even if you wouldn't own up to it in real life, the film caught you on a subconscious fear; a potential "what if" of dread...

But that was all far-off stuff that happened to other people, and the real humans involved were the sort of hairy drunken sorts in backwoods America who would claim to be abducted by aliens in the first place, or slick and scamming psychics who looked good enough for a TV show. The easy idea of an imminent threat in modern day life is never a quiet but determined organisation of men from your local area who were all well-groomed and held high-profile trusted jobs. Maybe for some horror about the evils of capitalism or climate denial, the sort of white rich man villain turned into the voice of our society's ills... Yet these guys were standing right on the edge of what wasn't real any more, where they couldn't possibly be ready to kill a young woman as a religious sacrifice, right? How did they get there at all? How did Mr Westcott, boring, pedantic authoritarian of our school, live a life as a teacher thinking that he might one day have to sacrifice one of his students?

It was all a layer under the lid of normality, and I had lifted it up. I'd expected to see gods and fairies and maybe some answers to my occasional visions, but never ever normal people that I could meet on the street in broad daylight who would honestly kill me with apparently no passion or particular hatred for me. Just a belief in doing what they seemed to think was the right thing. It was just difficult to get my head around the danger of it. That I'd been to Mr Westcott's office for innumerable reprimands and passed him in the school corridors even more. He'd been my French teacher one year! There was a sort of basic trust that he wouldn't turn around and kill me which had been my safety net for all the schemes I'd pulled which could have got me in trouble with him, and since he hadn't actually tried yet, I couldn't get myself to accept that he, or any of the cultists, would. Well, maybe the four we hadn't unmasked. They were the unknown.

Maybe Alana was right to be freaking out more than I was. How could I trust that the moment we left the house they wouldn't grab us, bundle us into the back of a van and we'd spend the rest of our lives trussed up and maybe even gagged: I sort of relied on a basic level of being able to manipulate people by talking to them; there'd be no chance to sneak off and find out what I needed to know so that when they confronted me I could spit their own secrets back in their face. They could take that all away just by being bigger than me and stronger than me, which wasn't hard to do.

Of course I was hoping that I'd have Alana with me, and that she'd do more than run around looking grumpy as she had done today: she was theoretically one of the more powerful members of our group. I wouldn't call what I did magic, and Ally was as useful as a potato, but Alana, if she could convince you she was a witch in the first place, had a pretty solid understanding of how to use magic to get her way. And with the cultists apparently firmly believing in the ritual they were doing, they couldn't afford to doubt this unassuming teenager was actually a witch.

And it helped that, for whatever reason, they hadn't considered her as a suitable candidate for slaughter and Alana was quietly assuming they wouldn't change their minds about that any time soon. We had never talked about it since, but I remembered the morning we were up by the motorway, before we caught the changeling. I remembered it far too often. I had my concerns about this girl and very few opportunities to crack open the door on them.

I supposed this then came down to being a trust exercise in Alana: no wonder she had been so insistent about having a plan. While I'd been quietly assuming I'd work something out on the go, she had been already seeing the problem that she, perhaps not the most accomplished thinker on her feet when Ally was a madcap dynamo and I had whatever cunning seemed to get me through most things in life and even Teb had a sharp mind and power to bully through a brick wall, was going to have to do all the work saving me, and I was throwing myself into being the damsel in distress.

"Tanya?"

Alana's voice floated out of the darkness, making me jump a little. I'd assumed she had gone to sleep long ago, given how tired she'd been.

"Yeah?" I asked, not bothering to pretend to be asleep. I welcomed the distraction.

"Why do you do it?"

"Do what?"

"All of it… I get that you're curious. But you're reckless and you have an agenda and none of it adds up to *just* Hermione being stoked to do her homework because discovering magic is real is the best thing that ever happened to her."

"You think I'm Hermione?"

"Nah, that's Ally. Which is why I'm confused about you."

I wanted to get into a proper debate about *Harry Potter*, since we'd all sorted ourselves long ago (Teb: classic Slytherin but wants to think she's a Ravenclaw so no one mistrusts her so she can get further in life; Ally: convinced she's a Hufflepuff but the bravest Gryffindor there is, so probably more like Neville if you had to name a character…) But my tongue got stuck in my mouth as I thought about Alana's purpose in the conversation. I couldn't deflect from it forever by dragging her into the Pottermore quiz: she only let me get away with so much.

"I don't really know, to be honest."

"You don't know?"

"I… A lot of days I feel like I'm coming back from a long illness. Or like I've just got back to town after being away for years. I don't even know if it's because I went to fairyland. I sort of felt that way always and it just got worse after seeing it all for myself. I'm wandering around trying to get my bearings, and I feel lost. Way too much. You know why I'm so excited about going to university? It's a total fresh start. Life here is a mess and I don't understand it, and as Ally's book hoard proves, there probably *isn't* a way to understand it.

Away from Troutespond… It feels like the real world. And it's got rules, with people in it who understand them absolutely. Maybe just because in different places, I don't *know* what weird stuff is going on and I'm not all caught up in all its twists and turns. I'm comfortably nestled onto the surface layer along with everyone else again. The course I'm signed up for is a course about folklore and fantasy and what it *means*, and that's why I decided there was literally nothing else I wanted to do with my higher education. I want someone to sit me down, set me a book list, and explain what is going on, the way everyone else sees it. The rules everyone else has decided for what's going on. And I can just write it all down and get the direction I need."

"Did you have an encounter with the fey at a young age? You do sound a bit like a textbook touched-by-fey case. It's the same yearning you get from eating fairy fruit, just not…" I think Alana gestured in the darkness, though I have no idea what the hand signal would be for wasting away from a devouring *want*.

"So there are textbooks?"

"Not really. I came into this all at such a different angle from you. I never really wanted to know all of this. The Piper has to constantly sit me down and explain, and all my research is just *oh god what am I dealing with today?* Not personal satisfaction. I want out. I'm never going to get out, but I didn't want in. All I know is the universe will never ever let me go now it's got its claws in me. I get by just telling myself I'm helping people, a whole 'try to leave the universe in a better state than you found it' situation."

"You really think that? It's sort of depressing."

Alana scoffed. "Welcome to my life."

"You shouldn't feel that way. You got given a long hard look at the world as it really is and decided to help people."

"Yeah, to fix my own fuck ups."

"I dunno. I think you're a better person than you think you are."

"Shut up."

I smiled to myself. "Not going to tell me anything different, anyway. You go on believing that and I'll go on believing what I do. We seem to work together okay, don't we?"

"You are one hundred percent getting us both killed tomorrow."

"Perhaps we need a plan after all," I replied, though the very thought made my nose scrunch up.

I sat up and fished my phone out from under the pillow.

"What are you doing?" Alana grumbled, emerging from under the blankets with her eyes all screwed up at the glare of my screen.

"We're going on a double date tomorrow," I giggled.

Sour Cream and Mackerel

Here's something you don't know.

I have become very close to being ineligible for a certain sort of sacrifice. When I was fifteen I managed to talk one of the sporty football-obsessed boys from the year above into going out with me (it's surprisingly easy if you pick a target who's single and you just go ask). We went on a few very low-key dates because the only thing worse than the thought of telling Teb about the weird people I dated was telling Ally about the *normal* ones I was interested in.

So after one particularly dull movie date (which seemed about the only thing to do in Bilsworth, if you weren't investigating cultists) I went back to his house, and after making sure his parents weren't home, we went up to his room. We kissed for a bit and I let him take my shirt off. Then he thought that meant he could take his trousers off. I didn't really have an issue with it at first, because I was only wearing a short skirt and jeans are sort of rough on the skin, especially from the outside (also I can be a moron sometimes just like anyone else), but then I realised he was getting really touchy-feely and I thought I had better stop things there for now. I kind of liked him, for one thing, and I didn't want to ruin it by letting things happen too fast.

"Hey, we should slow down," I said, gently untangling myself from him.

"What do you mean?" he asked in a weird voice, all distracted and turned on and probably not wanting to assume what he clearly should have guessed right away I meant.

"I mean maybe we should put some clothes back on and do something else for a bit." I scooted away, sort of meaning to look at the small collection of films he had on DVD.

"Are you saying you don't want to do this?" he asked, apparently convinced this was all or nothing.

"Um. Not right now. Maybe later. I've only been out with you a couple of times and it's not like we've seen each other much at school. I don't want to rush into things."

He got up and began putting his clothes back on in a really angry way, not looking at me anymore, and it was at that point that I finally realised that it *was* all or nothing to him: he didn't want to date me and sit with me at lunch, or hold my hand as we walked around school. The fact that I had wanted to be so off the radar with it in the first place had been encouraging to him because he thought I wanted the same, and it made it easy for him to not have a huge amount of fuss when he wanted to dump me. He probably even fancied someone else and thought I would be good practice. I didn't know how much people talked about me, but I'd already been on several dates with high-profile attachments to the weirder characters at school, so maybe there was a sort of semi-benign rumour that I was easy, at least, to ask out.

"You know what," I said, pulling my shirt back on, "I could probably just go. I'll make the next bus if I go now. Why don't you call me if you want to hang out again?"

Of course he never did. I suppose one good thing was that I got a black mark against my name so I never really got bothered for 'dates' by the more jock-like boys, and in return I was put off dating the sort who found it easy to get a girlfriend and had girls fighting over them. It left me much more interested in finding someone like my Warren, who would actually want to be patient and enjoy my company for its own sake.

It was the weirdest feeling to start *regretting not doing* ill-advised teenage fumbling in a nearly strange boy's bedroom, but there you go.

*

Morning dawned, and I woke up naturally… with a huge start. I had a feeling my dream had been portentous, but unfortunately it behaved like any other dream and drained out of my head even as I looked around wildly and reassured myself when I saw the army of dream catchers Alana had hung around her room. Well, they had done their job, if it wasn't one superstition too far, because aside from a feeling of shadows creeping in around me I couldn't say a thing about what my unconscious mind had been dwelling on.

I tried to get up quietly to go to the loo, but Alana made a great grumbling noise and emerged from the other end of the duvet, hair curling in every wild direction. "Why are you *awake*?" she groaned.

"I dunno," I said, not too keen on conversation either while my mind was still bleary. "Couldn't sleep anymore. Probably going to die today."

She collapsed back onto her pillow, and I dragged myself out of bed. My legs ached as I stood up: even my arms were a little sore, but the backs of my thighs screamed as I straightened up. I ignored them and went to wash my face and get changed, all the better to be bright and cheerful Tanya again, clearing away all my dark nighttime thoughts.

I returned with borrowed make-up on my face; Alana wasn't exactly my complexion and didn't flatter her own anyway so much as wore stuff influenced or even left over from her goth background, but I'd mostly wanted a bit of eyeliner and lip gloss that wasn't from her spooky phase. I nervously checked my phone while Alana blundered around trying to find clothes from the piles of fresh laundry stacked on her chair.

"Are they coming on the bus?" she asked.

"Um, I'm not actually sure. I managed to convince Warren to commit to nine o'clock, but..." I shrugged.

"So I have a question. How do we get *you* back out of the house then?"

"Oh, um... Don't you have any more fantastic ideas?"

"Well, I was thinking we could sneak out so we could wait in town, but then I remembered that you might be grabbed by cultists at any moment, so inside is still safer... And now you say Warren's coming to help us?" She looked extremely dubious that he would be any real use. "How do we get him to the house and away again without my mum seeing him and wondering what's up with *that*?"

"Well if we meet him in town, maybe we can go into one of the shops?" I suggested. "A shopkeeper would be as good as any other witness to make sure we're not abducted."

"That's providing the shopkeeper wasn't one of the cultists last night: there are still three, I think, we haven't identified."

"So we sneak out of the house when we know Warren's really close by... And just hope your mum... *mom*... isn't already awake?"

Alana glanced at her alarm clock, showing something horribly close to six in the morning. "She's up by seven. We're either sneaking you out now and hoping we don't get snatched by cultists, or waiting for him to show up and having to do a huge charade to get you out of the house. She's most active in the morning."

There was a tap on the bedroom door. I let out an involuntary squeak and dived under the bedcovers, like that would actually conceal me from view. Alana hauled me out by the ankle and I landed in a heap on the floor: she dragged me up and looked for a better place to hide me, eyes huge with horror as she tried to bundle me towards the wardrobe, but the door opened before either of us could make a move.

There was no one there.

No, there was one small person, peering in.

Alana let me go with a little shove as Jeremy sidled into the room (three foot tall again, unarmoured), looking rather alarmed himself at our panic.

"Are you okay?" he asked.

"No!" Alana hissed. "Shut the door! Now!"

He obligingly did, then came in and settled himself down on the sofa.

"Jesus, what are you doing here?" she groaned, sinking down onto the end of the bed, like she was already exhausted by today.

"I got the number that Tanya was asking for." Jeremy was looking between us with an extremely confused expression, almost wondering if he had done the right thing. He absolutely had.

"What number?" Alana asked me. She never liked to talk directly to the fey if she could help it. I'd guess it was a result of taking on the project manager position for Teb's Changeling Situation.

"Er... Mr Lane's," I had to confess.

"I assume you asked for that some time *before* we started working together on this?"

"Maybe. For all you know I was keeping it out of Teb's reach!"

"So you don't want it?" Jeremy asked, disappointed. The business card was in his hand, but he seemed to be on the verge of putting it back in the pocket of his oversized shorts that acted as trousers.

I gave my new goblin friend a soothing smile. "It's just... Things have changed a lot since the other day. For one thing, the cultists know who we are now, and we know who a couple more of them are. On the other hand, that means we don't need to try and draw Mr Lane out subtly and accuse him of being a cultist. He's more likely to have all his friends waiting to snatch us."

Jeremy groaned. "I told you not to get involved in it, Tanya!"

"Well you weren't freezing us solid to stop us running off to look when they showed up, so..." I shrugged.

He looked mortally offended that I was accusing him of not looking after me as well as Teb: I supposed his desire to protect people just ran very deep. "I warned you! That was me trying to protect you! You can't keep running into trouble. You will get gravely hurt."

"Do you *know* that?" I asked sharply, suddenly worried that I wasn't the only getting premonitions. That felt like the sort of comment you didn't brush aside when it came from one of the fey.

Jeremy looked tortured. "Not now, but... I don't want Teb's friends to get hurt!"

"He's lying," Alana said.

"The fey don't lie."

Alana folded and refolded her arms, scowling. "He's doing the next best thing and it's killing him."

"Jeremy, how can you protect us now? We have to leave before Alana's mom wakes up, just, you know, out of niceness to Alana, who has to live with her another month, but our hired protection won't get to town until nine…"

"I can walk you into town!" he said, suddenly beaming, delighted at a chance to prove he could look after us.

"No offence," Alana said, meaning it completely as offence, "but you're tiny. Teb's little brother would be better…"

"We don't necessarily need someone huge and burly to look after us: it's more that the cultists won't try taking us while there are witnesses who theoretically know nothing about it. Walking down the street with a goblin is less defence than Teb's little brother because *he's* not supposed to know magic exists. Obviously a goblin does, so the cultists aren't going to have qualms about behaving outside of social norms around him."

"Tanya, can you actually finish a sentence without sounding like a total boffin?"

I shrugged. "No."

"How about Teb's dad?" Jeremy put in, before we could start fighting.

"What about him? I think he'll find it very weird if we phone him up and ask him to come hang out with us for a couple of… *Woah.*"

Suddenly it was like Mahesh was in the room with us: Jeremy had copied him right down to the crinkles in the corner of his eyes, the white specks in his hair. "Lose the house slippers," I told him, much more relaxed about seeing the transformation than Alana: her eyes were practically bugging with a suddenly realised horror.

"Did you steal his name? Did you *changeling* him?"

Jeremy looked horrified: "No! No no no. I've seen him a lot lately. I've always been good at casting glamours. It's all Jeremy underneath." He shimmered and was the little goblin again: not a transformation, just, implausibly, a trick of the light which made a tiny creature look exactly like a man I considered a sort of second father. "I just know this man's shape quite well at the moment, after watching the house for weeks. He should do for your purposes: he's big, like Alana wants, and mundane, like you think, Tanya."

I nodded. "Meet us outside as soon as we leave the driveway; we'll walk you into town, and you can sit with us until Warren meets us. We'll buy you a treat in exchange for your time."

"*Will* we?" Alana asked. "Someone here has nothing but their phone on them."

I grinned. "If I don't die by cultists then I will totally pay you back."

The walk into town was surreal: after escaping Alana's house unnoticed, I found myself much more distracted by the way I kept having to remind myself Teb's dad wasn't walking with us. I constantly checked myself from saying strange things, before remembering that, yes, I could say them and I wasn't around a man who knew nothing of our supernatural shenanigans. To be honest, if we were to include a second parent after Ally's mum in our inner circle, Mahesh did seem the most easy-going of our collective pool of parents.

I had a feeling however chill my dad acted around me, he was always a bit too close to a panic attack to let him know what was really up.

Alana seemed much more concerned with the goblin, rather than the man he was impersonating. "Aren't you supposed to be guarding Teb right now?" she asked as soon as we were on the road and had safely made it out of sight of her house. We took a steady pace and I at least was consciously trying to walk like nothing strange was happening.

"I have my sister watching her," Jeremy explained, using the usual lighthearted voice I'd come to expect from the goblin in a friendly mood. It helped to hear Teb's dad talking in that high-pitched voice: it made it easier to remember it wasn't him. "She is far better at fighting than I am. But I expect no one will come to hurt Teb. It was your involvement I was guarding against."

"Why though?" Alana sounded more than usually grumpy: she clearly had not liked having magic used against her, her mood souring as she remembered our last encounter with Jeremy.

Jeremy made Teb's dad pucker up with confusion. "You do understand that you are walking into grave danger? You have recruited me as a bodyguard yourselves just for a short walk. Why do you think it is strange I will try to protect the goddess I have sworn myself to from walking into the same danger?" He gestured the trees around us like an army of cultists would burst out of them.

Alana scoffed. "Yeah, but Teb has a ten foot long spear, a magic bow and arrows that she apparently can't miss with, a gold chariot with enormous spikes on the wheels and massive fairy warhorses pulling it. Look at how squishy me and Tanya are in comparison. You can see why we might want her along with us?"

Jeremy shook his head vehemently. "She isn't *ready*. They can't know about her! All they do is poke and prod and pry… I have been to the grey town recently and it's half empty: no one goes there to trade. People are leaving. The grey castle sends out an evil feeling into our world, poisoning it. And these people will be too happy that she exists. She is not trapped in this town like the Green Man and Lady. She's not dead like the swamp gods at Severstrong or untouchably vague like all those elves in Ransley. She's a living, breathing human with a huge magical thumbprint right across the valley *and they will notice*. They are always looking for a sign the Other is there, and she's it!"

"Wait wait wait," I interrupted. "They're always looking? They're doing a big magical ritual right now in town with *perfect* knowledge of the Other."

Jeremy waved a hand. "Those cultists are a crazy offshoot, a secret Order in the secret society. No one else at the grey castle thinks what they do works. Most of them don't even know the sect exists within their ranks. Some of them don't truly *believe* but protect other secrets that hide the Other beneath; others have the certainty that *only* their thing works, and then some search for answers without knowing the question they are really asking, as you do,

Tanya."

"Well they're doing *real* magic. The Piper—"

"We know that!" the poor goblin was sounding extremely stressed now. "We were hoping they didn't. But if you interfere, there's no way they're *not* going to know that the stuff they do is having a real effect on the landscape. If they meet an organized resistance, with a witch and a goddess and a seer standing in the way of what they're doing, all they're going to feel is vindicated that they weren't wrong and use you as proof that their experiments have borne fruit. They don't care about what's good or bad, just doing what they think they were born to do, same as any one of the Other people, but it's bad when they act like us. Bad for our world, I mean."

"So, what, you think they'll start sacrificing people more often if they know it works?" I realized we were already reaching the main road and reminded myself to speak quieter. Our walk so far had been eerily lonely, but I didn't like taking chances.

Jeremy shrugged unhappily. "Maybe. I don't think this sacrifice happens often, but the others from the grey castle aren't sure that what they're looking at is real. If this cult goes to them and says it is and have proof they never had before, well… Those people have been waiting for some version of that news for a long time. Once they believe them, once they know where the boundaries are to push… The methods of those in the Grey Castle will spread. Their knowledge will be shared. The world will be changed and we will all be in danger."

"What else do you know about these people from the grey castle?" I asked excitedly.

Alana seemed to realize too late that she was letting me ask anything I wanted about the cults to someone with apparently full knowledge and a contractual obligation not to lie and cut across any chance Jeremy had of replying with, "I think this other big organization is none of our concern at the moment: just the little 'Order', as Jeremy put it, that is troubling us now. We're in town now, so let's pick a place to wait and hope your boyfriend gets here sooner than any of these cultists." She put a hand on my back, the better to steer me with, and headed towards the nearest café, using members of the public as a defence against me blabbing on about magic and goblins and Other things.

I was about to protest about where she was leading me, but we arrived too soon for me to not make a scene, and it didn't seem that awful to be there when the choice was go along or make a fuss. Roberta's had just opened: Bobbie herself was washing the windows from the inside, and 'open' seemed mostly to suggest she was in the shop rather than settled down and ready to serve a stream of customers who wanted ice cream for breakfast. She looked rather panicked to have three of us show up at once.

Alana finally gave me some agency in my movements again and let me pick my seat, and I chose the chair I'd sat in on my date with Warren, the better for watching the street. Jeremy quickly took the other chair at the table but recoiled from the cast iron, ending up weirdly perched so he was only in contact with the cushion. Alana patiently waited for Roberta to hurry back around to the correct side of the counter then ordered three vanilla ice creams. I wrinkled my nose, but Jeremy looked thrilled to have a human treat with lots of sugar. Perhaps his head would explode if he knew what the house special was.

"Don't goblins turn cream sour?" I murmured while Alana took a moment as she paid above-average for the ice creams to glare over her shoulder, I think having caught a whisper of the G-word in public.

Jeremy chuckled. "Only if we want to," he replied in a low voice. Alana turned around and glared again, perhaps thinking we were talking about her since I had mistakenly caught her eye, so I leaned back in my chair and watched the street and tried not to be too thrilled about the company I was keeping. My list of things I would love to have discussed with one of the fey had grown exponentially since my brief stay over in the fairy world in March, and if Alana hadn't been glowering at us so much I would have been deep into it now I'd finally been granted an interview with Jeremy, who was much more inner circle than Cathy. If only Teb would share.

Alana grabbed one of the rickety chairs from another table and put it right in the narrow passage between counter and door for the sake of sitting at our table; she leaned in to insert herself between Jeremy and me, making an awkward silence that lasted until Roberta showed up with three small bowls of ice cream and a pursed look on her face about Alana creating a health and safety hazard in the middle of the shop.

When Bobbie had retreated to the back of the shop, I ate my first spoonful of ice cream almost tentatively, like the raw sweetness might strangle me. "This is the most decadent breakfast I've ever had," I giggled.

"I'm not normally a breakfast person," Alana admitted, and after barely tasting the ice cream, she pushed hers deliberately away towards Jeremy. He had already devoured most of his own. I felt rather greedy keeping my own ice cream after that, so I handed mine over after eating a tactful half of it.

The silence came back, except for Jeremy's clinking spoon. When my phone trilled a text alert I almost jumped out of my skin.

"Warren's asking where we are," I summarised while hastily tapping a coded response even a dunce couldn't get wrong unless he had literally sleepwalked through our last date.

Bobbie returned from the back of the shop and took away the two empty bowls. I slipped my phone into my lap until she had gone, suddenly feeling anxious and paranoid. When she had left us alone again, I hissed at Jeremy, "Eat slower or we'll be kicked out with nowhere to go until Warren gets here!"

He nodded, eyes downcast.

I went back to adding a postscript for him to get to the café as soon as possible. I sent the text and got on with unhappily staring around, waiting for anything to happen. I didn't like the town still looking normal. Troutespond could bore for England... Quite literally, I'd seen it in an informal list of "most boring towns" somewhere on the internet. Of course I should have been expecting it to carry on being surface-level dull, but even so the waiting was killing me.

I was just beginning to mildly resent Warren for not replying instantly to my text when the first random passerby of the day stopped to peer in the ice cream shop window, eyes screwed up behind thick-lensed glasses as he tried to work out if I was in there for real.

It was almost impossible to stop a goofy smile appearing on my face as I waved at Warren, signalling him to come in and join us.

He slipped into the shop and scurried up to us. "Um... hi?" he said, catching sight of 'Mahesh' with us.

"Hey, Warren. This is Jeremy, a goblin. He's been looking after us, and in no way should you assume he's any relation to Teb, however he appears."

Jeremy put his spoon down, ice cream finished, and stared at him, eyes narrowed and looking him up and down, like it seemed Mahesh was evaluating my choice in boyfriend and not approving in a fatherly way.

Warren just nodded, vaguely intimidated by Jeremy's look but otherwise like, okay. I loved best about him that he usually just accepted weird stuff I told him and got on with things. "So are we going?"

"Yes, the sooner the better," Alana said, standing up with a huge screech from her chair. "Jeremy, thanks for the company. You don't want to...?"

Jeremy shot me a rather grumpy look, that much more telling because it came from Mahesh's face, and I knew those looks so well. "I should get back to guarding Teb. I only meant to slip away for five minutes to give you the number."

"Hop to it then," Alana told him, sounding teasing.

Jeremy didn't seem to take it that way: he scurried away before we could exchange any more pleasantries. I felt strange and sad that he didn't meet my eye again on the way out, or say goodbye properly, though perhaps that was just fairy custom.

"Shame," I said. "He could have been useful to keep around."

"I'm not sure there would have been room for him," Warren replied before Alana could give me any scowling attitude for questioning her dislike of having goblins following us everywhere.

"Room?" I asked.

"Well, yeah. I thought if I came on the bus it's half an hour until the next one, so I called up Mack and got him to drive me over..."

"You brought Mackerel!" I cried, delighted. I'd known we'd meet him in Bilsworth as our hired muscle, but Mackerel driving us was definitely a best case scenario. No threat of being stuck on a bus with cultists then.

Warren grinned, even as Alana began shoving him by the shoulder to get him to leave the shop. I turned to compulsively check I hadn't left my bag under the chair, thrown by the lack of weight on my shoulder where my bag still lay on the floor in my room. Of course there was nothing there, but as Alana stood by the door, giving me the hurry up, I found my eyes sweeping the back of the shop. Maybe I knew before I saw it: maybe the prickling feeling that had made me uneasy and anxious since we got to the shop had been a warning, or a sense... A cloudy face peered from the back of the shop, half-hidden by the frosted glass in the door to the kitchen, but in just a few days I had learnt the look of that face well. It was Mr Lane, shrinking back into the shadows as my eyes turned his way, and even if I only saw him for a fraction of a second I can say with certainty it was him.

The aura he gave off was just too familiar.

*

"They've seen us," I moaned in horror as Alana grabbed my elbow and set us off on another strained jog. As she pulled me away from the ice cream parlour I felt a stretching: a sort of thread tying me to it, a moment that snapped as we reached the corner, leaving me free to run. I didn't know if Mr Lane had tried to trap me, to drag me back, or if I had sensed something greater, a moment when one possibility ended and another began. For that moment every instinct I had told me to run back into the shop.

"They can't know where we're going," she replied tersely, giving me another friendly nudge to get me to cross the road, which she did at a sharp angle. I wondered how she knew which way to go when Warren was trailing behind us, but then I saw a looming friendly giant, standing by the most beat-up student car you could imagine: the body was mostly faded blue, with the left side's doors in brownish red. At least on those doors it disguised the rust creeping from the wheels up. People had probably died in that car. It was more than likely haunted, because a vengeful ghost would be the only thing powerful enough to keep it running.

I waved rather urgently at its owner: "Okay, not that I'm not delighted to see you this deep into the summer, Mackerel, but I really think we ought to hop into that deathtrap—car—and get on the road." I clambered into the front passenger seat out of grabby habit. I didn't dare make a fuss to rearrange us so that I was sitting next to Warren: I was busy buckling myself in and steeling myself for a hazardous drive. As I looked around to make sure they were getting into the car with all due haste, I caught Alana and Warren exchanging a look through the back windows of the car. Their concern was exhausting but it was the one thing they had in common. That and curly wurly hair.

Mackerel heaved himself into the driver's seat; I felt the suspension groaning as it tried to deal with four people at once, one of them a six-foot giant of a boy.

My initial fears disappeared as the engine started and Mackerel proved that not only his car worked but that he could drive it, both dubious points considering I hadn't even known he drove, so he'd probably passed the test in the last month or so: any Bilsworth kid who drove to Troutespond for college became the focus of intense adoration from the other Bilsworth residents in case it meant no more bus for them.

Once we were facing down the main road out of town, I felt my tongue loosening, about the same time Mackerel had relaxed from his nail-biting start to the drive (I never said he was good at un-parking a car, just that he didn't wreck it in the process).

"So what—"

"I saw Mr Lane in the ice cream place!" I blurted over his unnecessary question, refusing to give up my right to speak even though I had started second.

"What?! We should go back there," Alana said, leaning forwards between the front seats: I saw Mackerel freezing up at the added stress and I pushed her back as gently as I could while convinced he was going to swerve into oncoming traffic.

"Do you *want* me to stop and turn back?" he demanded, sounding more stressed than I've ever heard him. Mack was about the most good-natured person I knew, always chill and ready to listen and offer up that big shoulder for a chat.

"No! Going to the museum is a better plan than going back and cornering him. For one thing… We know he won't be there because he's back in town!"

"A better plan?" Alana protested. "Sometimes I think you just want to sound like you're smarter than everyone else."

"I can *feel* it."

"Well guess what, you're not the only one in this car with extra senses— no, not you, Warren—and I don't see why grabbing Mr Lane would have been a bad thing."

"*Grabbing*? How would you have gotten him out of the shop? What, you hoped to lure him out and overpower him somehow? We can't rely on Bobbie being cool on us nabbing the guy lurking in her back room: I'd assume she knew he was there *since she went in there*. Oh god, she has a flat for a lodger on the top floor. She *told* me that months ago. He's been living in the ice cream shop. There's a cultist infiltration in my favourite ice cream shop."

Alana had clearly reached her Tanya-limit for the week: she was almost snarling as she replied. "Your plan might be to 'snoop', but I know you mean 'get caught', because that's what we discussed before suddenly your boyfriend was in on this, and now Mack as well? Just because you told them something different doesn't mean you think it's going to end any other way once we try going in there. At least we can be honest with them about that."

"Well at least then we'll be caught in the right place!"

"The ritual is in *Troutespond*."

"So? The museum has all the information."

"No it doesn't! There is no display on cultists throughout history that we all somehow missed on the boring school trips we took through that place. Mad new history doesn't spring up just because you know a little more about the world than you did the last time you visited the place. So what do you plan to do when we get caught there?"

"Well that will give me some time to interact with the cultists, maybe snoop around..."

"Tanya, they are not movie villains, and the only reason we're not entertaining the thought they'll immediately hand you over to the police is because we're working on the assumption they plan to kill you later. Which, incidentally, if you get caught they are not going to risk you getting away."

"I just need a chance to find out some more about them..."

"From *what*, Tanya? What are the chances we go in there and they hand us all this wonderful missing information on a plate?"

I shrugged. "It's amazing what you can find out from just a glance."

"What on *earth* are you two talking about?" Mackerel suddenly interrupted. "Is this conversation a *joke*?"

Warren decided to summarise while Alana and I seethed at each other: "Mr Westcott is in a cult that wants to sacrifice Tanya for the good of the town. One of the cultists saw them getting ice cream, so now we're going to the museum to find their lair and hope that more of them are in Troutespond looking for her than there are at their secret base."

"But," Alana interrupted, "now that Mr Lane saw us leaving, he can make a call and as soon as we get there we'll be captured, so Tanya is basically walking into a trap that she's set up for herself."

"Do they know you're definitely going to the museum? I mean, if you were a bit more... careful, you'd leave town and get the hell away, right?"

I wished I didn't have to argue with Mackerel: I agreed with him on a common sense level, but this was an uncommon situation. I had to take my own angle on it. "Well they only know what we know if Bartholomew, the curator, who is a cultist, knows we were eavesdropping from a hidey-hole in the church yesterday. If not they don't know that we know that they have that connection. But I have a long history of being caught snooping there before I even knew so that's... something to deal with."

"Maybe they think you're just coming back to finish off the mammoth for good," Mackerel chuckled.

"It happened once!" I complained, laughing a wee bit hysterically at my school-level reputation following me into this scenario.

"Look, I'm not sure if you're playing a game or if this is deadly serious... I can't tell with you and Warren most of the time! But if you want me to help… I can pull a fire alarm, go in with you… something. I'm the same size as everyone else in the car put together, if there's a fight."

I looked to the backseat, where Alana just shrugged.

"He's got a point," I told her.

She folded her arms, sunk down in the seat and fumed.

Way too soon we were standing in the museum car park at the rear of the building. Bilsworth's dull office buildings squatted behind us, the noise of the main road muted until it felt almost like we were in a wilderness, a brick and concrete wasteland. The car park was small: six bays for staff parking, twelve for visitors, and like most parking in the centre of town it was a pay one. I hung back while Alana grudgingly went through her purse and found some coins for Mackerel, silently sulking about having to fund terrorism.

I stared up at the back of the museum building, a place which sat so much more heavily on the landscape than all the buildings around it. I was trying to imagine it in grayscale, trying to see what the goblins saw. At first it was hard to filter the colour away, but then it was like the building melted, smooth as a dozen marshmallows blending into one solid mass on the surface of hot chocolate, so the brickwork softened. When I saw the front of the building in my mind's eye I understood that I was being shown rather than seeing. A great cave yawned in front of me, the door to the museum filled with gnashing teeth and a darkness that drooled out between them.

"Tanya?" Alana nudged my shoulder.

"Right. Right! Warren, as we discussed. Find a fire alarm, pull it, then *leg* it home. Mackerel, follow him into the building at enough paces to not look like you're together, and get good and lost in the exhibits before any bells start ringing. The curator, if he's here, will have to be out and about if the museum is potentially burning down. Get your eyes on him, stay hidden, and text me if or when he heads back to any staff-only area. Alana and I will take the back door when the alarm goes. Got it?"

The boys nodded. Alana folded her arms and tried to look stern and ready to go.

I impulsively hugged Mackerel, enjoying one of his amazing hugs, then planted a kiss on Warren before he could squirm away, embarrassed at people watching us.

"Let me know you're safe as soon as possible," he told me.

"Of course. Got my phone right here!"

"Enough love-in already," Alana butted in.

I nodded and stepped away from Warren, freeing him from a subconscious snare he'd been in since I first grabbed him by both shoulders. The guys headed off to the footpath that led around the building, Mackerel giving us a big cheery wave.

Alana nodded to the museum and we set off. "Well, this plan of yours is holding up so far."

"Shush," I told her, marching off ahead. There was a dull "staff only" door that looked out onto the car park. On arriving on their back step I found a week's worth of cigarette ends and a key code panel for the door.

"Well, that's great," Alana groaned, stopping behind me.

I keyed in the code and turned the handle: the door opened without complaint.

"How did you do that? Why aren't you *waiting*?" she hissed, helplessly following me into the building. There was a bland white corridor beyond, lined only with a few sparsely filled noticeboards. Beside the door was a pot plant and a statue of a foo dog, its weird snub nose turned up, grinning happily. I patted it absentmindedly as Alana shut the door behind us.

"Okay, are you going to say how you did that?" she demanded, tripping after me as I headed down the corridor. "Why aren't you *waiting* for the signal from Warren?"

"It was the date that Ransley Castle burned down. Those key code locks aren't very secure: you don't even need to put the numbers in in any particular order. But they can't duplicate a number *within* the code for the sake of security. Once you press one of the numbers you can't input it again. So think about the dates we have connected to the museum: there's two fives in the date Severstrong Abbey got done in. Two ones in the date the museum was built. Two sixes in the founding date of Ransley Manor… I can go on. They're surprisingly limited in what secret codes they can use, if they're going to be all self-referential."

"And the fire alarm?"

"Pfft, they have automatic smoke detectors which link directly to the fire station. There aren't any the general public can smash: the stewards can radio down to the front desk where they have a panic button if the smoke detector fail. But Warren's going to find it a nightmare to set anything off."

"So now we've established I'm trusting your most alarming alternate personality, what does Super Spy Tanya suggest we do?"

"We need to head upstairs. This floor is all staff offices." I gestured the nearest door, a Professor M. Kingston. "The downstairs is a basement full of historical goodies and priceless texts. You can't let me in there or you'll never get me out and I'll ruin the mission. But no one has ever written down anywhere in existence what is on the top floor, even on original plans and stuff. So. We go look."

"And get caught?"

I shrugged. "If the cultists think we genuinely skipped town out of fear, they're not going to chase us. They have a backup candidate who is almost certainly wandering around looking for them today."

"Shit. Ally."

I rolled my eyes. "*Now* you see why we're walking into the dragon's mouth. I just felt if we could get caught on our own terms, the better for us. I would never have hid and let Ally be the one in danger."

After that I was allowed to lead the way to the stairwell in silence. I'd won.

The offices were quiet in turn: no telephones or murmured conversation, no TV or radio sounds leaking out. It made me uncomfortable to think of the building being deliberately cleared out, but it was still early in the day. I couldn't imagine the day-to-day business of keeping track of the past was very surprising for the majority of the staff.

On the stairs I got a good look at the sign pointing down to the "Archives". A faint whine fought its way out of my throat as I put my feet on the stairs leading up. Alana nudged me, and I moved.

The door to the first floor was as bland and officey as the ones downstairs, yet for the first time since getting here I felt a prickle in my fingers as I pushed it open, the sensation of hairs rising on my arms and head accompanying my normal magic-sense. I don't know if it was excitement or particularly strong magic.

"Here goes nothing," I whispered, stepping out into what could have been plain sight. I glanced around the ceiling: no sign of CCTV. "Hmm."

Alana followed me in, her shoes scuffing barely perceptibly on the plush red carpet that lined the hall. "Not exactly the Death Star, is it? Are you sure these aren't just offices for more important people up here?" The wood panelling on the walls and local landscape portraits hanging regularly at eye level certainly seemed to suggest the genteel luxury of an expensive public building.

I tiptoed a little way down the hall and inspected the first door that I had come to. It was solid wood, with a shiny brass handle. Not office standard any more. "Maybe not."

Alana had no sense of the need to sneak: she strolled up behind me. "'The Elm Room'," she read off careful lettering on the door.

I nodded. "Read that already." I reached for the handle, but Alana stepped heading to the next door. "'The Oak Room'. Hey, do you think these doors are made of the same wood? They're not the same colour as each other at all under this polish."

I shrugged. "Most likely if it *means* something."

"Well there are two more doors right at the end of the hall. Let's go check."

We went down and read 'The Rowan Room' and 'The Ash Room'.

"They're definitely into tree symbolism, if this isn't about Pokémon professors. Wonder what it all means?" Alana asked.

"That we go into the Ash Room," I said, decisively answering her rhetorical question.

"How do you know that?"

In response I poked her bare arm with a prickling finger. I almost heard the crack.

"Ow! Was that static?"

"Magic warning pins and needles."

"Maybe you have poor circulation."

"Maybe I can ground it on you because you're as receptive as I am."

"Why aren't I getting any special tingles—oh don't giggle."

I bit my lip. "I'm more in tune to this scenario. It's my life on the line after all."

"You going to open the door?"

I brushed the handle with my fingertips and had to pull them back: something repelled me, like I had the wrong side of a magnet embedded in each of my nails. "I'm not sure I can."

"What?"

"I just *really* don't want to open that door. Unnaturally so."

"I thought you were gambling everything on finding out what was behind it?"

"Well yeah, I'm madly curious. Open the door for me."

Alana rolled her eyes, grabbed the door handle and pushed it down. "That wasn't so hard, was it?"

"It was." I tried to peer around her as she eased the door open an inch.

"Why could I open it then?" she asked, her voice dropping to a whisper.

"Maybe you don't care so much about what's in here."

She gestured an all clear and stepped into the room. I followed her, feeling another shiver as I passed through the door. I got the feeling the very wood of the frame was telling me to back off, not to enter.

Inside we found a surprisingly small, muffled room. Wooden panels of the same ash wood lined what walls weren't taken up with bookshelves. The carpet was thicker, dotted with Persian rugs. The curtains were heavy red velvet, the furniture polished wood, all dark hues and stateliness. The books were fairly uniform: they looked like they must have been made specifically for this room, though there was a clear sign of ageing as I looked down the rows from the door to the window a hundred years or more settled onto the leather of their covers. There were no titles on their spines.

Alana wandered up to the big table in the middle: seven chairs were placed around it, six at the sides and one at the head. She stopped, looking deep in thought, and rested her hand on the back of one of the chairs. "This is a meeting room, isn't it?"

"I'm guessing for those cultists, yes. Which means this is their nerve centre. These books must have everything they need to know. The spells that kept the Piper out... What the ritual will be and what for. The *history* of it."

"There must be nearly a thousand books here. Where are you going to start? We don't have time to do an Ally all over the room."

"No... But..." I walked up to the nearest shelf and brushed my fingers along the spines in front of me.

"You sure that's going to work?" she asked as I walked down the row.

"I'm never sure anything I do is going to work. I can only find out by trying."

Alana sat on the edge of the table and put her feet on the chair in front of her. "Let me know when you have a book you need me to pick up."

Sacred Orders

Here's something you don't know.

The book Alana liberated from the shelf for me was almost a relic in itself. The whole bookcase by the window was full of texts which looked like the first print run. But the pages were much older than the already faded leather covers. As I stood with my fingers humming impatiently towards one book, I could see that the pages in all the books of the shelf were strangely irregular. All were a little brown, but there was a uniform shape that fit the books properly, the real pages, and between them many pages that were strangely cut or folded in to fit, expertly bound together to include the different pages seamlessly, like extremely boring scrapbooking of books together. The book Alana handed me when I told her I'd found it was another example of the mixed media books. While the ones on the bottom shelves had looked like they contained vellum and parchment, this one had a section of papery thin pages, and when I opened it the pages contained within it were, at times, considerably older.

Gingerly I flicked through the first pages to see what it was that could possibly be contained in such a book. I'd barely taken in chapter headings on generic terms or obscure names and Latin text when we heard the sound of someone approaching.

"Is the door closed?" I hissed, whirling around. It wasn't. We'd blundered in like fools in a movie who stand around conspicuously wrongdoing through the large crack in the door that should have been shut. I could almost see the shot of us framed from the hall: no, a flash of someone else's eyes about to be on us. Foresight. Seconds extra for us to use.

Alana grabbed the book from me and threw it under the table. I snatched two more off the shelves and crammed one into her arms, letting the one I held fall open in my hands.

The curator came in, looked at us for maybe half a second and then closed the door behind him, slowly but firmly, making very sure it clicked.

He turned to face us again. "Tanya Pomphrey."

"Bartholomew," I said, peeved not to have a last name. If he worked for the museum in an official capacity then he *had* to be on their website somewhere. I should have looked him up. Maybe the name thing only worked if someone gave you the name out loud.

"And this is…" He gestured Alana, his brow suddenly furrowing.

"Ally Guardian," I said.

He didn't look perturbed: nothing fey about him. Even the most piddly little sprite would have known I was lying when it came to names. Wouldn't have been able to do anything about it, but they'd have known I was lying.

Alana slowly closed the book in her hands. I didn't have to look at her to see the pissed off face she was pointing at me. Rule one was keep Ally out of it. How did she not realise that was what I was doing? They already had her name, thanks to her blabbing it to Mr Lane the other day. No one had Alana's. Maybe now they'd think they had Ally and not go looking for the real thing.

Bartholomew strolled towards us, his steps perfectly measured like he was just making the introductions in a run-of-the-mill business meeting. "I am curious, Tanya, about how you have ended up here."

"Ah, well, my friend Mackerel has a car."

Bartholomew was not the sort of person who smiled. Ever, as far as I could tell. He didn't even have an inside smile at that. "You have zeroed in on this… *situation* with incredible accuracy. That night at the stone circle, your friends looked to you for orders. My associate tasked with recruiting you reported that you stumbled into him somewhat intentionally, and again it was you eavesdropping last night. Given your record here at the museum, I can't doubt this character assessment. You have found your way to us three times over and I know you have been trying to get at the truth for months before the Order was even assembled. I want to know how. I want to know what it is you know that keeps bringing you back here."

"Well if I'm going to tell you anything, do you think you could give me some trade secrets in return?" I asked.

That got the slightest eyebrow quirk from him. Amazing. Human expressions. It could have been surprise. Probably not admiration. "I think not."

"Does it matter? You're going to kill me anyway, aren't you?"

He shook his head almost imperceptibly. "Your knowledge is too important to crack your head open any way but figuratively. And you have brought us the second candidate."

I felt some important cards slip between my fingers.

"Goddammit, Tanya," Alana hissed in my ear, feeling the sword swing her way.

I shrugged, swallowing back the flare of guilt that Alana had caused. *This wasn't like prom.* I could manage this. After all, I knew that it was Alana, not Ally, here with me. None of them had Alana's name. "So you're keeping me alive? Won't I start finding out your secrets anyway? The least you could do is be upfront."

He gave a laugh that wasn't really a laugh. "You think you can walk in here and just demand I tell you some of the most closely guarded secrets we have? Secrets we've been protecting for a thousand years? And we'll just open up to some curious girl who can't keep her nose out of things?"

"Well I assume none of the people who knew the secrets a thousand years ago are still alive to protect them. The rest of you had to find them out somehow." I flashed him a little smile, mostly I think on an instinct to try and coax some expression out of him.

He took another step, right into our personal space. I tried not to flinch but he only took the book from my hands, then Alana's. She quietly handed hers over; I gave my book one defiant tug before relinquishing my grip.

He stepped away, tossing the books rather carelessly down on the table as he produced a phone from his pocket.

Alana was rounding on me, ready to hiss some furious warning about what she'd do to me if we survived this (probably), but my attention was caught elsewhere. As Bartholomew scrolled through his contacts the door opened.

"Don't worry, I'll handle this," a mellow, accented voice said, preempting Mr Lane's arrival in the room. *Dammit.* He hadn't stayed in Troutespond: not that he could have known where we were going, but I'd hoped his instinct wouldn't be to hare it back here.

Bartholomew lowered his phone. "How did you know to come here?"

"Please, I've been working on these girls for days. If they're here it's because I want them to be. You have a job to be doing, and they need watching until the evening."

"I'll send someone else to guard them with you."

"I don't need supervision," Mr Lane growled. "You keep forgetting how insignificant you are in all this, even if this is 'your' museum. You are here as nothing more than someone to fill an empty chair."

"For a while it was *your* empty chair."

"Well I'm back, and I outrank you by thirty generations, so why don't you let me do what is best for the Order and you go back to doing what is best for *you*, as I hear you always do."

Bartholomew narrowed his eyes, but even with this apparent insult and threat combination he wasn't going to suddenly start shaking and showing emotions.

He did, however, leave the room at a measured pace with no glances back. The door snapped closed behind him.

Mr Lane turned to us with a mild expression sliding back in to place. I still didn't exactly feel like he had saved us, although he seemed to think he'd done us a favour.

"Why don't you girls sit down?" he asked, gesturing the large table.

I glanced at Alana at last. She looked faintly sick. I took her elbow and guided her to the table. Mr Lane moved around to sit opposite us.

"Tanya. You're very hard to read," he admitted, settling down. "You have nothing to say about this?"

I gave him my cheeriest smile. "What's to say? We both know we've been spying on each other for one reason or another for days. There's no need for a shocked speech about how I trusted you or anything. You know exactly who I am, and I know who you are."

He nodded, understanding. He gestured a hand over at Alana, who was sitting next to me, mouth pressed in a thin line. "But I don't know you." There was a flinch again: confusion.

I waded helpfully in, remembering how baffled he'd been about our names thanks to Alana's little hiding spell when he'd met us. "You met her before. Ally Guardian." Worth a go.

"No, I don't think so. I was very confused about who you girls all were. When I saw you the morning after the stone circle there was an... obscurity. I can't keep your names straight in my head. I can't even look at her face!" He gestured at Alana with an uncharacteristic spasm in his movements; he was still looking directly at me, but like he couldn't make his eyes go where he wanted. "But I met Ally, I *talked* to her. And I-I think I know that you are Tanya, so why can't I find out her name?"

I glanced at Alana. Her eyes darted about like a cornered animal: I had no idea how this spell was meant to hold up in the long run, not now its target was sitting opposite her asking probing questions. The sensible thing would be to lean into whatever this spell was that was clearly befuddling him, Alana's power making our names repel from his head like two same magnets trying to push together, sliding away at every attempt. I could try to go one step further, tell him I was Alana. If he thought that, if it worked and her name was the key to the spell just as Teb's had been to her changeling spell, then he'd have Alana, the real one, there as Ally, ready to sacrifice her, except that he couldn't. Not when I broke the spell at the critical moment. And before that, while they thought I was Alana, someone off their roster, it would double seal me into not being sacrificed if both he and Bartholomew agreed I couldn't be killed, so long as they didn't confer and realise one knew I was Tanya and the other knew I was Alana. It was the perfect "Don't get murdered by cultists" card.

And I couldn't play it. Not when I looked at Alana and saw how scared she was. Short-term prolonging the inevitable be damned: I wanted her to *trust* me. I'd *rather* she did.

I shuffled.

I'd never asked about Alana's past, but she had never once seemed worried at the thought of herself being taken as the sacrifice, and I'd trust her not to be an idiot about it like I was: I knew full well that a wrong word would be the death of me if they wanted a virgin sacrifices. She had no denial, just a calm acceptance of the way round things were: I could bet she would offer herself up if it was possible and mean it. She seemed an idiotic heroic sacrifice sort of girl, pointlessly seeking some self-worth in throwing herself away. The fact she hadn't said a thing yet was more telling than anything. There was the fury of helplessness in her expression.

This was wildly dangerous. My whole hastily reworked plan depended on them thinking that Alana was Ally, therefore leaving me alone to snoop. Actually, my whole plan had sort of depended on them prioritising me over Ally for a sacrifice, but Bartholomew had made it really clear that I'd screwed up five seconds into *that* conversation. I was running on a hastily cobbled together plan B from the moment Bartholomew denied me information, and plan D next after this one was basically calling up Warren and apologising and letting him know how to *actually* set off the fire alarm for me, like some school disco prank was a viable way to save a friend's life.

I'd only said Ally's name because I'd been trying to throw them off looking for the real thing, but apparently the desire to shut me up was far less than the desire to wring me for information. The way he'd talked about me finding my way to them… Maybe they weren't as uninformed as Jeremy thought. Maybe I'd stupidly given away through my long history with them that I did know more than I let on and the only way I could have known it all was mysterious. If they were looking for proof of the Other then I was a walking talking beacon of it, if only because it was the Other that compelled me to investigate them.

I took matters into my own hands and pulled a card out of the deck that ranked down at plan Z or thereabouts. "It's because her name is Alana Susanna Larbie. But you knew that, didn't you?"

They both froze, neither looking at me anymore. Mr Lane's face fell open into the most readable expression of pure horror I'd ever seen. "You… You are…?" he managed to stammer.

"Come on, you suspected it," I said irritably, since Alana was still totally freaked out, not sure how to react to this at all, since his reaction had been so strange. Now his eyes refused to *leave* her. Her sense of betrayal that I'd blurt out her whole name was clear enough. She grabbed my arm like she wanted to shake me for a different answer, too late after the words had fallen out of my mouth.

He forced his attention back to me. "What do you want?" he demanded, conceding that my bargaining chips were incredible.

"Bartholomew doesn't want to kill me, but you can't kill Alana. Sort of need you to override his decision at the last minute. I made a mistake. I hoped I was sealing my position on the sacrificial altar when I came here to protect Ally, but instead he decided I was worth more alive. I'm done triple-bluffing. Let's try honesty."

His reply sounded dragged from far away. "H-he's not like the rest of us. The society put him onto the group months ago to keep an eye on them. When I got back they had lost another member, so he stayed. But he's not got a legacy. He's not *one of us*. He answers to his bosses at the museum far more than our own leader." Mr Lane gestured around. "This space has always been ours by right, but he holds us hostage with it being under the museum's roof and it's given him an unnatural power within the Order. I'm not even sure he *believes* the reasons we do it. Why do you want to exchange yourself for Alana so badly?"

"Tanya, *what are you doing?*" Alana hissed, her nails digging into my flesh.

I rolled my eyes. "Telling the truth."

"*Why?*"

"Mr Lane is going to help us now."

"How can you just *know* that? Why would he?"

I glanced at him and figured I might as well lift the other half of the name spell since he wasn't getting around to it and this would run so much smoother once we were all on the same page. "Because Mr Lane isn't his real name. His name is Gregory Larbie, and he's not dead."

His intense stare at her cut off at once: he looked down at his hands, unable to watch her expression as my words sunk in.

I wasn't afraid to watch it though.

I was deeply concerned for Alana, but there are very few chances in life to see what a nonsense soap opera moment looks like in real time. In the end she barely reacted outwardly: a flinch, and then her face drained of feeling, her eyes hardening as she drew inside herself. I think the worst bit was how she instantly accepted it: she trusted me by now, at least on some matters, and she knew I wouldn't joke about something like this at a time like this. What I was watching was not her wrestling over whether this could be true or not, but with the real question:

"*Why did you let me think that you were dead?*" She spoke in a cool tone that would have made Teb alarmed at the lack of emotion. It was a deadly stab nonetheless. She leaned forwards a little, resting folded arms on the table, and I could see that she was trying to stop the shaking in her shoulders spreading any further. "Why did you let us think you'd killed yourself for all this time?"

Mr Lane—*Mr Larbie*—took his time answering, though he really ought to have prepared some flash cards for this situation the moment he rolled into town. It was only after much gnawing of his lip that he could get out a response. "Sometimes when you do something very bad you keep running forever because you can't ever face up to having done it. I never intended to come back. I wasn't going to see you again."

"But now you're here."

"It's for the ritual. I messed up early on into my exile. I used a bank account the Order holds to transfer some of the money. I thought because of their security and secrecy it was a perfect crime. Perhaps the authorities didn't catch wind, but *they* did. They've been keeping tabs on me, and when the time came they called me back."

"That's it? That's all you have to say on the subject? 'I wouldn't have come back into your life, but my secret cultist past caught up with my sketchy criminal past, but it's fine, I didn't intend to come see you anyway?'"

"Alana…" Her name caused a pronounced catch in his throat before he can speak again. "I used you and dropped you when I heard the law catching up with me. Your reaction is exactly why I couldn't think about reaching out. I've wanted to, every day since I left you. I considered turning myself in, but… But you would have hated me whether I was alive or not, so I thought it would bring you more peace to at least hate me on simple, uncomplicated grounds and think I was already in Hell. No need for you to feel obliged to reach out to me. No need to feel like a bad person if you chose not to. No need for me being alive to weigh on you."

"Are you actually trying to apologise?"

I understood her incredulity: I could barely believe he was saying this, and it wasn't meant to impact me on any emotional level. I got why he was saying it, but it didn't seem like the right reply. Though in this situation there probably wasn't a right reply. The right reply possibly would have been *never stealing all her money and faking his own suicide in the first place.*

He examined his fingers for a moment, but to my surprise met her eyes again. "No. I don't deserve it. And I didn't come here for it. I'm not going to ask for forgiveness just because you stumbled into my path."

"*Stumbled?* You were stalking my friends!"

Mr Larbie's smile in response sort of killed my heart right then and there. I don't think anyone could say he didn't feel bad about what he'd done, because I'd never seen anyone cover up so much pain in their lives. He was still a total arsehole who'd put my friend through the wringer, destroyed her childhood, stolen her inheritance and ruined her life rolling on from there, but the trouble with magical empathy is you can't just shut it off when someone is feeling something wholeheartedly, because realising they genuinely mean what they say is inconvenient to your worldview. "Of course. The reason I am back in Troutespond at all. Safe ground for us to discuss, I suppose. Tanya is right: I would never kill you."

"So why did you come back at all? What's going on here? Why are you *involved?*"

He shook his head. "It's a hell of a story, but I can summarise so much as this has been in our family for generations. I grew up in the village and only moved to America as a teenager. I think you still live in the old family home, don't you? My father told me everything about the Order when I was a child, made sure I knew what was expected of me. I was a brainwashed zealot like all the rest. I suppose it's why your mother liked me so much. We met through church friends. Not that I would ever have told her about the sect I was in. The trouble was, going to America just made me more liberal: hanging around in Hollywood, a million miles from the dusty libraries and cold stone crypts from a thousand years ago I'd been brought up treating as hallowed spaces made it all seem so ridiculous when I could see the same in a plywood set and see how the magic of the movies created these scenes as hollow stories. I drifted from the faith. You wanted to be an actress, your mother got fed up and took a trial separation, refusing to come back with me to America after one of our winters in England, so I stayed out there with you while she wrote angrier and angrier letters trying to get you back. But you had a career, and it was making me rich, then it was making me *illegally* rich, and I forgot everything about the life I'd been brought up in. When I had to start a new life under a new identity I shed every idea I'd ever had crammed into my head when I was young…"

"So why are you back here helping the cult?" I demanded, butting into someone else's story before I could help myself. I mean, come on, I was still in the room with them, and this was fascinating.

"Because of Alana. Their first contact with me was to remind me that it was the seventy-fifth year and that I had a teenage daughter right here in the town. I came back to do *anything* to stop them from choosing her as a sacrifice, as they clearly intended if I did not return. It was probably the easiest blackmail in history, but at least Alana will never be hurt by them."

"You wasted your time," Alana said, leaning back in her chair, arms still folded but now in a way that was more like hugging herself. Her eyes drifted off to the shelves in the corner. "I don't fit the criteria."

Disappointment and relief mingled together in his slanted frown. "I see."

"So," I said, leaning forward and trying to inject some smiles into proceedings. "What are we going to do about the sacrifice? If they won't use Alana you're pretty much free of your obligation to help them, aren't you?"

That did not make Mr Larbie's frown any less grim. "You don't understand what the ritual is for, do you?"

I shook my head. "But nothing can be as bad as killing a girl, can it?"

"Every seventy-five years for nearly a millennium people have done it. Do you not think that there were times like this? That there were people in the past who said it was wrong to kill? Every generation there will be someone who doubts the purpose, but I have to trust that those who find themselves in the Order at the time of the sacrifice have, historically, made the decision to do it because it was the right thing when they came up against the very same challenges. It's our family history. I disavowed it when I was young and liberal, but now that the time is here I find it harder to say that it should never have been done before without condemning our whole bloodline."

"You can't use the 'everyone in the past did it so it has to be good' argument!" I complained.

"I'm sorry, Tanya. Why don't you read the book that you've hidden under the table? It will help you to understand why we have to do it."

He stood up suddenly, and I only got as far as, "Wait, but you have to—" before he was out of the room. The door closed behind him and I jumped a little as it locked.

I jumped again when I turned and found Alana's eyes fixed on me, fierce and redder than I'd ever seen them. *"How long did you know?"*

"S-since this morning. At the ice cream place. I felt it then. He felt like you."

Alana leaned back a little, though her intensity didn't dial back. "You've known longer than that."

"I *suspected* longer than that. *You* were the one who freaked out and cast a glamour on yourself the moment you saw him. I think you suspected something too."

"I thought he was a creep. Guess what? *I was right*. And you didn't tell me your suspicions. How did you even *know* about him?"

I shrugged. "It's sort of obvious something happened with your dad. Your house is a shrine to him without a single picture. Guy about the right age shows up and throws you completely off your game? I could feel a connection between you at once."

"And again... You didn't *warn* me?"

I didn't know what to say. I'd been too caught up in the drama; obviously it was someone's real life, someone I cared about to boot. But it hadn't seemed *right* to start throwing around theories like that. I mean, I was known for my mad theories, but I never told my friends things like how I'd always known Ally's mum was doing *real* witchcraft since childhood, or dared tell Teb that it had been any sort of destiny because I didn't see her as *missing* anything without her name, that she'd swapped it for something that seemed to fill in a gap she'd always had. You can't just *tell* people where their life story is going. Alana's obvious crack in her armour had always been her dad, and it had always sort of hovered in my mind that we'd see that addressed *eventually*. I'd never known how, but seeing Mr Lane had filled in the gap as surely as Ally's sudden *comfort* with magic post-Fairygate or Teb's new bearing since she sold her name. If we came out the other side of this, there was something broken deep down in Alana that might finally work again. Even if it was only peace because she knew the real story, and she never had anything else to do with him. My soppy side wanted reconciliation, though my logical side was being pretty loud that that seemed just a bit of a stretch right now.

I ducked under the table and scrabbled for the book instead. "Look, we're locked in here, your dad is gonna sacrifice me for the greater good in a few hours and we're surrounded by books, so let's do an Ally and get reading."

When I straightened up she didn't look any more relaxed. "You're unbelievable sometimes."

"What? I didn't put the cultists here or drag your supposedly dead father out of the woodwork. I'm managing the situation we have here. At the moment the situation is that we have no way to avoid me or some other poor kid they grab off the street being stabbed in the name of mad quasi-religious *something*. Mr Lane can talk Bartholomew into using me instead of you using his cultist seniority, perhaps, and we're back to the first steps of plan A, but he's not going to let us go free and I'm still going to die or disappear into their world. The only way we're getting out of this is if some random other girl gets sacrificed in my place, and now I'm here I can't let *that* happen because that will be my responsibility. And plan A was all about getting in, getting to this room and finding out what the hell is going on before it happens. We've been coming up against this for actual *days* and we're none the wiser. So. Reading."

Alana got up and walked into the corner of the room, moving stiffly, not looking my way. I couldn't force her to read, so I plopped the book down on the table and took a steadying breath as I inspected the plain leather cover again, preparing myself for the words inside.

I heard a sob from the corner. *Crap.* I'd been wondering how Alana had been holding it together so well. It turned out that she wasn't.

With the least hesitation I could manage while still giving the book longing looks, I got up as well and hurried over to crouch at her side, since she had apparently leaned against the wall before slumping down like someone had cut her strings.

My touch to her shoulder was hesitant: for all I knew she hated me now. But her hand came up at once and curled around mine, gripping so tight my fingers splayed under her grasp, and I could see my fingertips turning red. I didn't argue, just settled in next to her and took her weight on my shoulder as she sobbed it out.

I gave her ten minutes to move through awkward sobs to ragged breaths mixed with hiccups and finally a defeated slump forward to rest her head on her knees, where only the slightest trembling in her back betrayed that she was still working it out of her system.

"Do you want to talk about it?"

"Not in the slightest. Go read your fucking book."

I gave her back one last rub so she'd have a lingering sense of comfort and got up to get to the reading I seriously, urgently owed myself.

Research Trip

Here's something I didn't know:

It all began a thousand years ago. A village long troubled by supernatural ills, Troutespond fell under attack by a vicious dragon, which took to living in the hills, stealing down in the night to consume livestock and to ravage the countryside. The Lord of Ransley was away on the crusades, so many heroes came seeking glory in our quiet corner of the country. All failed to kill the dragon. Most were likewise devoured as if there were no difference between them and the sheep that the dragon largely preyed on.

Finally Lord Ransley returned with his dozen bravest knights. Before they had even made it down the road they found themselves beset by villagers begging them to do something about the monster that attacked them.

Lord Ransley sent his men into the woods to flush out the monster, assuming it would be as easy as any hunt, and he himself rode hard for Ransley Castle to collect his father's lance and sword, since he had shattered both of his own in the wars. He understood that this was his family duty: that maybe the dragon had come because he had abandoned his land.

He rode back across the Hill Road, that same one with those standing stones I'd investigated just days before (which explained a hell of a lot about those visions), hoping to meet up with his men by the shortcut. Before he reached them, the road took him past a little cottage where a woman the villagers claimed was a witch lived. She stood in the middle of the road and stopped him passing her; his horse was too afraid to continue and reared up, because of course horses can tell a witch just from looking and are, apparently, deadly afraid of them since they tend to curse people's livestock dead if they're in a bad mood.

"Move, witch!" cried the brave young lord. "A dragon attacks one of my villages, and I must slay it before it lays waste to the whole valley!" (I'm paraphrasing the text but this is almost certainly the kind of overdramatic way they'd have talked and you can't tell me otherwise because this is my story and my source material didn't have commas, let alone speech marks.)

But the witch just cackled and stood her ground. "The dragon cannot be slain, foolish knight! To kill mindlessly is not always the answer! The beast has awoken but it can be made to go back to sleep!"

"That will only delay the problem!" he said, forcing his horse to ride past the witch (who didn't make it fall dead underneath him, although to be honest he was pretty rude so I'd totally understand if she had). He came to the woods above Troutespond. But before he could call for his knights, who he knew were hunting there, he heard a terrible shout. When he rode to the source he found his knights had gathered at the sound of the scream; all but one, who had met the dragon and been slain by vicious claws as sharp and deeply-biting as the curved swords they had fought against in the East. (There's, like, a page of racist ranting about the Crusades after that and honestly this timeline makes no sense because they kept saying it was a thousand years ago but that all happened later. I think someone rounded up for dramatic effect and no one ever did the maths. I suppose blurry historical confusion maketh the myth.)

They buried the knight at the Church of St Troute (I'm not even sure Troutespond *existed* yet except for that one building; we probably weren't big enough for a proper place name until like the 1400s) and mourned for him for like a page and a half, for he had been a brave knight and none of them had expected any of their number to be slain, and so soon on returning, on home soil.

That night they patrolled the edge of the woods and prayed that the dragon would not come. And in the morning another of the knights was dead.

Deeply enraged, Lord Ransley swore he would not eat nor sleep until the dragon was dead. He rode off into the woods to hunt it alone, but instead came again upon the old woman, standing in his path.

"What do you want, crone?" he demanded.

"I too am a servant of God," said she. "I do not suggest evils, only a way to make dragons sleep. Hear me out, my lord!"

But he spurred his horse on and rode past her without looking back.

For three more days he unsuccessfully hunted the dragon, and three more nights one of his men died. Three more times he encountered the old woman and she entreated him to listen to how to rid the village of the dragon.

Finally, when he had only six men left and himself, he was growing tired and near miserable of the hunt. And when the old woman met him on his ride, he got down from his horse and knelt before her to ask, "How may I be rid of the dragon, goodwife?"

And she told him.

His knights drew back from the woods and ended the hunt. They held a vigil at the church for their fallen brothers, and said the prayers that she had taught them. (It helps to remember that Witchcraft wasn't all wicca and paganism back in the old days—especially in rural areas it tended to be supplementary to Christianity but with a bit more practical magic and herb lore, rather than some wicked crone in her cottage casting spells. I'm seeing her more as Ally's mum but *Christian* and having not had a bath her entire life. All the stuff about consorting with devils is A: them consorting with Christian demons, and B: propaganda to really get the Witch Hunts going when these sort of women would generally be equally feared and respected in their community. Sorry, this is bothering me because this story really wants you to think she was the Devil Incarnate by the end, tricking him with this fake humble child of God act, and okay, this is completely dodgy because she recommends human sacrifice, but you have to give her a chance because who tells the story but the crusty old white man? Like, at least cast Meryl Streep to play her in the adaptation to bring some depth to the role and make sure she's fully fleshed out.)

Lord Ransley met his men in the graveyard of the church, between the five graves of his fallen knights. They formed a circle and said another prayer that the old woman had taught them, and they took one virgin girl from the village (who had been promised to a nunnery to give her life to God and went willingly with her lord, not thinking that he planned to murder her) and shed her blood.

The dragon vanished and the village became safe again.

For the next seventy-five years.

And then it rose again, and once more the current Lord Ransley, now the original's son, only aware of his father's deeds as a bedtime story he'd been told, gathered six of his most trusted men and set out to repeat the ritual entrusted to the most secret records of his father's time…

*

I looked up from the yellowed page with a shiver and found that my eyes were drawn to the clock in the room. It was afternoon already. Alana was sitting on the floor in the corner still.

Alana was not just clocked out and sitting catatonic all that time – she was listening to music on her phone, eyes closed and head tipped back to rest on the wall. It was only then that I realised that Greg hadn't just left us with the storybook I'd so hungrily devoured… Alana was beyond sensible action, but now that I had got what I came here for, I had to take stock. Even just looking at my phone and seeing that it was well past noon grounded me back to reality.

As did Teb having sent me some memes while we'd been running around, oblivious to our peril.

There was something surreal about having been left with the opportunity to call for help, and choosing not to scream. For the sake of keeping my other friends safe, sure, but still in a daze from reading a history I'd been seeking for years, I couldn't really say either that I chose to send Warren a thumbs up emoji and put my phone back in my pocket just because I had been yelled at by Jeremy to keep Teb out of it. Finding a sense of belonging right then and there was the weirdest sensation, but it happened. A feeling of actual calm and purpose, of relief. There really was a cult with a secret book with a hidden history and I had been the one to find it.

I wasn't hungry at all and I couldn't imagine Alana was either, but time was marching on even if it was going unmarked by meal times. I suddenly felt sick to the core, gripped with panic and indecision about my next moves as it hit me that my plan had been to get us this far, but I'd been so determined to do that, I hadn't put a sliver of the energy into our next moves. Soon it would be my turn to shed blood in the name of God, apparently.

None of the men now in the cult had been there the last time they'd killed, and maybe it always worked out that way with that huge time between sacrifices, so that no one had to bloody their hands twice unless they were extremely long-lived. It was almost neat.

Mr Larbie knew about this—but did he *really* believe that there was a dragon?

(A *dragon*.)

Did I believe it?

Did it really matter, when tonight they were going to try and kill someone— probably me right now if Greg did what was expected of him to keep Alana safe and my current situation didn't change dramatically—and it was really pedantic to fuss about whether there really was a dragon or if there wasn't and this was all done in vain, if they were only accidentally wishing it into existence by feeding blood sacrifices to the idea that it existed. Could my fear all by itself conjure the dragon? What, in fact, was a dragon in the first place?

No, I had to keep my priorities in order. Now I knew the core of their secret, the thing that bonded this Order together year in, year out was this blood pact. Only it wasn't their blood. It would be mine, as it had been the blood of a dozen girls before me.

They had to be stopped.

And, it was worth noting, they had the Piper as an enemy. But he existed to maintain balance and order, and to oversee rituals. It was on his orders that Teb was supposed to do the Wild Hunt in the summer. It was his job that had even brought him into our lives, as he oversaw the summer rituals in the town.

Was this so much out of the natural order that even he couldn't let it continue in good conscience? Or was it something he begrudgingly had to let happen, that the presence of the curse bags containing his own pipe (which they would need to source every time) was a way for him to have plausible deniability? To be forced to look the other way? Was there any difference to him, an immortal, a being beyond comprehension in power and existence, condoning the death of the star boar for Teb's Hunt to my death here?

(Was this falling on me because I'd set that poor creature up to be hunted, even though I knew it would be reborn the next time the stars aligned a certain way?)

No. He'd been angry. He knew who they were. He knew they didn't want him there… But nothing had happened to the cultists. He hadn't raised a hand against them in the two days since I'd removed the blockade around the town.

No, he'd put Alana on the case. And me.

He needed a spanner in the works and we were his plausible deniability so that he didn't have to directly do something that contradicted his nature. He was Justice, yes, but he was Balance and Order, and sometimes bad things happened in the natural order; he was bound by arcane rules beyond human morality. I'd seen enough nature documentaries to know that the cutest critters were eaten by predators who were only doing what they had to do to survive. And if their hunt seemed cruel, who were we to argue with the ethics of an orca tossing around a seal carcass or an eagle smashing a tortoise from a thousand foot drop when the next scene might be a sad baby whale or little fluffy chicks to remind us that our heart should go out to all creatures?

Stopping these cultists was going to be throwing chaos into an ancient pattern, and the Piper wasn't meant to create that.

Fortunately, chaos was something of my speciality.

*

Alana unhooked an earbud and looked over at me as I sat there completely stumped.

"I can tell you're done reading. What's the verdict?" Her voice was flat, a sort of emotionless get-the-job-done state settling on her.

"It's a dragon."

"Are they summoning it?" She didn't even *blink*.

"Protecting us from it. It's banished by virgin sacrifice."

"So we have a motive. Any ideas how to get around it?"

I had to shake my head. "Not yet. Not until…"

"*No.* No more waiting. I don't care anymore, okay, Tanya? I'm done caring. We're going nuclear."

"You're…" She was messing with her phone. "You *can't* call Teb—Jeremy said…"

She put her phone to her ear and surprisingly got an answer immediately. "Hello? We need the police. And the fire service. Someone's started a fire in the Bilsworth Museum, on the second floor, one of the offices. We-we're trapped in a room." Ah.

"Alana! What are you doing?"

She raised a hand to shush me as I scrambled up from my seat, meaning to run to her side and stop her. Wrestle her phone out of her hands if I had to.

"Sorry, I can't stay on the line, my phone battery is almost gone. Please, come quickly. There's so much smoke.—We can't last much longer!" She hung up.

"Are you kidding me?"

"Do you know what they forgot? When they left us our phones? This is all some huge game to them, but it's not to the rest of the world. *Human* captors, Tanya. Human. Our rules. I was this close to just calling in a kidnapping, but this is quicker." She struggled to her feet and began pulling books off the shelf next to her.

"Wait, no. Don't you dare."

"You know what else they didn't think about when they didn't take our phones? What else I might have in my pockets."

"Alana, *no*. Think about everything that's written in here!" I grabbed up an armful of books from the floor, but Alana was busy sweeping an entire shelf off in one movement—it was pointless.

"You know what? I don't care. It's my fucking legacy apparently, so I can do with it what I want. Who do you reckon gets here first, cultists or fire engines?"

The room was so muffled to the outside world I couldn't hear anything on the street yet. I hadn't seen any cameras in the room either.

Alana knelt beside her pile of books and flicked her lighter—probably for the first time since I'd met her, the flame caught on her first try, and she held it to one of the pages of a book that was lying pathetically open and trampled. The parchment curled and blackened and withered at the touch of the flame, and I watched in horror, Alana in anticipation, until suddenly she had a new flame growing in the middle of the pages. She moved to setting the next book on fire.

"What if the cultists don't come for us? What if they leave us in here to burn to death? They still have Ally..."

"Don't try playing that card with me right now, Tanya. Open the window. Do you think the curtains will burn?"

"If you throw them over the fire it'll put it out probably. Isn't that what fire blankets do?"

"I knew you'd come around."

"No, I just apparently can't stop being smarter than you."

Alana glared at me from the other side of what was quickly becoming a proper indoor bonfire.

I retreated to trying to lever the window open. Which was easier said than done: they were old, single-glazed windows, but they'd been sealed shut with layers of paint—the air was still and stuffy, probably for the sake of the books, and while I hadn't seen cameras I had seen vents, so this room was presumably air-conditioned and climate-controlled and they did not want the unreliable factor of British weather to interfere.

"I don't know how to open it," I complained.

"*Honestly*," Alana said, and a moment later I felt a tug on my arm pulling me back, and a hard-bound book came flying past me. The window shattered and the book disappeared outside, secrets protected by the cult for a thousand years landing unceremoniously in the car park.

The fire had taken pretty well to the dry books: the pile Alana had made was crackling with flames reaching a foot high, and she backed off to start kicking the burning books towards the curtains.

"Hang on, wasn't that so they would be able to rescue us through the window?" I asked. The sound of sirens was now reaching us. We might actually be saved. The smoke was starting to build up around the ceiling; the room stank of burning leather, but it was still breathable—we wouldn't suffocate *just* yet.

"Nah, just so they see the smoke and believe us and come inside. Why do you think I called the police?"

"So we actually are going with the scenario where we're left inside the room to possibly bake to death like jacket potatoes if the cultists would rather let this all burn than admit what we're up to."

"Shut up and help me get more books on the fire. At the very least we're taking this cult's history down with us."

"You don't care about the police not finding this?"

"They kidnapped us. Whatever they say about their reasons, they're adult men who locked two girls in a room for an afternoon after telling them they'd kill one of them. To be honest, burning this shit might just undermine their brainwashing defence at trial and make them more culpable. Probably. I'm not a lawyer witch. Stop standing there and *help*."

I stood by the table, arms crossed, still horrified that she was burning books, watching the flames, waiting for them to jump to the table or to run wild across the carpet, frozen with indecision, throat dry with the smoke in the air. This was the riskiest thing I'd ever been involved in: we could probably survive the fall to the ground out the window...

The sirens were on the same street now—the firemen would be outside pretty much immediately. I untensed a little: unless we were very unlucky, the authorities were here. We probably wouldn't die unless we were stupid or something unpredictable happened. Even the jumping out the window scenario would have official supervision and hunky firemen who could catch us if the door stayed closed and we were left here to burn.

I looked over my shoulder.

And *finally* the door opened.

It was Mr Larbie, who took one look at what we were doing and his face dropped in horror. "Alana! Get away from the fire!" He strode into the room, not sparing a glance for the flames crawling up the curtains and lapping at the bookshelves. Alana spun around, folded her arms and stood her ground.

"I'm taking this all down with me," she spat. "Fuck your cult, and fuck you, *dad*."

"Alana!" I yelled. "Don't you dare make this some suicidal mission thing. Let's *go*." I didn't trust a lot of things about him, but I did honestly trust that Greg had come here to save Alana from being picked on by the cult, and that the risk of being discovered as a previously thought-dead guy who'd be immediately wanted for massive theft and fraud was probably high enough to suggest he honestly would protect her with his life. His intentions towards her bled open emotion.

Alana backed away towards the fire as he approached, cautious like he was creeping up on a flighty animal. I couldn't let them do their whole terrible father/daughter bonding thing though: I leapt in, grabbed Alana by the arm and tugged her towards Mr Larbie. She made herself extremely heavy, but at least my movement inspired Greg to come forwards and actually try and help pull on Alana. She reacted by squirming past him—thankfully in the direction of the door, and I think we herded her out more than anything.

I could hear the firemen outside—the sound of someone calling through a megaphone presumably to try and reach us if we were able to come to the window.

"The police are outside the front," Mr Larbie said as Alana backed off towards the door to the stairs. I breathed in deeply for the first time in five minutes, almost too relieved not to be in a room filling with smoke to really focus on the situation around us.

"Good. I'm going to go tell them exactly what you are all doing here." She turned and strode away, kicking open the door at the end of the hall as hard as she could. I scurried after her: there were people coming up the stairs, and despite me still being back in the hallway, I didn't think she had noticed them before I did.

It turned out she hadn't—I shoved through the door and landed right in the scene of someone in a rather important looking police uniform coming up the stairs with two more normal policemen ahead of him. Alana froze,—glanced to her right like there was a serious possibility she'd try jumping down the gap in the middle of the stairwell,—squared her shoulders like she might actually try fighting three policemen who were all a great deal taller than her—and then deflated.

"Is this the arsonist?" the important looking policeman asked.

"And her accomplice," Mr Larbie said just behind me, and his hand fell on my shoulder.

Yeah, I'd said I trusted him not to let Alana (and me by extension) die. I'd never said I trusted him any further than that.

*

I'd ridden in the back of a police car a couple of times—mostly just getting a lift home, to be honest. I'd never had the whole experience of being handcuffed and yelled at to keep quiet any time I made so much as a comment like pointing out we had human rights or that virgin sacrifice was highly illegal.

They'd finally taken Alana's stuff and my phone, so we were utterly resourceless. We hadn't even thought to do the cool girl spy thing of putting our hair up with pins so we'd have lockpicks, and at the moment I was feeling like the biggest failure ever just because that was my favourite empowering trope of girls who kicked ass and looked good doing it. Not that I exactly knew how one was meant to get the hairpin off the back of your head and into your hand, especially when your partner in crime wasn't talking to you.

I looked over at Alana in the back seat next to me, and she curled her nose and looked back out the window.

We were riding just with Chief Inspector Singer, our latest representation of old white guys in charge of creepy old cults. He'd told his presumably non-culty men he'd take it from here after Alana and I had been loaded into the car, with the background noise of the fire engine and people being evacuated from the museum. I'd have thought he would have been pissed about us burning down their sacred library, but either he hadn't been updated on just how much damage Alana had done with her lighter before we left or he was holding back until he got to ritually sacrifice one of us, which would have been a great stress relief, I supposed.

Which was unfortunate, because high blood pressure related things like a stroke or heart attack were pretty high up on my list of ways to successfully escape from this. Say he flipped the car into the hedge, it was much more unlikely randomly called ambulances would have a cultist in charge. It was just poor luck that they represented authority figures from all around the local area, so *of course* on the day of the sacrifice, when there was a huge disturbance at Bilsworth Museum, he would come in person to see what was going on if Gregory hadn't just called him as soon as he left the room and he'd adapted to our emergency call.

At least it was obvious that he wasn't taking us to the police station—he turned the police car down the very familiar main road out of town and back towards Troutespond. I hadn't exactly thought we'd go anywhere else, but it was weirdly reassuring. Because if he was taking us back there to the ritual and not being whisked away to some middle class English countryside Guantanamo cultist place we couldn't burn down so easily, then that meant I was still the best candidate and they were continuing to keep Ally out of it. And it also meant that Alana's actions had liberated us from that room and, in the way of random crazy unpredictable happenings and personal failings, we were exactly on the sort of path of chaos I most valued and worked best under pressure in. She may have rejected that path out loud, but I was calling this a subtle win in our argument.

She had to be more pissed off about the thing with her father coming back out of the long-forgotten past to haunt her, but it couldn't help her that every moment rolling back in the direction of town was letting me win the argument.

And, okay, I still had no idea what to do next, but at least we were moving. Chaos was happening.

Detention

Here's something I didn't know until much later:

Way way back, what feels like a thousand years and another era of our lives, Alana didn't know us. Yeah, shocking, right? It feels like she's always been a part of our group. She was *meant* to always be a part of the group. I didn't find out for a long time how it really happened, but there's one incident from her first day that she knew us that never really got explained to any of us. Ally forgot it, as Ally is wont to do, but it bothered me when I was trying to work out a timeline of everything that had ever happened to us and why, and eventually I got Alana to fill in the gaps:

The Piper came to her with a job. She sassed back at him. He handed her an acceptance letter at the school. She called the school a hellhole full of mouth-breathers who smoke on the bus and think they're edgy because they don't have to wear a tie (she was very clear on that point even if she was fuzzy on some other details). She made a more eloquent point that her homeschooling was practically killing her, but it was only a few months before she could take the exams and be done with the whole process, fly the nest and start a new life free of her mother's influence. (Seriously, we basically all asked her why she was bothering to switch schools so late within a day of knowing her without getting a proper answer. Even once we knew she was here because the Piper asked her, it wasn't really the *full* answer.) Basically, why, when things were in an almost reasonable balance and she'd learned to cope with what was on her plate, would she inflict a huge upheaval on her life that would only be for two months of school?

But then he told her, and this is pretty much what he said in a long tetchy back and forth with Alana, sorted into a coherent motive: "I pulled in some serious favours to get information that's made me *want* to put you in the school: I was curious about a student. There's something significant about her and it has unsettled me. But what is more... I found out that you will meet her. And not just casually. If I had not saved you when I did, you would have met her as you went down that path. If I *had* but not done this, there is still a clear future, in fact, the one currently in place if you refuse to go to the school, where you meet her anyway. At the moment, when you, as a homeschooled student, take your A Levels, you will have to go to Troutespond Comprehensive to sit them. They have the facilities and staff to deal with home-schooled students: this is a fact. You are taking History, same as she is. Another fact. What I found out was that in your History exam you will be sitting on the end of a row at the back of the hall, and this girl will be seated next to you. She'll see something in you, and she'll approach you. She will go on to be your friend, and she will draw you into her own story. All I can see beyond that is an incredible weight on the written future that's in her name. It's the sort of weight that won't change in the bigger details even if we change the finer ones. The fact I have knowledge of two scenarios where you meet her already written in stone as potential futures proves the importance. I'm making a third, where she doesn't have to save you, and you have a chance you would have missed to save her instead. She needs protecting. You need to be at the start of her story."

"So what are you doing, setting us up?" Alana asked.

He'd probably smiled mysteriously, as he does. And Alana had taken the job—she always made it out like she never had a choice to do anything the Piper asked of her, but I always feel she kind of did have some wiggle room, but she'd been genuinely curious.

And then she met Ally, in that fortuitous meeting in the office, and there's just something about Ally and her way of drawing you into her petty drama of the day, so Alana limpeted onto her and found a person very much in need of protecting: someone naïve of any potential destiny and confused, but very likely to go up and say hello to a near stranger. Alana trailed Ally everywhere that day until she had no more excuses to follow her. Until she was wandering around in the rainstorm that I'd just run through to find my portal to the fairy world, my bright future suddenly laid out in front of my eyes after the earlier incident where the Piper had accidentally taken me over there the first time.

The Piper, distracted with that, was completely failing to follow what was going on with his wayward apprentice. Alana was still lurking in Ally's neighbourhood looking out for what she had to protect her from, the Piper was hoping he didn't have to worry about me because Alana was supposed to be on my tail... and he suddenly realised I'd got away to the fairy world like I'd wanted to (oblivious to all this drama, of course). Once he realised what had happened, about the moment I crossed between worlds again, he knew Alana had messed up at once, and some song and dance followed of taunting Ally out of the house and into the rain, the end result of which was that the Piper narrowly missed sacrificing Ally to the fairies to get me back, bumped into Alana and got all caught up with her interpretation of events, took her to task for all the confusion and the fact they'd (both) screwed up the protection detail, and said to her, "Why were you not doing your job to protect Tanya? Now she's run away to the fairy world!"

(And that was where Ally caught up with her again, screaming with fury that they'd been so befuddled by the March madness that had fallen on the town, the same madness I was celebrating with glee had taken me on my first true steps of learning about the fairy world first hand.)

*

The school was deathly silent in the summer: the main gates were padlocked, the windows all dark, and it was probably around the time of day the playground should have been filled with students leaving, the pavement outside a solid stream of escapees heading into town to buy sweets or catch the bus.

The teacher parking was still unlocked—there was a smaller gate to the side, up what was practically a muddy country track between the school and the last houses on the row, and the gate at the end had been left mysteriously without its normal padlock. There were a couple of cars in the car park, only one of which I recognised as a teacher's car: Mr Westcott. Of course, we'd done a charity fundraiser car wash once, so we'd spent a lot of time complaining about who had the worst car.

Anyway, it wasn't exactly surprising to see Mr Westcott walking out to greet us as the Chief Inspector pulled into the spot normally reserved for the head teacher.

I rolled my eyes at him while he still couldn't see me through the back window.

Alana surprised me by speaking once Chief Inspector Singer had gotten out of the car: "I should have realised I was right when I said that transferring to your shitty school would be what got me killed."

"You knew that?" I teased.

She gave me this deadpan look. "I knew something or *someone* here would be the death of me."

It wasn't exactly forgiveness, but it was a start. She would come around and see that this was not my fault but Greg's, and not Greg's fault but the cult, and perhaps if she went really bigger-picture, the fault of whatever cosmic forces found it so much fun to toy with our lives. The Piper first.

The Chief Inspector opened the door on Alana's side.

"Get out," he ordered.

"What, is the school kid jail now?" she snapped.

"Get out or we make you get out."

The door on my side opened and Mr Westcott reached in. Despite my attempt to yank my arms away, he caught me by the handcuffs' chain and hauled. My wrists would be bruised to hell no matter what, but I scrambled out of the car so I wouldn't be dragged around like a dead weight between two broken wrists.

"Oh I bet you're enjoying this," I spat at Mr Westcott.

"It's an unexpected perk of the job. My office. Now."

There was a scuffle behind me—Alana had taken an opportunity to try and scramble across the car to get out of my side, since Mr Westcott couldn't manage both of us at the same time. Chief Inspector Singer lost his composure trying not to manhandle Alana, as if he'd get accused of police brutality in his official capacity, and grabbed her by the leg. She was kicking at him when Mr Westcott gave my restraint another tug, forcing me to follow after him. The back door to the school was close by, so that the teachers didn't have to walk far on a rainy day with folders of important homework over their heads as makeshift umbrellas. I was hauled into the building before I could see the resolution of Alana's fight. The Chief Inspector was old, but big. She was small, but fought dirty even without witchcraft to back her up.

And then I was being pulled through oh so familiar school corridors, the bland retro look of the administrative block. Mr Plebsy's office, where I had spent countless hours. Mr Westcott's, ditto. He shoved me in and slammed the door. By the time I had staggered to a halt and turned to rush back to the door the lock rattled. I'd lost my chance to try forcing the door.

"You coward!" I shrieked. "At least stay in here and look me in the eye! You owe me that!"

"I owe you nothing, Ms Pomphrey," his boring voice droned from the other side. God, how many times had I walked past him teaching in classrooms and heard it muffled in just the same way? This was unreal—too familiar. It was the uncanny valley of hostage situations.

I kicked the door as hard as I'd always dreamed of doing, enjoying how it juddered in its frame (but ultimately looked much stronger than I could kick down in a day). I listened, panting hard but trying to get my breath under control so I could hear him walk off and leave me be.

Okay, so I was handcuffed. But I was left unattended for who knows how long in an office. I mean, how stupid did he think I was? I didn't have the option of calling the police, since Chief Inspector Singer would almost certainly radio in at once that he was here and had the situation under control—unless I fessed up to all our sneaking around and wrongdoing that had led us here and then fingered him as the one who was holding me captive. Could I blow his cover like that and get away with it? Surely they had to treat all accusations seriously, and surely this was not actually a huge conspiracy that permeated all levels of society, but was only the domain of the seven cultists involved, plus a few museum personnel who were in the know, if not in the belief...

I lifted the receiver on Mr Westcott's desk phone and the empty noise of no connection greeted me. I slammed the phone down and crouched to look under the desk. The phone connector had been yanked out of the wall, wires exposed and snapped. I was good, but not, like, Tony Stark good. I couldn't repair that in what I assumed were the four or five hours I'd have until sundown. Not in handcuffs with no materials or tools to my name.

I sat in Mr Westcott's desk chair and span a few times just for the anti-authority hell of it, since that was also something that I'd never got a chance to do—he'd never left me unattended in his office before, since there was an antechamber for all miscreants outside the reception that these offices branched off of. And he certainly wouldn't have trusted me to be in here alone even long before there was any chance I'd have known about the whole cult thing, since one of my first big misdemeanours had been industrial espionage on the school network.

There were no paperclips on his desk, his desk drawers and filing cabinet locked. It was an end of term emptiness, a sorted and cleared look of a desk no one intended to use for another month, a fresh start.

I wished Alana and I were closer—mentally and physically for all I knew, since I hadn't heard them bring her up here and I figured she'd have been doing about as much shrieking as she was when I left her. If we were more in sync I'd have a chance to try and reach out to her, make some sort of shared consciousness with her. There was no way in hell it would work with Ally, who was receptive as a potato, and Teb may have been extremely magical but she was so prickly and defensive, even ignoring Jeremy's defence of her, that she would probably take so long to 'hack' it wouldn't be worth the energy. But that moment with Alana, Ally's mum and I had had a frisson that showed the potential. If only I hadn't pissed Alana off so much, I would have had a fair chance of reaching out to her after all our bonding of the last couple of days. At least I could have got a feeling of how she was doing while we were united by this shared trauma.

But, alas, nothing, no matter how hard I thought about it.

I really could not blame her for closing herself off after the last couple of hours and how they'd treated her.

I curiously tried feeling for Hester on the wavelength we'd shared, but she sort of subsumed into the general feeling of the town—as she skipped around the shops or went for her afternoon walks she wove her protections and blessings around her. The problem wasn't exactly sensing her, but sensing what was *actually* her.

I was stumped for that approach, but it had given me a rather more mundane idea at least for how I could pass my time while I was trapped in here.

I booted up Mr Westcott's computer as I sat there swivelling myself just back and forth a few degrees in frustration, too dizzy to make any more spins. It was really just something to do—something to look at as my front brain distraction while I thought things through. Unsurprisingly a login screen appeared, telling me to enter a password that was one of the few things that I had never managed to discover in all my years at this school.

On a whim I clicked around to bring up the admin login, since I had a good amount of knowledge about how to be IT support—probably in some areas more than the people who were actually in proper jobs *doing* IT support here. For obvious reasons the computer wasn't on the network right now, but if I was lucky then the admin password would be either Admin or TPComp (a popular one I'd discovered when messing with things like trying to get free printing in the library) and not require any external validation.

It was TPComps. Nailed it on the third try—I wasn't even going to have to wait out the fifteen minutes after accidentally deactivating the login screen like I'd been dreading if I kept getting it wrong. The bland teal background of admin mode loaded up, and I flexed my fingers in anticipation, trying to shake off some of the pain in my hands from the mistreatment in handcuffs, get myself all lined up for using the computer with my wrists held so close together, metal bracelets jangling on the desk as I moved.

I searched for files stored on the hard drive, but ran into Mr Westcott's personal password again. Apparently it applied to anything you tried to access that was in his account. On a whim I brought up the command box and tried accessing the drive through that, but was challenged with the password again. I changed tack and headed to try and change the admin controls on the computer, hoping to find a way to override the request for a password in the first place.

It was awkward, dragging one hand after the other to use the mouse, hovering it like a dead weight over the wrong side of the keyboard, but at least they were close enough together that the handcuffs were merely painful and annoying rather than truly restrictive.

It took me half an hour of more and more creative solutions that were getting into stuff I'd read on seriously creepy websites, but *finally* I was looking at Mr Westcott's personal files. There was a whole lot of teachery stuff— reports, minutes from meetings, actual work for the lessons that he taught. He was also still reliant on an email program rather than accessing them through a browser, and regularly backed his emails up onto the hard drive, because of course he did and occasionally once in my life something worked really well in my favour. He was the sort of dinosaur who probably didn't even have a computer at home or use his phone email, so if he was going to be doing any weird cultist stuff over the internet, the chance of him using the computer like an overcautious grandparent played into my hands.

The email program would helpfully open saved emails much like Word would open text files, so without having to log into his account or work out how to convert them to a readable format I started clicking through some of his recent emails, looking for a pattern and excluding stuff that genuinely seemed to be school related.

It was harder to resist peering into gossip about my fellow students—my life was literally on the line and I was never even going to see them again, even if I survived, but unfortunately those were both also really good arguments for why I should satisfy my curiosity and have a look-see.

The afternoon was wearing on outside, the sky taking on that dreamy summer afternoon look, with little fluffy seeds and insects drifting interchangeably in the air and catching the light. The office was much hotter than the cultists' library (at least, before Alana had started a fire in it) and sweat was prickling at my hairline, sticking my t-shirt to me. It wasn't like they needed me more than a day—I already had figured back in Bilsworth that they weren't going to bother feeding us while they had us captive, but I was starting to feel a bit sick from skipping lunch. Which was presumably how they wanted me so I'd be easy to handle.

In the end my search for knowledge was getting too difficult with how unfocused and easily distracted I was, and I whacked off the monitor, leaving the computer running and hoping the hum wouldn't give me away if I just made a lot of noise. I pounded on the door again.

"C'mon! At least let me out to pee!" I yelled. "I'll go in your rubbish bin if you don't!" I mean, not like he seemed particularly precious about his own office if he had been the one to rip out the phone line, but then again he could always call maintenance and play dumb. Maybe stage a robbery on school property and throw insurance fraud into their crimes. Or pretend a mouse had eaten through the wires or something.

My threat of defiling his office worked. The door opened within a minute and Mr Westcott bristled at me as threatening as I'd ever seen him.

I grinned at him.

"No funny business," he warned me before frog marching me to the nearest ladies' room. There was no drinking fountain, but once I'd washed my hands I steeled myself and took a few sips of the tap water out of the palm of my hand. I regretted helping spread the rumours that when the old janitor had been replaced overnight and was never heard of again it was because he had fallen into the water tank on the roof.

Like, that was two years ago, but how long did it take for a body to decay in cold water?

I barely made it back to the toilet before I threw up.

Nerves, I told myself, shaking and hovering over the toilet, dry-retching. You did not seriously squick yourself out over an imaginary dead body so much that you puked. It's because you're in danger yourself.

Actually, given my past form, I had a pretty hard time believing it.

The toilet door opened and I looked around to see that Mr Westcott had come in after me.

"You shouldn't be in the girl's loos, pervert," I muttered, scrambling to get up so it wasn't quite so obvious that I'd just been spitting into the toilet to clear the taste of bile from my mouth.

"You were taking too long."

"You sent me in here with handcuffs on. What if I'd needed to change a tampon, huh?"

Okay, *that* one never failed to turn an old dude pale. Ten points to me. (A thousand points still to the cultists holding me captive, but I'd take the small victories.)

I stalked over to the sink and washed my hands again, splashing my face. I suddenly wasn't feeling very thirsty though.

"I don't get it," I said. "You were always kind of a jerk, but I thought that you cared. You're not actually a bad teacher. But human sacrifice? That's a steep curve into cartoon villainy. Why?"

"You've always been good at your little research projects. You must know we're doing this for the good of the town—the town that I *know* you love more than every other student I've ever taught, if your projects are reflective of your emotions. It's not personal. Well… It *is*, but not more than the fact I don't lament that it has to be you. I don't regret that our relationship ends this way." He held open the door for me, almost gentlemanly. I considered running, but when we got out in the hall I saw Chief Inspector Singer blocking the one route I could have taken that wasn't a dead end where Mr Westcott could easily corner me again, even if I was presumably a far better sprinter, even with my hands bound in front of me.

"Did you always know?" I asked instead. "As the guy on the inside from the school—you knew that the seventy-five years were going to be rolling around again while you were still teaching here and started weighing up what students you did and didn't like. Was your Oxbridge club of nerdy girls and straight-laced kids whose parents forced them to study instead of date a good way to thin down your options and find the perfect candidate? What a sick abuse of power."

He didn't, surprisingly, splurge his entire supervillain back story with his spare time cultist activity and motivations to me, his old nemesis (shame—I could have written a good redemption arc to rival Snape, but this was just underwhelming). Instead he huffed and cleared his throat and finally said, as we got back to the offices, "Let's just say that after a point it wasn't hard to find someone's name who I didn't mind putting forwards. It made it an awful lot easier to deal with you when I could think about your fate."

"Disgusting," I said. "I should have peed in your bin."

He shoved me back into his office and locked the door. I listened closely and this time was in a clearer state of mind to hear him knocking on another door—down in the general direction of the heads of department rather than back up towards Mr Plebsy's office—no idea if that implicated someone else or if he just had stolen a key—and I heard the rumble of his voice offering Alana a bathroom break. I breathed out again. When I heard Mr Westcott leading her past me—it was obvious from their dialogue that she was digging her heels in—I thudded myself bodily against the door. "Alana!"

There was an answering thud. "Tanya!" she squawked. A scuffle followed, and I could only yell a meaningless reassurance at her, then the sound of her struggle disappeared down the hall. I wished her the best of luck with a potential escape plan, and I went back to reading Mr Westcott's email.

*

Night crept up slowly, as it does at the height of summer. Daddy wouldn't worry about me—not yet. He knew that I was with Alana (and in a way I still was). He knew that when I hung out with friends sometimes we would disappear to each other's houses for days at a time away from home. That Teb and Ally and I had spare toothbrushes at every one of the other's houses. That it was just as likely later in the week—if this was a normal week—that our house would invaded with laughing, shrieking girls, spreading over the living room, eating pizza and watching a movie on our largest shared TV that wasn't frequently taken over by Avi's cartoons.

I felt a sudden wave of grief for my dad, oblivious to the loss and suffering he was going to go through, a process that already would have started if only he knew where I was.

No. I could beat this.

The Piper had limited foresight, enough to know when there was a problem and what to throw at it.

But he hadn't even known all this was happening. He'd been successfully blocked out by the cult and I couldn't help feeling he was scared of them or even at a disadvantage, no matter how powerful he was supposed to be.

And so my brain looped on and on over all the data we had and all the things I didn't and couldn't know. I sort of knew that I was wasting my precious final hours absorbing the extremely boring correspondence of my least favourite teacher, but it wasn't like there were any games on this account, so I really had nothing else to do unless I wanted to read some of his books on teaching. At least this felt sort of productive, like there was something more I was doing towards my own case. And I was letting myself think and think, waiting for my brain to stumble over some loophole or possibility that I hadn't considered yet, some way that this could all be magically made right in a fraction of a second and no one would die and everything would be fixed just like that.

Night was almost on us and I was getting bleary, my arms exhausted from the weird mantis way I had to hold them over the keys, and I mistakenly clicked on a PTA email from last month and read it for lack of anything better to do:

"Mr L refusing demands. Meeting @ 7, board room, to discuss terms.

Bring AL's files & school photo.——Mr S"

"Bingo!" I hissed. Apparently I'd stumbled right onto the blackmail plot centring around dragging the Larbies into this mess. And Mr Westcott's place in the school was the obvious way to profile us, but also how to get information about Alana to send to Greg (although I supposed her criminal record might have worked; grim mug shots weren't as emotionally compelling as school photos). Greg might not have even known for sure where Alana was until he'd got the message that would have resulted from this. In fact, if he'd known she had been placed in St Troute's school, presumably that was where he was an alumni of, and while I'd have more likely suspected that old, creepy, religious school to be a hive of weird pseudo-Christian cultists, if he had known that Mr Westcott was their cultist embedded in a school, he may have thought that Alana was safe and that they wouldn't know about her. More shame her for getting expelled and transferred to our shoddy murder-cult school.

I scrambled to find the other emails from the "PTA" (this was almost more cunning than I would have credited the small-minded and mean head of sixth form to come up with on his own, but then maybe one of the more technically minded cultists could have briefed him on how to do it). The more recent emails were much more urgent——I needed information that was up-to-date on their plans, at this point if nothing more than for my peace of mind when I went into said plans.

My best bet on times seemed to be:

"PTA meeting——15th Aug 11:11 PM STT."

Which was today, so presumably if this was the actual Parent Teacher Association then Mr Westcott was going to have one hell of a scheduling conflict. And I didn't think it was likely they'd be having a meeting at eleven at night. In the middle of the summer holiday. Yeah. I was thinking cult stuff. Nice to know exactly when I would die.

I exited out of everything and turned the computer off. I figured there wasn't really anything so incriminating I could read to help——most of the messages were vague people-managing and arranging meetings. Things like the stuff about Alana and Mr Larbie I could only determine because I had so much insider knowledge on it. I didn't even know who all the other cultists were. If there was dirty laundry to air, I wasn't going to find it here in the emails. And it was eight o'clock by now and I was getting bummed out by all this frustrating reading.

I spun some more in the chair, thinking over everything one last time. Trying not to panic. My methods of just flinging myself at a problem were still the only real option I had, but an option which had been pretty successful before in the past. All I could do was act like I had it under control, try to fake that I knew what I was doing, that I had a plan, that they wouldn't kill me because of some brilliant thing that I hadn't done yet.

"You can beat this," I said out loud, listening to the sound of my voice. I said it again and again until there wasn't a single wobble and I could probably convince myself if I heard it from someone else.

"You're going to win. You always win."

*

Mr Westcott returned at ten o'clock to collect me. I didn't fight it as he led me down to the police car that was still waiting in the car park. He slammed the door and disappeared off back into the building.

It took another twenty minutes to return, which I spent counting my breaths and not thinking about anything at all. He emerged with Chief Inspector Singer, both of them hauling Alana with a hand each under her arms. I guess they'd earmarked more time in case I fought as well, or had constructed a rudimentary trebuchet out of office supplies and launched an attack when they first opened the door. Alana struggled all the way until we were back in the car together.

"Fancy seeing you here on a night like this," I said, winking at her.

Small wonders, her face cracked into a smile. She stomped it down as hard as she could and looked back out of the window on her side, but I'd caught it and that was more than enough to keep me going as the car shook with the two men getting into the front. The engine started and we pulled out of the school carpark slowly, as if he were trying to drive inconspicuously.

It wasn't far to go: we were taken into the town centre, now dead and empty, and the car pulled up outside Bobbie's.

"The ice cream place?" Alana said disbelievingly.

"They're in league, remember?"

She looked like she really, really had not intended to remember that. Shame, really. I was sad I'd never be able to eat another one of the big sundaes again.

Chief Inspector Singer turned in his seat. "We're going to get out here, and if you scream, so help me, I will make you suffer for it."

"How?" Alana shot back. "How can you possibly ruin my life any more than it already has been today?"

He glared at her. "You have other friends."

The door to the shop opened and a red-cloaked figure came out. Maybe Greg trying not to cause an incident with Alana. Maybe not. He opened the car door and immediately clamped a hand down on Alana's mouth before she could try screaming anyway, and Chief Inspector Singer got out of the car to help him half-carry Alana into the shop.

Mr Westcott addressed me: "Will you come quietly?"

I squinted through the dark shop windows; there were other cloaked figures in there.

"You know what? I know when to pick my battles."

He opened the car door for me, and with just a hand on my shoulder he led

178

me inside.

We were taken up a wonky, creaking staircase that betrayed the age of the house, then to a slim hallway with two slanting doors. One of them opened and light flooded in, revealing the brown floral painting on the wall and the scruffy carpet. Bobbie peered out, her normally cheerful face looking pinched and angry. Did she know what was going on here? Unless she was perhaps a wife or something to one of the red-cloaked men, she could just have really disliked having men in weird cloaks clomping up and down her house late at night. I tried a "help call the police" look at her, but then I was shoved through the door and Alana was already sitting there on a natty velvet sofa in front of a TV playing golf on low volume, gagged with a women's scarf in her mouth, and I figured Bobbie had at least got accessory to the crime status.

I came in and sat quietly next to Alana when Mr Westcott gave me a push on my shoulder. Alana scowled at me like *why aren't you gagged and being dragged in here?* I pulled a concerned expression and went back to watching the cultists crowding at the door. Only Mr Westcott and the Chief Inspector were out of their robes.

"Get ready for the ritual," another (obviously male but otherwise unidentifiable) voice ordered. "We'll make sure they don't go anywhere."

Greg had to be in the gaggle: I'd counted all seven by the time we were in this aggressively maroon sitting room. So he was back to passively letting this happen, though I suppose with the renewed reassurance that Alana was not going to be sacrificed.

I took a gamble: "Greg! You going to be brave enough to be the one to stand guard over us?"

There was muttering. Two of the red-cloaked figures stepped forward, one ushering Bobbie out, and then the door closed and it was Alana and I on the sofa with a cultist either side of the door.

"Is one of you Greg, then?" I demanded.

Alana kicked me, rather painfully I might add, in the ankle. She did not want the agitating I intended to do to take place. I felt sorry she had to go through this—I had questions because I cared about her, but maybe questions she wouldn't care to hear asked.

"I'm here," his unmistakable accent (at least in these parts) came from the left-side cloak.

"So there's two guards either side of the door, and one always lies and one always tells the truth…" I started.

"Do you have a point to this?" the other cloak barked at me. "Otherwise, be quiet."

You know, I recognised his voice. That was the MP for Ransley: he tended to get into scandals and have to cover for himself on the news when pretending it was totally normal for the rivers to fill up with weird oily sludge from some business he allowed to practice nearby. So that, weirdly, meant that Greg by process of elimination was the guard who told the truth… No, I didn't like that version of reality. He needed shades of grey. But I was hoping for an honest answer here at least.

"So when you've killed me, what are you going to do about Alana? You're not going to suddenly be a magically perfect father-daughter team. You're not going to walk back into her mother's life. That much is obvious. But let me tell you, it does *not* seem unlikely she will sell you out considering she already burned down your headquarters after she found out who you were and called the police on you. But if they've brought you back here with a promise not to hurt her… What happens to her?"

"I thought I might have to take her back to America with me. At least for a while." He sounded uncertain.

Alana made a hugely enraged gagging noise from beside me.

"Yeah, so good luck making it through airport security with her," I said.

"That's *enough*," the other cultist cut in. "Mr Larbie, go to the graveyard and help with the preparations there. We will join you when everyone is ready."

I saw a long hesitation. But then the hood shifted like he was nodding, and Greg opened the door and left. A minute later a second figure came in. I thought I recognised the tummy as Dr Oathill, who had been treating all our families all our lives, but I did not want to commit to the idea that the man who had been giving me lollipops after every injection I'd ever had now intended to murder me in cold blood.

"Is there anything I need to do before the sacrifice?" I asked insolently.

"You will be absolved of all your sins when you are offered to God. There is nothing you need to concern yourself with in this world anymore."

"Geeze, religion is a bummer," I muttered, glancing at Alana. She looked like she still hadn't forgiven me for trying to get some private conversation with Greg, and didn't smile at my joke.

Another cultist cracked the door, muttered something, and then Dr Oathill (dammit, it was him) asked me to stand.

"Are you just leaving Alana?!" I cried.

"Do you *want* her at your sacrifice?" the MP for Ransley (Tory, I might add) asked, somewhat disbelieving.

"Hey, if it's as purifying as all that, she should be honoured to witness it," I said flippantly.

"Fine. Just don't make a fuss."

"Fuss is all we do," I muttered, and *this* time Alana's eyes softened a little at me. I grinned at her, but then I had an arm on my shoulder hauling me to my feet, and once again I was being dragged around.

Sacrifice

Here's something you don't know. (And, to be honest, like with the music thing I'm still not totally a hundred percent sure about.)

There was a traveller once, hundreds of years ago, even before there was a dragon in Troutespond. In fact, there was almost nothing there: three or four buildings by the bend of the river, a farm which ended about where the pond began, in a murky miniature marsh, squelching over the land for dozens of feet more than it does in the current day. The place wasn't even worthy of the name of a village. There was an old barrow mound, from back when this had been a place worthy of a name, but a name that even in this long ago time was forgotten. It was a burial site which had come to mark the crossroads between the Ransley road over the hills and in the other direction, the London road that in the present day had been absorbed into the six-lane flow of the motorway and where those crossed the one road to the little market town of Waitington, now the main city that this county was named after, and a thin path on the final branch that led to the lonely monastery of Severstrong (and Ransley if you wanted to go the haunted way).

People said there was something odd about the barrow, that ghosts of the old king and his men lived there, and his wife, Glynnes, wandered the hills, angry she had not been buried with him, always trying to find him, and, because people in the Dark Ages loved a horror story as much as we do now, it was said she mistook the humped roofs of thatched houses for barrows and ripped into them in violent storms. (I wonder if Glynnes became the dragon.)

And also the fair folk would get you if you sat by the pond.

The people who lived in those parts were very suspicious of the family who lived in the farm next to the barrow and the pond. (They just called it the Barrowpond, creatively enough.) Despite plenty of warnings, and a great deal of suspicious staring and muttering, the family never moved or did anything to even pretend they were worried about the barrow right on the edge of the property. They continued to plough the damp earth, even when strange bones or rusted, useless weapons surfaced in the muck, and seemed to live in no fear at all that Glynnes would come destroy their house in her fury.

"Well, she's got lost, hasn't she?" the father said, if someone ever worked up the nerve to question him directly. "Seems like her man's barrow is the last place she'd stumble across if she's supposed to never find her way home. I'd worry more about your own roofs."

And when they tried to warn him about the pond he didn't listen, and he didn't stop his daughter going down there every day and picking the wildflowers that grew by the edge.

So that's the way things were when the traveller came by. He was a young lad who went by the name of Troute at that point. A wanderer who fit in nowhere and belonged to no land. His family was dead and he'd been driven from the land, left without a thing to his name, so he walked instead, going from place to place never really knowing what he would do until he got there. Though there was usually work for someone as strong as him, the pay was just enough to keep him alive and nothing more, usually just his meal for the day.

He'd heard that the farmer down by the Barrow Hill had some work that needed doing, and he'd walked seven miles that morning from across the valley from some place that's of absolutely no importance, to another place he had thought would be of absolutely no importance once again, as was every place he went to.

He came to the little farm and stopped for a moment by the fence to see what sort of place it was, since he was probably going to spend the next couple of weeks or even the season working there if he were lucky. Though he would accept what they had no matter what, he wanted to have the right words when he approached the farmer, since he was conscientious like that. A compliment of the pigs the farmer kept or some well thought-out advice about a problem with the land might just be the thing to get him hired for the year.

But as he stood resting, singing caught his ear, a beautiful voice that carried on the breeze, and he found he was drifting down the road towards the barrow. The road became even more of a muddy mire than even a Dark Ages man was accustomed to and a pond spilled out over it. Sitting on the lowest slope of the barrow (around about where I nearly fell into the pond that one time), amongst thick grass and many wildflowers, was a girl of roughly his age, small and with copious amounts of coppery-red hair, looking the perfect ideal for one of those Victorian Romantic paintings. In the way that these stories often go, young

Troute was captivated, and knew at once, whether he was set clearing the field that ended in this swamp or not, he was going to feel like he was shovelling clouds while he worked on this farm. Blah blah, love at first sight, as it happens.

She looked up, her eyes widened as they met his, and she stopped singing.

And then she abruptly squealed, tumbled over nothing from her sitting position like she had been grabbed and fell headfirst into the pond with a disappointed wail but not even a splash. Clearly something else had been enjoying her singing as well and was not pleased that she had stopped, perhaps jealous that she had immediately started making the same heart eyes back at Troute.

Troute wasted no time and flung down the sack that contained all his worldly possessions and dived in after her to save her from what he presumably just thought was drowning in the spur of the moment.

He emerged in a strange twilight-green world where the stars drifted about low overhead and monstrous trees loomed along the horizon, surrounding them in the primal forest that always threatened to swallow up a village with its vines and thorns and creatures like dragons that lurked in the safety of its shadows. The barrow had a huge door in the side, all carven wood inlaid with gold and painted bright colours. From inside it glowed like hundreds of fires burned, and the roar of people and the sounds of a vast feast escaped from within: the old King and his court living a merry afterlife beneath the hill (Glynnes was probably just annoyed that she hadn't been invited to the party).

But it was the fairies who had taken the maiden by the pond—this Other world was a space filled with more than just one creature, it was the space in which things crossed over, and he could see them dancing away with her up the hill. He gave chase and roared, a lad with strong arms and wide shoulders, a monster to the small folk who had taken the girl. He laid into them with his bare fists, frightening the strange, nearly demonic creatures he perceived; he was too wrathful at them taking her to worry about what exactly they were.

The fairies scattered in fear and let go of the girl. He grabbed her hand and ran back for the pond.

"Oh, but they were promising me wonderful things!" she cried, bespelled and confused. Though she had shared a smile with him when he had interrupted her singing, she was rather less happy to see the strange farm hand than the beautiful creatures she had perceived.

Her shrill protests drew unwanted attention: some of the warriors were drawn out of their barrow, and now they saw the girl. "It's Glynnes!" they cried, mistaking one girl with red hair for a fearsome queen who had died hundreds of years before. The cry went up and more and more warriors poured out of the barrow—all the King's men for three generations— drawn by the shout of the name of the lost queen. They tried to stop Troute from passing before the King could return and claim his wife back. It wouldn't be seventy-five years, the fairy curse on that pond; it would be an eternity locked underground.

Perhaps the girl would have liked the party in Valhalla, but realistically it's not a very healthy relationship to be kidnapped by a ghost king forever even if they are going to treat you like a queen.

Troute didn't really know all of this: he just found himself once more surrounded by monsters, who were once more trying to capture the girl that he had met less than five minutes ago and had already valiantly tried to save once. At this point he had no other option but to try again. He fought them all bravely, although they were already dead and, unlike the fairies, had swords and shields and all the fine armour they had been buried in. In fact, his jabs at them passed through their ghostly flesh, while their blades, of bronze and gold, were as sharp as they had been in life and cut him fiercely.

Finally the old King came out from under the hill, in his jewelled helm and golden jewellery heavier than his armour. Troute was bleeding and quite dazed and frightened, slowly beginning to understand how far from home he was and how strange the world he had found himself in was. But he was a decent guy and the girl was more scared than he was, horrified by the fight that she had watched. He had his arms spread to stop the warriors from grabbing the girl, who huddled behind him, terrified.

The King marched forward, and, I mean, I've seen how tall the Piper is, but he loomed over Troute, pushing him aside with a shove that threw him to his men dazed enough they could catch hold of his arms to stop him fighting. The King pulled the girl up by her arm so that she was standing and examined her closely, lifting her hair to peer at its curls, tipping her face up with her chin caught between two immense fingers.

"That is not my Glynnes," the King proclaimed, finally, dropping her face. She crumpled to the floor, too shaken to hold herself up. "Take her from my sight!" And with that he stomped back into the barrow to get back to his post-death drinking.

The loyal warriors stopped playing with Troute: one of them shoved him down with a final sharp blow to his side while another grabbed the girl. They threw her bodily into the pond, and she vanished through without a splash, returned to the human world (there's no record of if the curse still worked on her—she never left the town again, but in those days people didn't tend to leave the town in their lives anyway.—It's rather more of a modern concern that the curse affects you on both sides of the pond).

Troute pulled himself up, glad that somehow things had sorted themselves out, and then realised it had not been just a push: the front of his tunic was stained red with blood, a much deeper cut, an intended killing blow. The warriors of the barrow thought as much: their eyes ran over him with no more violence in their faces, just a sort of acceptance of him, a welcome of another fallen warrior to their number. They turned and went back to their feast while he was left bleeding beside the pond, to choose which path he would follow. Not dying immediately, but he knew a wound that deep could not be fixed: if someone bandaged it, almost certainly it would turn foul and kill him from inside. But he didn't want to die in this strange dark place. He didn't want to join their party and drink as one who had fought them bravely and earned a seat at their tables. With what little energy he had left he crawled to the pond, and he fell through it back home.

When he woke up he was in a church—no, the hospice wing of the small monastery, a good thirty miles from where he had started. He hurt all over, and his fear of dying slowly of a putrid wound resurfaced—better they had let him die on the road and that he would already be in the ground, his soul departed, than suffering for days or even weeks in this unfamiliar room.

A silent monk was sitting near him, and when he saw Troute coming to consciousness he got up and left. A few minutes later, another man came in: a strange man, tall and wild-looking, with oddly black eyes—too black, the darkness seeming to take up all of his eyes. He wore a monk's attire, but it was split down the middle: half black, half white, more like a jester than the member of a venerable order. And the man's hair was untonsured, but looked wild, long and braided in places with leaves occasionally twisted in, only a thin line between looking like he'd done it intentionally or slept on the forest floor. He knelt beside Troute and checked the wound.

"You don't have long to live, boy," he said. "I can keep you breathing for a few more days, at most, but you will not enjoy those days. Without my help, you'd already be dead."

"I am ready to die," Troute replied, trying not to sound too much like he was asking for the favour, though he hoped if the man had any compassion he'd see the question. "I thank you for keeping me alive so you could administer last rites, but do not bother yourself to keep me here longer if it will trouble these monks to nurse me."

"Ah, boy, you know nothing of death or being ready to die..."

"I'm willing to learn," Troute replied desperately.

"You will. But not until you have walked around the world with this burden. And it will grow greater as time passes."

"It doesn't have to."

"But it will. I want you to understand that before I make my offer to you."

Troute didn't really know what to say to that. He had pretty much nothing to give this man in exchange for whatever it was he would offer. Lying in silence just made him more aware of how much pain he was in, so he struggled to ask. "What offer?"

"To walk with this burden in my place."

"What... is that burden?"

"To do the right thing. You seem to know what that is, if the story of your heroics is true. In this world there are many times when the right thing has to be done, and someone must be saved, not always for love or honour, but just because the world needs them to be safe. Sometimes there are things that must be punished for threatening the safety of those who need protection. In your heart you are already aware of how to make this distinction, and, I think, have been given a hard lesson in the dangers of this world."

"So what do you want me to do?"

"Not die... Not ever. At first, that is all that matters. The rest will come to you."

"That's easy to say," Troute replied, trying to gesture the bandages across his stomach but moving was so painful he may as well have been paralysed. He fell still with an agonised groan for his attempt to be snarky. (I sympathise—I feel I'd be the same on my deathbed.) "If you can save me, truly, why are you doing this? And for *me?*"

"I need a replacement, and fast. I have waited too long to choose one, though I have met thousands of people in my travels. Now I find myself here with my power waning, and all there is in front of me is a dying boy who was stabbed by a ghost's blade. You have not doubted what you have discovered so far of the world. Let me expand upon it some more... Or you could die if that's *really* what you want. I can't promise your spirit will pass easily with a wound like that. I hear those killed by a ghost's sword tend to become the restless dead themselves."

He held out his hand to Troute, and for a moment the lad was confused, but then he saw that this strange man was trying to give him something: a beautifully carved wooden pipe. It was painted in a flurry of reds and blues and gold.

"What do I have to do?"

"For now? Live."

*

Since the graveyard was moments away, they didn't have any special transport lined up. Feeling ridiculous by association, in the middle of a big circle of the red-cloaked cultists, one of whom was carrying a box of presumably sacrifice-related supplies, another of whom had the sword in hand, we walked across the village square. The only person around was the man who perpetually stood in the garden of the pub with a big, mostly empty glass in one hand, a hand-rolled cigarette in the other. He was the old bearded drunk of the village, and whether it was the alcohol or just seventy years of living in Troutespond where this shit happened all the time even if it wasn't exactly this specific shit, he didn't bat an eye at seeing our odd group pass but watched with a glassy stare until we'd passed. I heard Bobbie close and lock the shop behind us, staying inside herself. Her sinister acquiescence to this whole thing had put me off ice cream for life. Provided life was more than just the next few minutes.

The sounds echoed a little in the utterly still night air. I could feel goose pimples rising on my arms, not sure if it was that the summer weather had decided to take a night off or if I was just too scared to appreciate the warmth. I shuddered as we walked under the arch of yew trees at the side gate to the church. I didn't see the priest there—maybe he was staying home pretending none of this was happening. Now he was someone who could call the police for us and maybe get a response, so along with ice cream I had to write off organised religion and seemingly kindly priests if I ever survived this.

I felt rather less sympathy to the dead under my feet, knowing that there were generations of murderous knights down there too, all of whom would have happily approved my impending murder. I was walking almost in a dream by this point, and I knew it was bad. I was unfocussed and I *needed* to be sharp so that I could come up with a way out. My plan had literally just been "I'm smarter than them" and fear and hunger had reduced me to having a blur around the edge of my vision, thoughts drifting to all the victims who might be buried here, all taken and killed in mystery to their families.

And now I'd potentially be joining them.

Okay, that still made a sick shudder run through me. How much would I do not to be a corpse this evening?

In the dark the ground seemed invisible; the air was lit by the now-distant street lights, but that ended with the gates of the graveyard. The darkness began in a jagged, blocky outline of black headstones. The fractured, delicate outline of one of the trees that grew at the end of the graveyard loomed over us, backlit by the lights of houses—that was my street, I thought dimly. My house was only a dozen away from here—I could make out the roof in daylight. I could see, if I leaned out of my own bedroom window, the church tower and the top of the hill. I doubted Daddy would be getting a breath of night air from my window and spot what was going on, but it lent absurdity to the moment.

I wondered how this looked from the road. Not many people came this way, with all the shops closed and the pub in its last ten minutes, unlikely to be filled with more than the aforementioned drunk. The village fell dead after dark; maybe one car would pass through on the way to somewhere better, but the driver would be thinking only of home, and if they looked at all it would be a second take in their rear-view mirror, even as the graveyard vanished behind the trees or church and we were hidden again, the cultists free to continue their ritual.

Even though I was intimidated by the cultists and terrified they'd hurt Alana or go after Ally even in these final minutes, I felt like I was letting it happen. It didn't help with how disassociated and weird I felt about the intimidation. It was my fault for always making myself the one in control of a situation or making a play to be in control of the situation, even when I really, blatantly was not, responsibility for it all soaked into me. I couldn't help but see that somehow or other I was the one leading the cultists, rather than them leading me.

The cultists did the actual, ridiculous Gothic horror trope of producing a length of rope and tying Alana to a gravestone—one with a cross at the top she couldn't just wriggle her way up the stone and pop off the top. I guess it lent a little extra irony to her situation, being the lapsed Catholic of our acquaintance and all.

They led me to what I knew to be the exact middle of the graveyard, something ingrained in my useless knowledge after circling it five times while I was measuring it for Greg. There was a big tablelike tomb dead in the centre (bad choice of words). It sort of came into focus slowly, but then I realised as I stared that there were six graves around it in a circle, old and weather-beaten, lichen creeping over them but probably no more than a few hundred years old, a later contribution to the mythos of this cult. No way they were original. From this angle the graves looked monolithic and almost like the standing stones from up the hill recreated.

"Sit up there," one of the cultists who wasn't Greg croaked at me. He was scared—I could feel it dripping from his voice. We were all grappling with the fact I was going to die, except for the fact that I would *actually* have to die and they'd be able to tell themselves it had to be done because it was tradition, for the good of the town.

It seemed ridiculous to think of Mr Westcott fervently believing in dragons all the time we'd known him.

He'd yelled at Ally for doodling dragons on the front of her exercise books.

As I clambered up onto the big tomb I forced myself to relax, to open my mind and try and feel again.

I wanted to know that all the cultists were frightened, not just at the thought someone might wander down the road and stop to watch they were doing, mistaking it for some street theatre. All their years of running around feeling superior in their special little cult had never actually prepared them for having to go through with the full ritual that they practised for. The feeling I got was mixed; some minds I just couldn't know because I didn't know who was under the cloaks. Others seemed pretty set on it—the curator from the museum really did not give two shits about me. Mr Westcott was more complex, but ultimately he had had the longest contact with me as a sacrifice and talked himself into it maybe even years ago, face with name and all. But there was uncertainty and fear in the group.

Their fumbling in the dark ended with them getting seven heavy-duty candles lit, big enough that they had probably been borrowed from the church. At first six points of light flared up, and I could hear the desperate clicking and under-the-breath swearing from the photographer, who generally seemed to be more of a disaster than the others, if the little jog we'd seen him on was anything to go by, but his lighter finally worked and his candle burst into life as well. Maybe, I thought, he'd borrowed Alana's dodgy lighter.

They stepped back and though it was only a little light it was still better than nothing, and I could see what was going on in the dim flickering glow.

The church was a dark square against the sky, where a crescent moon was not making a very good show at bringing us any more light. I couldn't see the pond, but I could feel it as an almost physical tug of darkness. Somewhere thankfully beyond the realm of bones that this graveyard was built on. Something with its own dark power stirring inside it. I heard the water bubbling slightly, and it brought back sudden strong memories of another lake earlier in the summer.

The cultists didn't have much else to prepare, so didn't take long to organise themselves to begin the ritual after that. They were getting into a very organised looking circle, the candles at their backs to add to the creepy lighting that just made them silhouettes again.

"So, you're seriously going to do this," I said, sitting up straighter and swinging my legs from the tomb.

"Lie back or we'll tie you down," the MP cultist ordered.

"You do all, you know, *actually* believe it's going to work, don't you?" I asked, trying to keep my voice conversational. "Does it even work if one of you doesn't? Bartholomew doesn't believe it. He's watching you all like an anthropologist. Or I dunno, Jane Goodall. Greg's here on coercion and you're probably going to have to kill his daughter afterwards, since I know Alana won't let this go, and he's more scared of that than killing me. Ten to one he grabs her and runs while you're distracted trying to dispose of my body. And——"

"Shut up!" Mr Westcott barked at me, echoing between the graves in a way vastly different from how he shouted to make himself heard on the echoing playground. Same voice though.

"As for you, *sir*, you're just settling old scores. You're not scared of getting caught. You're not scared of killing me. You're scared of *me*. You ripped out your computer's internet. You've taken our phones away. But how do you know I haven't written down everything I learned or told my boyfriend everything just minutes before we went into the museum?"

That caused a murmur—not the one I had expected. "She has a boyfriend?"

"Her medical history was clear that she's never been to the nurse for… anything like that," Dr Oathill said.

I almost laughed. "Hey, I never said I was smart *all* the time."

"She's stalling," Mr Westcott said. "Her boyfriend is a nerdy little runt who's scared to hold her hand. I've seen them together. I don't think we have anything to be worried about."

"Hey!" I protested. "You don't know what we've got up to in our own time. Not unless you've been invading my privacy even *more* than you already have going through my records like that. But if you have to know, one of our favourite date spots is under the big oak tree in the meadow."

"What if we sacrifice her and the ritual doesn't work?"

"Virginity is a stupid, heteronormative patriarchal idea anyway," I contributed. "What if I were a lesbian?"

"Tie her down and gag her."

"What if she's telling the truth?"

"She's *not*; she's posing ridiculous ideas to make us uncertain. She's not gay, she's had dozens of boyfriends."

Mr Westcott did not seem to be backing up his point very well. I was winning. It wasn't exactly the showdown with him I'd pictured, but hey, give me an arena. We all have that one teacher we would gladly fight if we had the chance.

I rolled my eyes. "I'm being perfectly sensible. You can't know, the whole concept is stupid, and I could be extremely impure and unchristian while still technically being a virgin. If the whole point of a virgin sacrifice is to offer up someone of untouchable purity to underline how important the sacrifice is, the fact at least two of you are using this to settle a personal vendetta against me is—mpff!" One of them moved forwards and I had a whole lot of red velvet (and not the cake) in my mouth as he practically crammed his sleeve into my face.

"Tie her down. We don't have much time before the dragon comes."

I shrieked as best I could and lashed out, trying to scramble free before they could grab me. I fell off the tomb, winding myself, and only managed to get to my feet before hands were grabbing at me and I was hauled back into place. They were coming at me with more rope…

In the next moment they stopped, and I had no idea why, at first, as I continued screaming against the hand over my mouth and thrashing my legs. But then I caught a sound as I stopped for breath, stifled with my nose half-covered too, and the sleeve damp with my own spit.

Impossibly, a tinny version of the *Bananas in Pyjamas* theme song was playing nearby. Dread filled me as the ringtone abruptly cut off, and then there was a moment where no one was moving at all. In the stillness that followed only the sound of Alana violently struggling and groaning behind the gag in her mouth filled the night air. She knew what it was too.

"Who's there?" a cultist demanded.

I honestly thought she wouldn't do it. I kind of… really, really wanted her not to do it.

I heard movement, and then Ally's shrillest voice echoed between church and pond: "I'm here to stop you!"

My hero. My poor, silly hero.

I frantically reshuffled the cards in my hands while the cultists laughed. Time for a plan which I had been idly running my thumb over for days, but rejected each and every time circumstances suggested it for being our worst gamble. The only way to avoid it had been to play along with Alana's whim to keep Ally out, but here she was, and in the darkness I could feel the presence by the pond taking shape, giving us an urgent deadline. There was no *time* for anything safer.

"Take her phone," the Chief Inspector—ah, that was who was pinning me down—ordered. "Find out who was calling her."

"Wait—don't!" Mr Westcott yelled, and I was confused about why until I heard a crack, rather like a boxy old phone getting smashed against a gravestone, if I had to take a wild guess. Ally whimpered in horror at what she'd done, and then the cultists went for her, and she was dragged into sight, tall as the two cultists who held her but spindly like a stick figure between them. She looked helplessly at me, her face aghast at the scene she'd stumbled onto.

"How did you find out about this? Did Tanya tell you?" Mr Westcott snapped.

Ally's eyes bugged out of her head. "*Mr Westcott?*"

"Mmmph," I said, rolling my eyes, since it was important to express to her somehow or other, with extreme sarcasm, that this was old news and she was wildly behind the times.

"Answer the question."

"*Dr Oathill?*"

The cultist on her left shook her arm slightly. "Does anyone know that you're here?"

Okay, she didn't know the museum staff like I did, thank god, so the round of befuzzedly naming all the cultists was over. "I—I read it in a book. I found out it was tonight, so I came to see the dragon. And, um. Save my friends. Which, *for the record*, I did not expect! Are you *sacrificing* Tanya?"

"It's for the greater good."

"You have *got* to be kidding me. This is the plot of *Hot Fuzz*. Except there's no giant monkey."

Alana and I *both* made a synchronised annoyed grunt. I managed to take advantage of the confusion, and the fact that I had barely fought for a minute or two so Chief Inspector Singer had relaxed a little, to shove his hand away. I struggled to sit up as he shifted his grip to my shoulder, but I went pliant again as soon as I was where I wanted to be, not trying to escape so he wouldn't immediately start manhandling me back into being gagged and held down. He let me talk. "Ally!" I said, and she turned to look at me with her batty eyes. "There is a *dragon*. It's coming right now. I can already feel the line between the worlds drawing thinner. This is *exactly* like the prom. Except the dragon is coming anyway no matter what, and they're trying to stop it. They can stop it and save the town. That's what killing you is about."

"Me?"

"It's a trap," I said. "I'm the bait."

"We didn't set a trap to catch this girl," the MP for Ransley said, genuinely wrong-footed. I could *feel* Mr Westcott, one who knew my schemes best and understood me much better, draw back in horror without seeing him move.

I grinned. "No, I did. You're not going to sacrifice me tonight, not while Ally is here instead."

Ally's huge eyes turned on me again, looking utterly betrayed and yet somehow unsurprised. "You want them to *sacrifice me?*" she shrieked.

Bartholomew spoke: "It's as we agreed. Tanya is worth more to us alive. She's *proven* this by giving us an alternative sacrifice. Would you really want to squander a mind like this?"

"Ms Guardian, on the other hand…" Mr Westcott said, sounding like he was musing over the idea. I think he pretty much hated me forever and ever for saying this, so he'd have *liked* to kill me (and liked even more not to have me as a living breathing enemy).

"Hey!" Ally protested.

Chief Inspector Singer decided for the group—I don't know if he was necessarily in charge, since Mr Westcott seemed to have made more of the loud announcements, although it would make sense that he was picked to do the shouting thanks to his teacher voice. I felt myself being lifted up and unceremoniously dumped on the ground at the foot of the tombstone. "Bring her here," he ordered.

"Wait, no! You can't *actually* sacrifice me!" Ally shrieked. "This is a joke! I'm calling my lawyer! Give me a phone! I have rights!"

I glanced between the cloak hems to where Alana was on the edge of the circle. It was a pointless action—I just ended up getting the worst evil eye pointed my way.

I looked away as, right above me, Ally was dragged over and forced to sit on the tombstone. Her arm flopped down almost by my head, and in almost deliriously strong detail I looked at her ink-stained fingers, grey and blotchy from reading hundreds and hundreds of books. Who knew who had committed this ritual to paper, and in what forgotten tome, but Ally had found it—she probably knew more than me. And now she was its next victim, because she was the sort of nerd who stayed in reading books when she discovered there was an evil cult in town.

Focus.

I hadn't been lying about the dragon, anyway. I had doubted it until I got here, but now I could feel something drawing so close I could practically hear it breathing.

The cultists made quick work of tying Ally down, wrapping the rope around and around her and the tombstone—I was in the way, and they shunted me back, pushing me to the side. I ended up outside their circle, leaning against a plain gravestone, and even in the midst of all this horror my oldest fear reached up and grabbed me. I found my eyes skating over the stone, trying to read the name, frozen with the sick feeling that someone lay underneath me, that there was a grinning skull pointed right upwards looking right at me beneath where I lay. Dizziness and darkness closed in around my vision.

Somewhere behind me the cult began to chant some Latin prayer, the sound of which cut through my stupor. It gave me something to focus on—like playing music every night so that any time my thoughts got too self-defeating I could try and force myself to mouth along to well-known lyrics in my head, I tried to make myself listen, pick out the shapes of the words and understand what the chant was. I couldn't work out all the Latin, but the rush of magic that followed with it made me gasp like the air had been sucked from my lungs. It was happening fast. Something was coming. Something powerful and ancient, called down from the hills above the village...

I rolled over until I was sitting with my back to the gravestone instead of slumped over it, looking down, and took another sweep of my eyes across the scene: the cultists in a circle around Ally, the candles burned a third of the way down. Alana, a short distance away, desperately looking between me and the cultists, sending us equal amounts of hate with her eyes. I was still handcuffed but that wasn't exactly a deal breaker considering I wasn't tied to anything. With the cultists distracted I could easily have sneaked over and untied her, taken the gag out. If this was only a distraction, if I wasn't so overwhelmed, maybe that's what we could have done.

The water lapped noisily and my eyes went, drawn in horror, to the dark void where the pond lay.

The dragon appeared slowly. A glimmer of scales throwing the candlelight back at us... A ridged, barbed shadow drifting in front of the hooded figures... It dragged itself into the circle of light sluggishly, its back legs trailing, its head weary, its eyes half-closed. It was like a teenager crawling out of bed, still barely coherent, a long sleep clinging to it. What struck me was how small it was. A creature does not need to be massive to ravage a village of wooden-framed houses whose only defence is spindly fences and low stone walls and men with pointy metal sticks, especially when it can breathe fire (if this dragon could at all—there was no mention of it in the story that I had read). It was about the size of a sheep, though longer and lower to the ground. It had a furry, dog-like head, but human-ish golden eyes that betrayed its intelligence. Its scales were red, growing from tiny sparkling speckles on its nose to massive plates the size of my hand on its back and hindquarters. It was sturdy, thickset like the beefiest crocodile, with four legs that splayed similarly, but there ended the comparisons: the front legs ended in talons like an eagle's, horny and wickedly sharp. The back legs were once again dog-shaped, though still scaled, the claws long and wicked where they came from stumpy splayed toes. It likewise had massive fangs protruding from under its lips. Spikes ran down its back to a long, curling snakelike tail that ended in fins, swishy and vivid red like it was part goldfish too. And, of course, it had massive feathery wings folded against its sides, the same stunning red. The cultists looked almost black in the low light, but this dragon had an inner glow, something that made the redness stand out, though it cast no light of its own. Still, the graveyard seemed brighter for its presence.

It staggered towards the circle, and then I was struck with the second worst idea I'd had that evening—if Alana hadn't already gone through some sort of fed up with me event horizon she'd have strained something rolling her eyes. I reached out a hand and make clucking noises like I was trying to tempt a shy kitten, gently clicking my fingers and making soothing noises.

The dragon took a long, long look at the cultists, then ambled right up to me and the tomb I was reclining on. And then it encircled me and the grave, its tail reaching all the way around to under its paws, rested its head on my knees and closed its eyes.

I don't know if the dragon or I were under more of a spell, but at that point I lost all fear I had and reached down and stroked it, walking two fingers in the spot just behind the horns between its ears.

There was a sudden flurry of conversation a couple of feet away and the chanting broke off. All the cultists lost track of what they were doing and one of them even screamed a little bit when he turned to see what everyone was muttering about, but the dragon just made a rattling sort of purr and subsided further into my lap with a yawn that showed off a hell of a lot of sharp teeth. I withdrew my hand and it turned the rattle into a fierce growl. I hastily alternated my ear scritches with a hand scratching its belly (it would have been a lot easier to do without my hands still cuffed), but the dragon happily rolled a little to let me get a better go at it. There were no scales down there, just smooth red skin and soft red fur, the taut skin slowly going up and down with its sleepy breaths. Now that is how you wreck a ritual, short-term. Long-term was going to take some more work.

I looked up over my shoulder at the cultist I had a feeling was Mr Westcott. "Now what?" I asked.

"You... What are you... Why isn't it devouring you?!"

The cult were pretty much all edging towards me in fascination.

"Is the dragon normally meant to come out when you do this?" I asked as calmly as I could manage with had a huge, heavy and *hot* creature weighing my legs down.

They seemed completely stumped by that.

"We need to banish it," Dr Oathill said tersely. "It won't stay this tired for long if the stories about it are true. She'll probably be the first thing it guts once it wakes up a little more."

The dragon clearly sensed that they were drawing in too close and it made a "yip!" of displeasure, and I hastily got back to work rubbing it on the belly while all the cultists backed off. I thought it was rather obvious that it liked me—which is why they were definitely not so keen to get near it.

"You're right. The sooner we do the ritual the sooner it leaves. And the less chance of it waking up properly." Mr Westcott spoke with a wobble in his voice I had never heard before. In a very abstract way, it was almost comforting to find out his emotional limitations after all these years of fighting. Apparently when I brainstormed pranks I should have put "threaten with actual freaking dragon" at the top of my list.

The cultists clearly agreed without needing much more discussion, as they quickly reformed their circle and began to chant fast.

Well, most of the cultists did. I was watching intently, feeling the horror of having no time to come up with another plan, physically pinned down about as effectively as if they'd actually tied me, since I was agreeing with the doctor that I did not want to test how grumpy the dragon felt when it was shaken up a bit—it had already growled at me once so this was a truce brokered on petting only... And so I was trapped with only the inner circle to watch, my horror about what may happen to Ally growing as I realised I was getting absolutely no guidance on this, had nothing telling me what *would* happen. It was like when Teb ran away, or when I first went into the fairy world. It was just such a *big* event that I didn't get spoilers from the cosmos once I'd passed every marker of warnings that had been sent my way in the preceding days. Or maybe it was more that because I was an active agent in happenings, the universe could warn me of nothing more than that there would be a dragon, a week ago, and leave me to do the rest on my own, because anything more would just tell me what to do, and like everyone else... Sometimes I was uncertain.

I had a very uncertain moment then. Because my eyes skated over the cultists and something was clearly wrong. I needed another look before I realised. There were only six cultists in the circle.

The shadows moved behind Alana; she jolted in surprise, but didn't make a noise, as the figure behind her got to work unwrapping the ropes around her. The dragon lifted its head slightly, but the rope kept on unlooping, piles of it falling in Alana's lap like an inert version of the serpent I was playing host to. The dragon lowered its head again, as if seeing no threat at all in what was going on a few feet from it. Finally the cultist offered Alana a hand.

Without taking off her gag. A warning, I guessed, that this was supposed to be a sneaky exit from the scene.

She looked at him in horror, shook her head, gestured to the ritual with an incline of her head, the message clear that she wasn't leaving Ally.

"We have to go *now*," Greg hissed.

Alana struggled to her feet, almost toppling over from being sat so long uncomfortably, her hands still bound so she couldn't lever herself up off the back of the gravestone very easily. The dragon didn't even turn to watch this time.

Because, like me, it was watching the ritual. The sword had been produced and I was watching in hideous slow motion the tallest cultist raising it up ready to strike down at Ally, who was crying with fear at that point when I could get a glimpse of her face between the cultists.

"Ally, no!" Alana yelled, having yanked the gag out herself apparently, now that her arms weren't pinned in front of her. She lurched forwards as the sword began to fall.

A new tune mixed with the monotone chanting: one fast and shrill and furious.

The sword stopped. The cultist holding it juddered with the recoil of suddenly tugging at an immovable object. He pushed at it, leaned his shoulder against the pommel and leant on it with all his bulk. It stayed rigidly held like the air had solidified around it, the tip less than a foot from Ally's heart.

The tune kept dancing around us, growing louder, closer.

The Piper walked into the circle, his white eyes glowing with fury, his torn jeans scuffing on the ground behind his large boots, his recorder held to his lips. He walked right up to the tomb, shouldering into the space that Greg had probably abandoned, and blew a series of notes so fast I couldn't tell if the tune was going up or down, and then the sword just... melted away. Turned into dust and blew away before a crumb of it could land on Ally.

The cultists edged away with fearful murmurings, glancing between each other to check they had all really seen this.

The Piper lowered his recorder.

"Well met," he said.

Three of the cultists turned and ran. The dragon was off me like an arrow someone had loosened from a bow, off into the darkness beyond the candlelight. There was a scream. Not, I sadly noted, Mr Westcott's voice. Two more of the cloaked figures stood for a moment in horror, then also made up their minds and legged it while the dragon was distracted mauling one of their number, heading for the church, the well-known sanctuary. It occurred to me that if they were all prominent citizens, their disappearances or deaths would easily make the news and I'd discover who all the rest were in due course.

The other remaining cultist was backing away, hands raised. "I didn't know this would happen."

Bartholomew. So Mr Westcott was in the gauntlet racing a dragon. I wished him the best of luck.

"And you won't," the Piper said. He was bent over the tomb, hurriedly untying the ropes around Ally's limbs. She was looking at him with utter confusion and delight.

"What are you going to do?" Bartholomew asked.

"My job," the Piper said, and the next moment he was playing a song I actually half-recognised, but, for obvious reasons, a tune that never stayed in my head. It was the same song he'd played to make Teb forget when we came back from the fairy world for the first time. It was a lot faster viewed from the outside. We couldn't even see the spell effects. Just the cultist frozen in place, his hood slipping back to reveal a glassy expression on his bland face.

I resented that he was not going to get eaten.

"You will go into the church, and join the others there. By morning you will believe they worked themselves into hysteria thanks to their religious mania and serve as the rational voice of dissent to their delusions."

Bartholomew nodded and turned jerkily on the spot. He wandered off into the darkness.

The Piper carefully helped Ally to her feet and pulled her close. She grasped at the fabric of his t-shirt. "It's not safe to be here. Take Ally home, Tanya."

"What are you going to do next?" I said, seriously excited as the handcuffs clicked open all by themselves so I could finally shake them off (and keep them because come on, that's a trophy).

"My job," he replied. "Maybe one day I will be allowed to banish rampaging monsters for good *without* someone getting in my way."

"For good for good? Like the dragon will never come back?"

"This Order has been bothering and sometimes murdering the people of the village long enough. It is time this ended. It is not the way things should be."

I was quite happy to let him do his job. Or, not his job. Whatever he said, we both knew he had probably crossed a line somewhere by doing this.

"Go," the Piper repeated, pushing Ally gently towards me. Her eye landed on me with a hysteria I hadn't seen in a long time. "The dragon is still out there and while it has a taste for the men of the Order; you won't be safe for long."

I looked around. "What about Alana—" The Piper, Ally and I were the only people left in the graveyard.

"They'll be fine. They have a lot to talk about," the Piper said.

I gestured Ally with a nod of my head and scurried for the nearest gate, determined to get off hallowed ground and back onto the nice mundane road.

The Bigger Picture

Here's something I really ought to have considered:

We walked in silence, our steps fast with the thought of the wild dragon on the rampage, until we were back in the well-lit town centre and heading towards Ally's house. I would have to come back this way to get home, and at the moment it was much more tempting to stay with her for the night. There were certain issues troubling us, though.

"You do know I knew you wouldn't be killed?" I said, nervous of her reaction.

"How did you know he'd come?" Her voice was kind of wrecked from the screaming and shock.

"I had faith that he wouldn't let you die—that there was only one way he would intervene…"

"You… You manipulated all of this and put me in mortal peril so… so… you could stop the cultists? You *used* the fact he cares about me to get at them?"

"No! I…" This looked bad. "I mean, he wasn't ever going to ask you out on his own initiative. Having to get involved and save you…"

"This was you *setting me up* with him?"

"I mean just to look on the bright side… The cultists were already happening, and…"

"Tanya, remember how Alana was like 'we need to stop getting involved in all this magic and stuff for our own sakes'? This is exactly what she was talking about. You meddling with murderous cultists is not a *joke* or a funny way to 'help' your friends. I nearly died. People have been killed today. Because you meddled."

"That's not what I—"

"Alana is right. You need to leave well enough alone. You can't always be planning something, not with the resources you have. Do you even understand how dangerous it is?"

"Yes! I wanted to protect you. Ask Alana, we were—"

"Tanya, I don't care. At the end of the day you looked me in the eye and said you'd set a trap to get me sacrificed. You played with my *life*."

I groaned. "You're not looking at the bigger picture."

"I nearly *died*."

"The Piper—"

"I don't care. This is about you, Tanya."

And then, because this is a very small town, we were at her corner, and because her mum knows everything that happens here, Hester was running towards us and scooping Ally into a hug and dragging us both inside. "You're safe! You're safe! I was so worried about you girls!"

"Did you see what happened?" I asked.

"No, but I felt it… Oh, come in and have some tea…"

Ally gave me a quite horrified look at that, clearly wanting nothing to do with me while she sorted all of this through, and I tried to pull away. "I have been out long enough—I need to get back to my dad. He has no idea what's been going on…"

Hester, having manhandled us into the living room, found the same problem: Danny was there too and, since he couldn't know what was going on with the dragon, he was lacking the same relief that Hester had, since he didn't listen seriously to her panics until they'd hit some sensible proof they were justified.

"Please, just stay a minute," Hester begged me. I understood: she wanted me to be around someone relieved that I was okay after the ordeal, rather than the frankly isolating calm that Danny or my own dad would exude to me and Ally, even if those safe spaces were also very much appreciated. Being *understood* was more important sometimes.

I looked at Ally, who was inspecting her nails instead.

There was a knock on the door, and all three of us cluttering up the hall turned.

"*Oh*," Hester whispered, seeming to know who it was through the opaque door. "Ally, go sit down." She said nothing to me, so I hovered in the hall while she bustled over and opened the door again. The Piper, presumably having wrapped up all other business just in five minutes, was at the door.

"Good evening," Ally's mum said, sounding fluttery and nervous even for her.

"Well met," he replied. He looked over her shoulder: "Tanya, I have yours and Alana's phones."

I came over and took them from his outstretched hand, along with Alana's lighter and earbuds. I didn't ask how he'd got them.

"You should go home," he said, his expression kindly, all those storm clouds gone as he looked down at me.

I nodded, and he shifted aside so I could come past him.

He stayed at the door. "Hester, I was wondering if I could come in and talk to you and Danny for a minute. I have something to ask you."

Oh my *god*, what a gentleman.

I grinned to myself and scurried away down the drive.

Alana had said it would take something massive to get Ally to move on from the Piper, but I had to admit, I'd always liked the idea of them finding a way to come together again. She'd recover from how I had nearly set her up to die. And she'd finally have her long-awaited weird boyfriend.

*

It was as strange as I had anticipated to go home. Walking through the streets, I had my faith in the Piper that nothing would happen to me and that the dragon had been put to rest forever. Whatever it was, the air had cleared in the town and the sense of something about to happen that had been nagging at me for weeks before it did had gone.

I stepped through the door and my dad called vaguely to me from his office in a non-committed check to make sure I wasn't like a burglar that had just randomly let myself in.

I wondered how weird it would seem, but decided I didn't care and went to hug him as hard as I could.

He looked utterly normal and like he'd never worried for a second about me.

"You need to stop working late into the night."

He laughed. "I have a lot of work to do. Don't worry about me, sweet pea. Oh, thinking of work, I dug into that name you were asking about. There's nothing about a Mr Lane I could find."

"It's okay, Daddy. I'm not interested in being in any film anyway. Much easier just to watch them. Wanna put some old film on?"

"Sure. Let me just finish up here. Have you had dinner?"

"No, I'm starving."

"Me too," he admitted guiltily, like the fact he'd worked too long and skipped dinner was the worst thing that had happened in our family that day. I smiled fondly and rubbed his bald dome one more time for luck and went to go dig out some frozen meals.

*

I had a lot of missed calls from Warren that I'd been ignoring while all the drama had been happening before my phone was taken. I'd figured I'd have had a chance to talk to him sooner, but in the end when I was home and fed and wound down I went to bed and slept for thirteen hours uninterrupted (despite the nightmares I had dreaded), so I had even more missed calls when I woke up, many from Ally and Teb as well.

I cowardly phoned Warren first and told him how great he and Mackerel had been playing along with my game, and how of course we were fine—we had never really been in danger. I don't know if he seemed disappointed or relieved that dating me for the thrill-seeking was turning out to be such a letdown, but I promised to include him on the next adventure anyway, with a clause I added just for myself that it was totally conditional on what said adventure actually turned out to be.

He asked if he could come over again sometime soon and I agreed, thinking perhaps if nothing else I could do myself a big favour by crossing off "potential death by virgin sacrifice" from my list if I played my cards right in this relationship.

I caught myself staring out the window, feeling very disassociated and weird from Warren and startled by my own mercenary thinking, which just made me dread the other conversations I was due all the more.

My phone rang again before I could make up my mind: Teb. It seemed safe. She'd been like Switzerland in this whole debacle.

"Hello?"

"Tanya." I nearly had a heart attack at the sound of Alana's voice coming through the speaker. "We're down by the Green Man's oak."

"I have your phone," I said hoarsely.

"I know."

She hung up.

I scraped my hair back, put on some clothes that I strongly associated with good friendship moments for luck, and headed out the door.

I met Ally on the corner of the main road and the Green, which implied that Teb and Alana were freely associating alone, which was the most alarming thing. Ally was wearing the Piper's coat, despite it being a warm day, and she was holding it close around her like it was hugging her. She didn't look as bubbly as I'd hoped she would. She nodded to me, and we started off down towards the tree without talking.

At the oak, I found Teb sitting on the good low branch and Alana leaning against the tree, one foot resting behind her on its trunk.

"Hey," I said.

Ally carried on loitering behind me and despite the fact she's made of twigs I couldn't help feeling like she was the hired muscle keeping me in place.

"So, Alana caught me up," Teb said.

"Did Ally tell you that she's dating the Piper now?" I asked, trying to grin and make this a social situation instead of a trial without jury.

Alana's face didn't get much lighter at that, but she and Teb both looked surprised, so I figured Ally had been holding that one back for the opportune moment.

"You have my phone," Alana said, voice steady at the revelation.

I dug it and the other pocket junk out of my bag and handed them to her. She pocketed it all and sighed. "Tanya…"

"You're a menace," Teb put in. "I mean, it's why we love you, but you scared Ally. I have to take her side on this."

"We're taking sides?"

"Not unless you make it a big deal. We just want you to back off and say you're not going to do anything like that ever again."

"I saved the town! I unmasked a cult and managed to get Ally together with the Piper and banished a dragon…"

"No, you didn't. Other people did that while you manipulated everyone around you," Alana said.

"Look, either I was in control and did it or not…"

"It's *how* you did it that makes us worried. You're fun when you're not involving mortal danger or when your games actually look like games. You've started screwing with people's lives, and that's what we want to talk to you about."

"Actually," Alana interrupted, "the fact you think *you* did it all and that everyone was just your puppets to get stuff done is what's really making me uncomfortable. Life and death isn't a game. People aren't *toys*."

"You've reconciled with your father though," I said. "Aren't you happy about that?"

She set her jaw firmly and didn't reveal anything in her expression, but the fact was, I could see the weight lifted from her that had been on her the entire time I'd known her so far. A new, cold fury in her system, but it was far, far lighter than the previous darkness.

"Tanya," Ally said, finally weighing in, putting a hand on my shoulder from behind. I turned to face her. "*Please*, just say you're done. You've accomplished everything you wanted for us, right? Now leave off and promise you'll never toy with a situation like that ever again."

"I *saved* you," I said. "I've fixed everyone."

She shook her head. "It doesn't matter if we don't feel safe around you. Say you really, genuinely won't do it ever again."

"Or what?"

"Or we remove you from our lives so you stop feeling the need to do it."

I felt my head starting to swirl almost as badly as when I'd been stumbling around the graveyard. I turned to Teb, my partner in crime, who more than anyone had pushed that line—run away from us, rejected us, fought tooth and nail to tear herself out of our lives and not even cared that she'd loosed a changeling on us that had destroyed Alana's life in her desperation to fix her own. She shrugged, her expression much more helpless than her callous single lifted shoulder. She'd been here, but not in so many words. She did actually understand me. Majority vote and they'd got to her first.

I looked at Alana, who was much more resolute. I felt the sting of our brief but amazing friendship trickling away between my fingers.

"Okay," I said.

"Okay what?" Ally demanded.

"Okay," I said. "We're going to university at the end of the month. Things are running their course anyway, if they will or won't carry on from there... Time will tell."

*

Here's something I don't know how to deal with:

One new message from Teb: "We can fix it. Shopping tomorrow maybe?"

Three new messages from Ally: "Not if she's there." "Sry sent to wrong person meant not if mum @ shops not u. See you there." "Teb I mean not Tanya. See Teb there."

No new messages from Alana.

www.ingramcontent.com/pod-product-compliance
Lightning Source LLC
Chambersburg PA
CBHW030628190726
48286CB00008B/2441